THREADWOVEN

Book One – The ThreadCrafted Series

Hardcover Special Edition

Brynne Aisling-Rowan

Published by Woven Moon Press

This is a work of fiction. Names, characters, places, and incidents are products of the author's imagination or are used fictitiously. Any resemblance to actual events, locales, or persons, living or dead, is entirely coincidental.

brynne.aisling.rowan@gmail.com

ISBN: 979-8994083727 (hardcover edition)

For those who stitch light into the dark, and for those who walk in darkness searching for light.

PRONUNCIATION GUIDE

Ysolde — *Yuh-SOLD* ("Yuh" as in *yum*, "sold" as in *sold a book*)

Eira — *EYE-ruh* ("Eye" as in eyesight, "ruh" as in runner)

Anwen — *AN-wen* ("An" as in *sand*, "wen" as in *when*)

Caelen — *KYE-lin* ("Kye" rhymes with *sky*, "lin" as in *linen*)

Kael — *KAYL* (rhymes with *kale*, the vegetable)

Ines — *EE-nez* ("Ee" as in *see*, "nez" rhymes with *fez*)

Lysari — *lih-SAR-ee* ("Lih" as in *listen*, "sar" rhymes with *car*, "ee" as in *tree*)

Mirelle — *mih-RELL* ("Mih" as in *mirror*, "rell" rhymes with *bell*)

Varelda — *vah-RELL-dah* ("Vah" as in *lava*, "rell" rhymes with *bell*, "dah" as in *father*)

Varric — *VAIR-ik* ("Vair" rhymes with *air*, "ik" as in *pick*)

Brannoc — *BRAN-ock* ("Bran" as in *bran cereal*, "ock" rhymes with *rock*)

Darek — *DARE-ik* ("Dare" as in *truth or dare*, "ik" as in *brick*)

Elander — *EE-lan-der* ("Ee" as in *see*, "lan" rhymes with *man*, "der" as in *wander*)

Tauren — *TOR-en* ("Tor" rhymes with *door*, "en" as in *ten*)

Threadmancy → THRED-man-see

Leylines → LAY-lines ("ley" rhymes with "say")

Brookwyn → BROOK-win ("brook" + "win," not "wine")

CHAPTER ONE

FOURTEEN YEARS AGO

The workroom smelled of beeswax and a fresh summer breeze. Sunlight spilled across Ysolde's long table, turning the scattered threads and lint into strands of gold. Ysolde's hair, the deep copper of an autumn flame, slid forward over her shoulder until she brushed it back with the back of her hand. From outside came the clatter of wheels over cobblestones and the baker's singsong call offering up fresh baked honey rolls. She crossed the room to close the back door to muffle the noise.

Nine-year-old Eira sat straight, jaw set. Her hair was a vivid orange-red that caught glints of gold in the sunlight. Stray wisps had worked loose from her braid to frame a face still rounded with youth. Her skin was pale from long hours indoors, but her cheeks carried the faint flush of a girl in constant motion. She leaned forward, elbows on the table. A square of charm-cloth was pinned in an embroidery frame before her, chalk marks guiding the path of her very first stabilizing stitch. Beside it, a spool of glimmer-thread pulsed gently like a sleeping firefly.

"This will hold more magic than you think," Ysolde said to her daughter, settling another pin. "Intent steady from first loop to last."

"I can be steady," Eira said, sliding the threaded needle between her fingers.

From the hearth corner, Caelen, her mother's apprentice—older by four years and annoyingly good at everything—spun a needle over his knuckles. "You can be quick."

"Quick isn't bad," Eira said defensively.

Caelen always seemed older somehow, short dark hair kept neatly out of his warm brown eyes, his stillness like a stone set in a stream.

"Quick frays," Ysolde said mildly. "And frayed thread doesn't hold."

Footsteps pattered up the back step and Anwen appeared, pale braid wind-tossed. A basket of dye plants looped over her arm, stems scratching her sleeve and the sharp scent of green dye-leaf trailing in after her. "From Mum," she said. "And if you overboil the nettle again, she's not forgiving you twice."

"I only did it once," Ysolde said with a grin, taking the basket with grateful hands.

Anwen leaned toward Eira's hoop. "First stabilizer?"

Eira tried to look casual. "Yes."

"You'll have it perfect in no time," Anwen said, her belief in her friend as steady as the tide. Eira's shoulders loosened a fraction.

The back door eased open without a sound. Beck's grandfather stood there for a moment, eyes creased with pride as he watched Eira work. Then he stepped inside, satchels over his arm clinking with tools, and set a basket on Ysolde's table. His fingers lingered on the worn wood as if feeling the hum of the work there.

"Your repair held," he said.

"I'm glad," Ysolde replied, a smile touching her lips before she turned her attention back to Eira's hands.

Eira bent over the cloth, breath held. The needle slid; a flicker of excitement tightened her grip and the thread sparked—a thin ribbon of light darted across the surface, catching on pins and scattering like fireflies before sinking into the fabric as if it had always been part of it.

Anwen gasped. Beck's grandfather whistled, low.

Ysolde's hand came to Eira's wrist. "Breathe. Intent first, loop second."

On Eira's other side Caelen leaned close, voice quiet. "Loosen. Let it settle."

Eira obeyed, taking a deep breath and focusing. The light sank into the cloth and held. When she looked up, Ysolde's smile was warm, but her breath caught — the kind of pause reserved for moments that would be told and retold for years. Threads weren't meant to hold that much magic, yet under Eira's hands, they did.

Eira's eyes lit with accomplishment. She had a single, perfect stitch.

Then Beck crashed through the doorway in a tangle of elbows and barely-checked momentum. "It wasn't my fault—the chicken started it."

A round brown hen chased in after him, wings flicking in irritation and clucking loudly as if lodging a formal complaint.

Caelen sighed. "Beck."

"I didn't mean for there to be a chase," Beck said, attempting dignity as he pulled a leather notebook and a nub of a pencil from his pocket. "I was making important notes."

"About the chicken?" Eira asked, unable not to smile.

"About life."

His grandfather chuckled from behind him, ruffling Beck's hair. "You take after me more than you know."

Ysolde shook her head but left the door open. "Only until that hen finds her way out."

On the walkway across the street, a person in a dark Council coat paused, gaze lingering a heartbeat too long on the open workroom door before moving on, unseen by those inside.

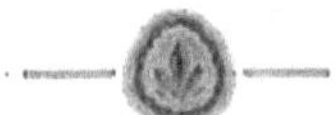

Ysolde believed learning magic began with listening. You could shape the natural world into threads with your intention, but first you had to control your intention — and to do that you had to listen and understand what was truly needed.

She taught Eira in small tasks that never felt small: mending a torn shawl while holding a memory steady; steeping dye until the color hummed the same note as the cloth; knotting a thread around a seedling and whispering patience into it.

"Magic doesn't begin with will," Ysolde said, binding Eira's finger where the needle had kissed it. "It begins with feeling. Intention only works if the thread recognizes it."

Caelen, seated nearby with a coil of flame-thread and a bowl of river stones, didn't look up. "And if it doesn't recognize it, it bites."

"It nips," Ysolde corrected, lips twitching.

Caelen flicked Eira a look—half teasing, half protective. "Don't make it a habit."

"I won't."

By week's end, Eira had three neat stabilizer loops, one scorch mark on the table that Ysolde pretended not to see, and a new ritual: when lessons ended, she, Anwen, and Beck sprawled on the back step while Beck read from his notebook.

Today, Anwen sat cross-legged on the worn stone step, unwinding a length of seed-thread from her wrist. It shimmered green with flickers of gold, faint as cobweb in sunlight, visible only to mage-trained eyes. She twisted it once around the stem of a dye-leaf in her lap. The leaf responded with a faint shiver, edges uncurling as if waking from a nap.

"Trying to make it bloom faster?" Eira asked.

"Trying to make it forgive me for picking it," Anwen replied, mouth curving. "Plants like to be asked."

Eira smirked. "And do they always say yes?"

"Only if you're polite," Anwen said, her eyes bright with the quiet confidence of someone whose magic always answered her call.

A soft rattle came from the front gate. Beck's grandfather stood there, one hand on the latch, the other shading his eyes. The breeze teased his long silver hair. His gaze was bright and fond

— but after a moment it slid past them, lingering on the far hedge with a puzzled frown.

"Wasn't there a well here once?" he asked, certain in the way people are certain of things half-remembered.

Beck's smile tightened at the edges. "That was at your old place, Granddad," he said gently.

"Ah. Yes, of course." The old man chuckled, but the crease between his brows didn't quite ease.

Beck rose and crossed to the gate. The latch stuck — a simple metal catch to most eyes, but to Beck it shimmered with lock-thread, a faint weave of pale copper lines curling through the hinge. He hooked a finger through the air just above it, tugged, and the threads loosened with a soundless sigh. The latch clicked open without him touching the metal.

"There we go," Beck said, swinging the gate wide. "Come sit by the lavender."

His grandfather let himself be steered to the sun-warmed bench. Beck gave his shoulder a squeeze before jogging back to the others.

"Entry one," he announced as he dropped to the step again. "Today I learned chickens can hold grudges, and that Anwen elbows hard."

"You ran into me," Anwen said, not looking up from where the leaf was now twining around her finger like a tame pet.

"Still counts," Beck said, flipping open his notebook. He scrawled a quick line, the paper dimpling where his quill tip skimmed too fast.

"What's in the book this time?" Eira asked.

Beck shrugged, though his glance flicked briefly toward the lavender bench. "Granddad says if I write the good bits, I'll keep them. If I write the bad bits, they'll stop gnawing."

Anwen's hand stilled on the thread. "Then you'd better keep writing," she said softly, "because you're going to have a whole library of good bits."

Eira didn't yet know what it meant to be gnawed by a memory. But she tucked the words away carefully, like a pin returned to a pincushion, and for reasons she couldn't name, they warmed her.

The trouble started the moment Eira touched the wind.

Ysolde had set a shallow bowl of river water in the middle of the worktable, sunlight pooling across its surface. "Threads answer feeling," she reminded, smoothing her own braid back. "So steady yourself first."

Eira tried. She truly did. But the idea of shaping breeze into braid set her fingers itching with anticipation. She slipped her needle into the air, coaxing for a thread, and the first loop caught — then bolted.

To non-mages, the room might have only filled with a sudden, mischievous draft. But to Eira's eyes, the wind-threads shimmered pale blue and silver, spinning away like startled minnows. They darted through the rafters, lifted Ysolde's hair free of its pins, and sent Caelen's notes pinwheeling into the air.

"Not… terrible," Caelen said dryly, squinting up as a page fluttered down onto his shoulder. Without comment, he reached out and steadied the bowl with one hand — his version of rescuing her without calling it rescue.

Ysolde laughed, a sound like thin porcelain gently tapped. "It wants to play. Give it a game with rules. We always have to set the intention."

Eira inhaled, exhaled, imagined braid instead of gust. She caught two of the pale threads between her fingers — cool, featherlight — and looped them slow and soft. The draft settled. The air-threads twined into a neat current that moved exactly as she asked - over the bowl, past the hearth, beneath the door, and out into the square.

"Better," Ysolde said. "Now, anchor it."

A small, ash-gray pulse warmed just behind Eira's left ear — weightless, but insistent. The air threads held, as if they'd chosen her back.

Caelen saw it; he always saw what she missed. For a heartbeat his brows drew together, but when Ysolde met his glance, he said nothing. He only reached up to pluck his last page from a beam, sliding it back into his stack with studied nonchalance.

Half an hour later, the front door rattled open just as Anwen arrived with a bundle of dawnleaf so fresh it still held a whisper of green-thread shimmer along the stems. Beck trailed behind, a round loaf under his arm and the self-satisfied grin of someone who'd just won a bargain.

"I didn't even have to pay for it," he announced, dropping the loaf onto the table. "Helped the baker's assistant untangle a storage charm in the flour bins, and she insisted I take this as thanks."

The faint glimmer of a lock-thread still winked across the crust — his doing, no doubt, to keep Anwen from claiming it first.

Across the square, a clerk in a black-trimmed Council coat lingered at the beeswax seller's stall. At their hip hung a narrow silver blade, its hilt etched with fine knotwork. Not the kind of weapon meant for open fighting — the sort carried for precision and quiet work.

"Does Ysolde still teach? The threadwitch?" they asked, voice too casual.

"Teaches carefulness," the candlemaker replied, unconcerned as she weighed out a block. "And patience. Never could get her to sell me that trick for keeping wicks from sulking."

The clerk laughed, but it didn't touch their eyes. As they turned away, their gaze skimmed the street — and paused for the barest moment on Ysolde's open workshop window, where the faint ripple of an anchored air-thread still shimmered in the frame.

CHAPTER TWO

TWELVE YEARS AGO

Two years can sand the edges off a child's face and sharpen the way they stand in the wind. Eira no longer tripped over her own excitement — well, not as often — though stray strands of hair still wriggled free from her braid and her boots bore the scuffs of too many adventures. She hopped from stone to stone along the path without thinking, skirts swaying with each leap. Beside her, Caelen no longer had the loose-limbed gait of a boy; he'd grown into his height, shoulders set with a quiet steadiness, his voice carrying the faint new depth of someone closer to manhood than childhood. Without seeming to notice, he adjusted his stride to match hers, as if the two of them had been walking this way for years.

Ysolde waited ahead, framed by the silver-thread shimmer of a leyline's edge. It rippled faintly in the air, like heat rising from stone, though Eira could see the threads for what they were — strands of light so fine they were barely visible unless they pulled tight. The air felt different here, humming with the quiet weight of old magic.

"This," Ysolde said, "is where the bones of our world meet its blood. The leylines carry more than power — they remember every hand that has touched them." She reached out, her fingers brushing the air until a faint arc of gold-thread light sang between them and the leyline.

Eira felt her fingertips tingle, her own threads tugging in response. Without thinking, she reached toward the shimmer. Caelen's hand shot out, catching her wrist before she could connect.

"Careful," he warned. His threads — soft blue, steady and warm — unspooled around her like a shield. "You don't know how deep it runs."

Eira tilted her chin at him. "And how do you plan to learn if you never test the depth?" Her own threads flared brighter, a blend of colors that bent and twined as if impatient to explore. They brushed against his shield, testing its give.

He didn't push back, but neither did he drop it. "I learn by not drowning."

Ysolde's voice cut in, firm but not unkind. "Both of you are right. But remember — the threads are older than your ambition and stronger than your caution. They will shape you as much as you shape them."

Eira and Caelen exchanged a glance, neither willing to yield the last word. The shimmer of the leyline between them seemed to pulse, as if it, too, was listening.

Eira's needle paused over the pale square of cloth, the tip catching the light as she considered the next pull of thread. The shop was quiet save for the rhythmic scrape of Ysolde's chair as she moved between shelves, sorting finished pieces into careful stacks.

She had meant to work on the practice scene Ysolde assigned her, but her mind wandered. The threads under her fingertips shifted, colors deepening into the hues of a day not long past.

The pond's surface flashed into her mind, green-gold with sunlight and ringed in reeds. She could almost hear the splash of Anwen's foot hitting the water, Beck's startled laugh, the lazy hum of summer insects. And then—Granddad's voice, warm and rich, calling them over. He stood on the worn path with a paper sack of sweet rolls tucked under his arm, the scent of sugar and spice drifting toward them.

He passed them out one by one, his weathered hands careful not to crush the flaky layers. Eira took hers, licking sugar from her thumb, and watched Beck beam at his grandfather like the sun itself had arrived. Then the old man paused, frowning faintly, as if a word he meant to say had slipped away. The moment lasted only a heartbeat, but in it, Beck's smile faltered—the briefest flicker, gone before anyone else seemed to notice.

Eira noticed. And now, with her needle and thread, she wove the memory exactly as it had been: the warmth, the laughter, the sweet taste of summer… and the faint shadow that had crossed Beck's face.

The stitches glimmered faintly as the truth of it sank into the cloth.

"Not just the happy parts," Ysolde's voice came from behind her. Eira startled, then looked up. The older woman's gaze was steady, thoughtful. “You stitched what was there—not just what you wished had been.”

She moved away without another word, leaving Eira staring down at her work, wondering why it felt so important not to leave anything out.

Winter crept in and the shop grew busier. Farmers brought in split harnesses and talismans with frayed edges. A traveling scribe asked Ysolde to bind the memory of a letter so it would not blur in rain. Eira loved those jobs most—the way intent and thread sat down together like old friends and refused to be parted.

“Some threads carry power,” Ysolde said one evening, lamplight soft on her hands. “All carry intent. They can be honest even when we are not.”

“What do the honest ones do?” Eira asked.

“They hold up a mirror.”

Eira felt the ash-gray warmth behind her ear again, a faint tug little as a heartbeat.

Caelen’s expression went distant, then sharpened. His fingers bore pale tracers of old threadburn. He flexed them absently, as if remembering—not pain, but promises. He knew his magic had a purpose.

“When would you ever need a mirror?” Beck asked.

"When you're about to lie to yourself," Anwen said, and sipped her tea.

Beck made a note. Eira watched the quick, clever movement of his hand and thought about keeping and losing. She remembered him saying, two years ago, that he wrote things down so the good wouldn't slip away… and so the bad couldn't gnaw at you unseen.

Now, with the memory of stitching Beck's moment at the pond still fresh, she thought about the danger in leaving shadows out of the record. Ignoring them didn't erase them; it only let them lurk, waiting.

Ysolde set down her needle and rose, crossing to a narrow drawer beneath the shop's counter. When she returned, she held something wrapped in soft linen. With a care usually reserved for spun-glass charms, she unwrapped the cloth to reveal a geode. Its fractured heart glowed violet—dim, steady, old.

"Stone hearts," Ysolde said quietly, "are repositories for memory—strong enough to hold a lifetime of it. The good. The bad. Everything in between. They can store what no book could bear and what no thread could safely carry. Stone hearts often carry the burden of old griefs"

Eira leaned closer, the glow reflecting in her eyes. "Why not use them all the time?"

"Because we don't fully understand them," Ysolde replied. "And power we don't understand can be as dangerous as it is tempting. A memory unbound from a stone heart can change the way you remember your life. Or the way you live it. Imagine being hit with all your old grief at once. It's a wave that could overtake a person"

Caelen didn't reach for the geode. He only studied it as if weighing the truth of her warning. Eira felt something different—a faint pull in her magic, like a door she might be able to open, if she wanted to.

Ysolde rewrapped the geode and tucked it away again. "Not every tool belongs in every hand," she said, and returned to her chair.

Eira threaded her needle and began a new square, one that wasn't beautiful but was *true*. The threads shimmered faintly—silver shot with shadow—as they settled into place.

The shop was still warm from the day's work, the air steeped in the mingled scents of beeswax polish, dried lavender, and the faint metallic tang that came from working raw thread too long. Afternoon light slanted through the high window, painting gold across the scattered tools. Ysolde had gone down the lane to fetch a tincture from Anwen's family apothecary, leaving Eira to "tidy the worktable" — a task she had quickly interpreted as "see what the copper thread could be coaxed into doing."

Caelen leaned against the counter, his shadow stretching long across the floorboards. He idly looped a scrap of dull silver thread between his fingers, watching her with the patient wariness of someone who'd seen trouble happen in exactly this way. "You shouldn't play with that without gloves," he said.

"I'm not playing." Eira grinned, her tongue caught lightly between her teeth as she teased the copper into a small, sunburst-shaped knot. The threads quivered under her touch, fine as hair yet shimmering faintly, as though they were alive. "I'm practicing."

"That's what people say right before they—"

The sunburst flared bright, the magic in it snapping like lightning across her palm. A hot sting bit into her skin, and she dropped the copper with a gasp. The fine line left behind was no deeper than a paper cut, but it burned as though it had been seared.

"—get threadburn," Caelen finished, his tone dry but his eyes flicking to her hand in instant concern. "You're lucky it wasn't worse."

He crossed the room in two long strides, the faint scent of pine resin clinging to his coat. Rummaging through Ysolde's small drawer of salves, he found a jar whose label had long since faded to pale brown. Without a word, he knelt beside her stool.

"Hold still." His hands were steady and sure, the calluses on his fingertips warm against her skin as he dabbed the cool, herbal salve over the burn. The ointment smelled faintly of rosemary and rain-wet earth. "It'll fade faster if you don't keep bending your fingers."

Eira watched the small furrow between his brows, surprised by the gentleness in his touch. "You've had this happen before."

"More than once," he admitted. "You think I got these—" he flexed his fingers so the pale tracer-lines of old threadburn caught the light "—by being careful the first time?"

She almost said sorry, but the moment didn't seem to need it. Instead, she met his gaze and nodded. "I'll be more careful."

"Good." He capped the jar, sliding it back into its place. Then, softer, with the faintest curve of a smile: "But don't stop being… you. Just maybe keep all your fingers attached, yeah?"

Eira's grin came bright and easy this time — and to her quiet satisfaction, he smiled back.

CHAPTER THREE

EIGHT YEARS AGO

The air smelled of rain-washed stone and fresh bread as Eira stepped out of the shop beside Caelen, the wicker basket on her arm brushing his sleeve when she swung it. Puddles dappled the cobbles like bits of broken mirror, catching slices of pale morning sky.

"Two stops," she said, adjusting her grip. "A packet of safflower petals from the dye merchant and copper glimmer-thread for Mum."

"And the latest news," Caelen added, arching a brow.

She didn't deny it. In Brookwyn, the market stalls were nearly as good as the town crier, and Ysolde had a knack for sending her out when the air felt ripe for chatter.

"Slow down," Caelen said, though his stride lengthened to match hers.

"You're the one dragging your feet," she replied.

"I'm walking like a normal person," he said, side-eyeing the way she leapt a puddle instead of skirting it. "You're walking like a heron chasing minnows."

"Herons are graceful," she muttered.

"Not when you're doing the impression."

Her laugh slipped out before she could stop it.

The market square was already busy, stalls bright with awnings beaded in rain. The scents of yeast, damp wool, and bruised rosemary tangled in the air. Traders called their wares over the steady percussion of boots and wagon wheels.

As they wove toward Ysolde's preferred dye merchant, they passed two women by the bread stall, one whispering far too loudly:

"...and the goat got into the mayor's garden again. Ate three shirts off the line before anyone saw."

Eira bit back a grin. Caelen caught her eye and they shared a quiet, mutual roll of their eyes before moving on.

Half a dozen paces later, another voice caught her attention — quieter, sharper.

"...acting strange again in the capital," a man said to the shawl vendor. "Spells slipping. Wards breaking without warning."

"Rumors," the vendor replied, though her tone wavered. "Tauren says there's nothing to it."

"That's not what Brannoc says. If the weave keeps fraying, he'll call the Council to session before summer."

Eira's gaze flicked to Caelen. He didn't speak, but his jaw eased slightly, the way it always did when he was listening harder than he let on. His hand adjusted the strap of the smaller basket on his shoulder — casual, but not careless.

They moved on without a word. The awnings above them dripped in uneven rhythm, and the sound seemed to follow them all the way to the next stall.

Ysolde's favored dye merchant was half-hidden behind a stall draped in bolts of cloth that shifted color with the angle of light. Between the displays, drying racks hung from the awning poles, strung with bundles of herbs, curling roots, and a fan of bright safflower petals that glowed like captured sunlight against the gray morning. The scents mingled — wet wool from a folded cloak, the clean sharpness of crushed mint, the honeyed tang of dried blooms, and the faint mineral bite of mordants stored in clay jars under the counter.

Behind them, the market hummed with life: the bark of a fishmonger selling the morning's catch, the slap of a rug being shaken clean, the laughter of two children chasing each other around a barrel of apples. The sounds bled into one another until they formed a steady, familiar rhythm.

"Ah, Ysolde's girl," he greeted, then glanced at Caelen. "And her shadow. You're in luck. Fresh safflower came in with the coastal traders this week." He ducked beneath the counter and came up with a neatly wrapped packet of petals, setting it beside a row of copper glimmer-thread spools that caught the light like fine-drawn fire.

As he reached for paper to bundle their purchases, something on the lower shelf caught his eye. "Oh — and have a look at this. Might interest Ysolde."

He pulled out a small satchel of weather-treated leather. "The lining's meant to ward against damp. Fine work when it behaves, but lately the threads have been… temperamental."

Eira accepted it, running her fingers along the inner seam. A faint, unsteady hum answered her touch — the kind of vibration that warned a stitch was near to snapping.

Before she could set it down, the magic gave way. The binding thread lashed upward toward her wrist, bright and quick as a snake strike.

Caelen's hand was there before she had time to flinch. He caught the loose shimmer mid-air — and something changed. Not just settling, but reshaping, the light bending under his fingers as if the magic itself had been coaxed into a new form. The unstable hum smoothed into a steady, anchored pulse before sinking harmlessly back into the seam.

Eira stared, her breath caught. She'd never seen thread behave like that without being cut and rewoven — and yet under his touch it had simply… obeyed. The magnitude of it pressed in, heavy with the knowledge that this was not ordinary craft.

Only then did she notice the size of his hand where it had brushed hers — broader now, stronger than she remembered — before he let go and the moment slipped away.

"Better," Caelen said evenly, passing the satchel back to the merchant.

The man inspected it with a grunt of satisfaction, already distracted by the next customer.

Eira, however, caught movement beyond the stall — a figure standing just at the edge of the square, half-hidden between two awnings. The dark coat marked them as Council, the silver trim catching the morning light. Their gaze was fixed on Caelen's hands.

When she blinked, the figure was gone.

The rest of the purchase was handled quickly. Caelen settled the packet of safflower petals and the copper thread into the basket, thanked the merchant, and steered them back toward the quieter side streets.

"You didn't have to—" Eira began.

"Yes, I did." His tone was flat but not unkind, and his eyes stayed on the path ahead.

They walked in silence for a few paces, boots scuffing on damp cobbles still slick from the morning rain. Somewhere nearby, a cartwheel creaked in a slow turn, the faint scent of yeast and warm bread lingering from the square.

"There was a man watching you," she said at last. "Council coat."

That made him glance down at her sharply, the line of his mouth tightening for the briefest moment before he smoothed it away.

"Probably just another inspector making rounds. Happens in the market sometimes."

"This one wasn't browsing," she said. "He was watching you. Your hands."

Caelen's jaw flexed, the rhythm of his stride shifting just slightly, but he only nodded once. "Then it's a good thing I didn't do anything worth their notice." His tone was light, almost convincing — if she hadn't seen the shadow still in his eyes.

The noise of the market faded behind them, replaced by the soft hiss of water dripping from the eaves into the gutters. Somewhere a door slammed, the sound echoing briefly through the narrow lane. Eira still felt the weight of the stranger's gaze on her back, like a thread she couldn't shake.

When they reached Ysolde's door, the morning light had dulled behind cloud. Eira stepped inside first, the familiar scent of dried lavender and beeswax wrapping around her like a familiar shawl. Ysolde looked up from the counter, her expression flicking briefly to Caelen before she turned to greet them.

Eira set the basket down, the petals rustling softly in their paper wrap, and busied herself with straightening a stack of folded cloth. Out of the corner of her eye, she caught Caelen lean toward Ysolde, murmuring something low enough she couldn't make out the words. Ysolde's fingers paused mid-fold, her gaze sliding toward Eira for the briefest instant before she replied in the same hushed tone.

By the time Eira turned fully toward them, they had stepped apart — too quickly, too neatly.

Her hands stilled over the cloth. She didn't ask what they'd been talking about. But the tension in the air was as tangible as any thread she'd ever worked, humming just beneath the surface.

And somewhere beneath it, she sensed they were both keeping her from something — something important — and that knowledge settled over her like the shadow of the Council coat still lingering in her mind.

CHAPTER FOUR

SEVEN YEARS AGO

The knock came at dusk — three firm raps that rang like a summons.

Eira looked up from the charm-braid she was finishing, needle paused mid-loop. Outside, the last light bled pale gold through the shutters, but something in the sound tightened the air inside the workroom. Ysolde froze mid-step, a ledger in her hands. Caelen's head came up from his work with the sharp stillness of a stag catching scent.

They didn't speak. They didn't have to. The look that passed between them was a conversation Eira wasn't invited to hear.

When Ysolde opened the cottage door, the cold air came in first, then two figures in finely cut, dark coats. Silver pins glinted at their collars — the Council's crest.

The man in front — tall, sharply dressed, gaze like a blade — swept the entryway with a glance that felt like a search warrant. Councilor Thorne. His voice was clipped, unyielding.
"Caelen Marrowind. We'll speak inside."

The woman beside him moved with a measured grace, her expression all warmth on the surface. Councilor Mirelle inclined her head politely.

"Miss Wynfell. Mrs. Wynfell. We hope this isn't a poor time, but circumstances have… shifted."

Ysolde's answering smile was thin. "I will speak with you, Councilor Mirelle, but not in my home. We'll go to the workshop."

She turned to Eira. "You'll stay here."

Eira's mouth opened — to argue, to ask why — but Ysolde's look stopped her. "The kettle's still warm. Mind the fire."

Without another word, Ysolde stepped outside. Caelen followed her, the Councilors falling in behind.

From the doorway, Eira watched their shapes cross the yard. The winter air hung silver in the fading light, frost catching on the edges of the stepping stones. Bare-limbed fruit trees stood like sentinels in the cottage's front beds, and across the open space, the workshop leaned nearer the street, its door angled toward the lane.

Thorne's gaze roved over everything — the flower beds, the cottage windows — as though cataloging it all. Mirelle glanced back once toward Eira and offered a pleasant, unreadable smile before turning away.

The shop door opened under Ysolde's hand, closing behind them with a muted thud.

Eira was left with the quiet tick of cooling hearthstones and the faint scent of winter air in the room — and a sudden awareness of how far away the shop felt, even when it was just across the yard.

Inside the shop, Ysolde didn't bother lighting the front counter lamps, steering them straight to the back workroom. "Please," she said coolly, gesturing to the long table. "Sit. I'll fetch tea."

Councilor Mirelle's smile was faint but constant, her eyes taking in every detail — the spools of thread, the labeled drawers, the neat rows of completed work along the shelves. Thorne didn't sit immediately, instead studying the table's surface as if looking for stray clues in the grain.

Ysolde returned with a pot and four cups, setting them down with a precision that might have been courtesy, might have been a warning. "You've come far. State your purpose."

Thorne finally took a seat, folding his hands before him. "We've heard reports. Observations from trusted sources. The young man under your care — Mr. Marrowind — possesses an ability rare enough to be mentioned in the same breath as legend."

Caelen's eyes narrowed. "What ability?"

Thorne's glance slid to Mirelle. She tilted her head, inviting him to go on. "Transformation," he said at last. "Not simple alteration of a thread-bound object, but complete reweaving — changing the very heart-thread into something new. Living or not."

Ysolde's voice was flat. "That's a dangerous claim."

"Not a claim," Mirelle said. "An observation. One that carries… implications."

Caelen leaned forward. "Such as?"

The two councilors exchanged a long, unspoken conversation in a pair of glances. Finally, Mirelle spoke, her voice quiet. "Guardianship."

Ysolde's brows rose. "Guardianship of what?"

"A sacred trust," Thorne said, and his tone made the words feel heavier than they should. "The most ancient archives, the deep-warded halls, the places that cannot fall. Guardians have always been… more than human."

Mirelle's gaze held Caelen's now. "You could take such a form. Become one of the sacred beasts — a dragon of the archives."

The words seemed to hang in the air. Caelen didn't move, but something in his expression shifted — wary, calculating.

"And what," Ysolde asked, "would be the cost of this transformation?"

Another glance between the councilors. This one was shorter, sharper.

"There are… consequences," Mirelle admitted. "It is not a gift to be used lightly. Some never change back. Some choose not to."

Caelen's jaw tightened. "And I'd be doing this where?"

"In the capital, at first," Thorne said. "And later… wherever the realm most needs you."

Ysolde poured tea without looking away from them. "And Miss Wynfell?"

"Versatility is her gift," Mirelle said. "She is adept at nearly every form of thread magic we've observed. It would be a disservice to leave her potential half-realized."

"She is my apprentice," Ysolde said evenly. "I decide what is realized."

Thorne's voice cooled. "We're not here to debate your skill, Mrs. Wynfell. Only to offer them the chance to serve the realm in ways they cannot here."

"In other words," Ysolde said, "to take them from under my care."

Mirelle's smile didn't falter, but the warmth in her eyes cooled. "To place them where they are most needed."

"They're needed here." Ysolde's voice was steel now. "You'll not have them."

Thorne's gaze flicked toward Caelen. "And what if the choice were his?"

"I'd advise him wisely," Ysolde said, "as I always have."

Caelen had been silent too long, eyes fixed on some point past the councilors, but now he spoke, slow and deliberate. "If this is as serious as you say, I'll need time. A week, maybe, to decide."

Mirelle inclined her head, but the movement was tight. "You have one week," she said. "Send a courier with your answer."

"And if I say no?" Caelen asked.

Thorne's answer came without pause. "Then for the good of the realm, and the safety of all its citizens, we will take you — and

Miss Wynfell — into our care regardless. Magic cannot be allowed to destabilize."

The last word seemed to echo in the quiet room

"If I agree to do this willingly you let Eira stay here." Caelen said eventually.

"Why would we agree to that, you're both powerful threadmages and should help your country," blustered Thorne getting red in the face.

"Forcing a child into service would be ill-received," Mirelle said smoothly. "Guardianship buys us time to consider other options while the Archives are secured."

"Hmph, I suppose." Thorne begrudgingly agreed. "But we will continue to -monitor- her development. You will send us regular updates Mrs. Wynfell."

Ysolde nodded and set down her cup with a sharp click. "Then we are finished here."

She rose, and though she didn't ask them to leave, the motion was so final that both councilors pushed back their chairs. Mirelle smoothed her skirts, Thorne adjusted his cloak.

At the workroom door, Mirelle paused to look at Caelen again. "Think carefully, Mr. Marrowind. The shape of your life — and hers — may depend on it."

They stepped out into the fading light, their footsteps crisp on the stone path back toward the street.

Ysolde didn't watch them go. She busied herself with clearing the table, movements quick and hard, the clink of porcelain louder than it needed to be.

Caelen lingered in the doorway. His voice, when it came, was low. "They're not bluffing, If we want to keep Eira safe and out of their control I have to go."

"I know," Ysolde said. Her hands did not stop moving. "And that's why we'll be ready."

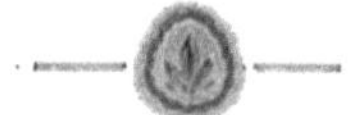

Eira was curled in the window seat with her mending when she saw them come back from the shop. Ysolde's pace was brisk, skirts brushing the path's edges, her jaw tight. Caelen followed a step behind, his hands jammed deep in his pockets, eyes on the ground as though he were counting the stones.

They didn't speak to her as they crossed the threshold — just headed straight for the small library alcove that held Ysolde's most prized tomes.

Eira frowned and set her work aside. "What's going on?"

Ysolde glanced up, the expression she wore carefully smoothed. "We have a task, love. Nothing to fret over."

Caelen was already stacking books on the table — bindings of deep green and russet brown, all stamped with the runes of higher working. Ysolde moved with purpose, pulling the lacquered box from the mantel and setting it beside the pile. She opened it, revealing the pale-veined geode she had shown them years earlier.

Eira's breath caught. "That's—"

"A safeguard," Ysolde said smoothly, as if the word closed the matter. "Caelen is being called to serve for a time in the capital. The Archives need protecting, and his talents make him… uniquely suited."

Eira turned to Caelen. "How long?"

He shrugged, but it was a tight, uneasy gesture. "For a while. Long enough."

Ysolde rested a hand briefly on Eira's shoulder. "We'll be sealing some of his memories, just the important ones. So that if—when—he returns, they'll be intact. It's only a precaution, nothing more. You're the best suited for geodecraft, so I'll guide you through it."

Eira searched their faces. Ysolde's smile was calm, practiced; Caelen's eyes met hers for a heartbeat before sliding away.

"Will it hurt?" she asked.

"Not a bit," Ysolde said. "Now — fetch your satchel. We'll need your silver thread and the moon-etched needle. This is delicate work, but well within your ability."

Eira went, but the air in the cottage felt different now — thinner, as if a door had been opened to something that could not easily be shut.

The snow had fallen all morning, soft as wool, cloaking the orchard in unbroken white. By late afternoon, the clouds thinned into bands of pale gold, sunlight stretching long between the bare fruit trees.

Eira spotted him at the far end of the orchard, leaning against the low stone wall, his breath curling into the cold air. He'd been quiet since the council visit two days ago, slipping away whenever Ysolde wasn't demanding his presence.

"You've been scarce today," she said, stepping through the drift toward him.

"Studying," Caelen replied, a faint smile touching his lips. "Trying to learn how to be something I'm not yet."

She stopped beside him, her mitten brushing his sleeve. "Something you don't have to be if you don't want to."

His smile faltered, the shadows under his eyes deepening. "That's not quite true anymore."

They stood in silence, the orchard breathing around them in the stillness. Eira glanced up at him — really looked at him — and the sight caught her off guard. He wasn't just her mother's other student anymore, wasn't just the older boy who teased and challenged her. He had just turned twenty; she was sixteen. Somewhere in the years between, he had become… more.

She blinked hard, and the edges of her vision blurred. "I don't want you to go."

"I don't want to go either," he said quietly. "But wanting doesn't change what's coming."

Crouching, he traced a circle in the snow, then etched the looping lines of a sunmark inside it. "So I don't forget," he murmured.

Eira knelt beside him, close enough to feel the warmth where their shoulders touched. "The geode will make sure of that, you said."

"It will… if things go as they should." He hesitated, then rested his gloved hand over hers. "But if they don't — if you ever meet me in another shape — look to the eyes. If they're still mine, you'll know I'm in there. Speak my name, and I'll hear it, no matter what I am. If they're not…" His voice dropped. "You run, Eira. You run and don't look back."

Her eyes stung as she studied him, every detail suddenly precious. "Caelen," she whispered, "you're more than my friend."

His breath caught. "And you're more than mine."

For a heartbeat, they leaned toward each other, the space between them warm despite the frost in the air. Her gaze flicked to his lips — his to hers — before he blinked and pulled back, the moment fragile as spun glass.

"I promise," she said.

He drew a second sunmark beside the first, a little larger, their edges touching. "Then we both remember."

The wind shifted, carrying the scent of woodsmoke from the cottage, and the world seemed to pause for them, holding their confession in its frozen breath.

The storm outside rattled against the shutters, but the hearth held steady, its flames woven with whisper-thread to keep them from guttering. Shadows wavered across the beams, stirring the bronze and obsidian chimes that swayed in soft, discordant notes — like reeds shivering in an unseen current.

Five days had passed since the councilors' boots had clattered down the path, leaving their words behind like a lingering taste of ash. Caelen had spent every moment since in preparation — combing the library with Ysolde, rehearsing protective sigils until his fingers ached, and walking the snowy orchard paths with Eira when they could steal the time. Each day had been one less he could spend here. One less before the council's deadline drove him to the capital.

Now there was no more time to steal.

Eira knelt on the rug her mother had stitched with memory-knot patterns, the colors faded from years of bare feet and spellwork. Spools of silk, bundles of flame-thread, and glass needles lay scattered between them in a chaos that only two mages could call organized. In the center, the geode pulsed with violet light, its cracked surface catching the fire's glow like an open wound. The beat of it was wrong — erratic, as though the truth sealed inside it was struggling to get free.

Across from her, Caelen sat, rolling his sleeves past his elbows. Pale, silvery thread-burn scars traced from his wrists to the edges of his forearms, testaments to the magic he'd learned too quickly and used too hard. His dark hair hung in loose waves that brushed his cheekbones, but his eyes — once the clear grey of a brewing storm — had begun to glint with something deeper. Something older.

She had seen that change before, in flashes when he thought she wasn't looking.

"We could still find another way," she whispered, though her hands betrayed her by hovering over the pattern they'd been building for hours.

"There isn't one," he said softly. "Not if I want to keep something of myself. Even if I forget… the memory will hold."

Her chest tightened. "You'll be gone too long."

He hesitated. "I'll come back. And I'll remember you."

She shook her head, eyes glassy. "I don't want to be just a shadow in someone else's mind."

"You won't be," he said, leaning forward. His voice was steady, but the flicker in his eyes told her how hard he was fighting to believe it himself. "You'll be the one thing the fire can't burn away."

The spell they'd chosen was older than the Archive itself. A binding of self, soul, and memory — stitched into flame-thread, sealed by intent, name, and love. Forbidden. The kind of magic only a geode could contain without shattering. And even this one, nearly as old as Ysolde's cottage, was already cracking.

Eira's fingers shook as she reached for the next loop — from fear, yes, but also from the weight of what they were about to do.

Her copper-brown hair slid forward, and she pushed it behind her ear without thinking.

Caelen's breath caught. Just beneath her hairline, an ash-grey loop of thread shimmered faintly, pulsing like a forgotten rune. He knew it instantly, though he had no right to. A sigil that saw truth instead of memory. Rare. Dangerous. Impossible.

He said nothing.

Not about the forbidden scroll he'd once seen in the capital that bore the same mark.
Not about what it might mean for her magic.
Not about how, if the council knew, they would never let her go.

Instead, he watched her. Quietly. Reverently.

Her hands steadied. Her green eyes locked on the final shape, looping the thread into the sunmark they had drawn in the snow two nights ago — their vow not to forget.

"If you forget me," she said, voice breaking, "how will I find you again?"

He smiled, soft and pained. "I'll be there, somewhere in the fire." His hand lifted, the backs of his fingers brushing her cheek in a touch that lingered.

"If I forget you, remind me gently."
"If I try to harm you—"
"Run," she whispered.
"And if I beg you to kill me—?"
Her chin trembled. "No. I'll find another way."

His eyes flared gold — not the gold of candlelight, but of molten metal — for just a breath. The dragon already pressing at the edges.

She pulled the final stitch.

The spell ignited, a low roar filling the room as the geode blazed from within. The memory shimmered in the stone, bright and alive — and beneath it, Eira felt something unspoken. The fear they wouldn't voice. The love they had barely dared name.

Caelen's breath hitched. His shoulders seemed broader now, the air around him hotter. For a heartbeat, she saw the ghost of wings.

"Eira," he murmured, and she knew — *this might be the last time he says my name with memory behind it.*

Then the dragon took him.

By morning, he would be gone to the capital.
It would be years before she saw him again.
Not until the Archive.
Not until the great black dragon opened his eyes…
and did not know her name.

CHAPTER FIVE

THE PRESENT

Eira's shop stood at the edge of the square, tucked behind a candle-maker's stall and shaded by a crooked tree that only bloomed during eclipses — a botanical oddity no one could explain, so they stopped trying.

The sign above her door read:

REPAIR & MENDING — CHARMED AND OTHERWISE
Discretion guaranteed. Payment negotiable.

The "otherwise" got her more customers than she liked to admit.

She left the cottage early, as always — lit the hearth with a flick of finger-flame, brewed a pot of ashroot tea, and laid out her thread in neat rows by spell type: flame, frost, wind, whisper, memory. Each shimmered with its own resonance — threads that sparked when touched, threads that hummed like taut wire, threads that softened into silence when gathered in her palm. Then there were the threads she still didn't quite understand. The gray-silver threads. The ones that didn't hum or spark, but pulsed like something alive.

She told herself the ritual helped her focus.

Truth was, it kept the silence from pressing too close. And with silence came the memories she'd been trying to forge into something useful, or at least distant.

Some days she almost believed she'd succeeded.

Outside, spring rain tapped gently against the shutters. Inside, her magic hummed — quiet and tightly coiled, like a storm waiting for its name.

Eira stitched a glove cursed to summon bees (a prank, the note said), reset the truth-binding on a merchant's ledger pouch, and untangled a tattered shawl that once belonged to a woman who could no longer remember why it mattered.

But as her needle passed through the final thread, the hum of the shop changed.

Just slightly.

Like something waking up.

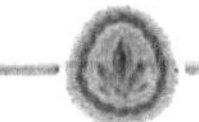

Around midday, Beck showed up - tracking mud, carrying trouble, and grinning like he hadn't just nearly fallen into the river again.

He held out a scarf. "She lives."

Eira took it. "You tried to set fire to a water charm again, didn't you?"

"I didn't try," Beck said, leaning on the counter. "It just happened. Like destiny."

"Destiny shouldn't smell like singed wool and desperation."

She started inspecting the damage while he flopped dramatically onto the bench near the back and began scribbling away in the journal he carried at all times. It seemed like Beck always brought a strange kind of warmth with him - loud, impossible to ignore, and safer than it should've been.

"You should come out with us tonight," he said casually.

Eira raised an eyebrow.

"Anwen and I are going to the North Barrow. Thought you might want to breathe for once."

"I breathe just fine here."

He shrugged. "Suit yourself. But the trees miss you."

She didn't answer. Didn't need to. Beck had known her long enough to stop pushing when she went quiet.

He waited until she handed him the newly repaired scarf, looped it once around his neck, and gave her a two-fingered salute.

"Don't start any fires without me," he called, already halfway out the door.

He paused for just a moment with one hand on the door frame like he was going to add something else. But then he shook his head and let the door close behind him.

Her mother came in an hour later — quiet, wind-chilled, wrapped in her usual dusk-colored shawl woven with threads that caught the light like mist over stone. Ysolde's hair, streaked now with silver, had softened from the deep copper of her youth to a pale ember's glow that was pulled back into a neat bun that spoke more of steadiness than vanity. The fine lines around her eyes deepened as she looked at Eira — not with judgment, but with the kind of careful tenderness that only comes from loving someone too much to ever stop watching.

She never stayed long now that she had retired, but she always brought something. This time it was honey. Thick and dark, with the scent of wild bramble.

"You haven't slept," her mother said gently, her expression folding into that soft, practiced concern Eira had known her whole life. Not a question.

"I've been busy."

"You've been dreaming again."

Eira's hand tensed slightly over her work. Her mother saw it. Said nothing.

Instead, she stepped close - just close enough to rest her fingers near the back of Eira's neck. Over the place where a faint, ash-colored threadloop curved just behind her ear.

"It glowed last night," her mother said softly. "You didn't notice. But I did."

"It's just old magic. It hums sometimes."

Her mother didn't argue. She never did.

"Use the honey for your tea," she said, already turning toward the door. "And if the wind shifts? Lock the wards."

By dusk, the shop was still and dim. The rain just stopped. Drops from the roof still ticked gently against the windows. Her tea had gone cold. The only sound was the whisper of her thread as she worked a stabilizing rune into a fraying traveling cloak– the kind used by couriers and storm runners to ward off unraveling winds and magical interference.

The silence felt earned.

Deserved after a longer than usual day at the shop.

And then-

The bell above the shop door jingled, a high, familiar chime. Eira didn't look up from her worktable. Her hands remained steady and true. She knew the sound of every footstep that passed her threshold, at least those of the regulars, and this one was new.

She brushed a finger across the pale thread she was stitching into the frayed edge of a tattered charm bag. Her hands moved with practiced ease, wrapping memory into thread. The bag's faded lining fluttered once, then settled, its magic smoothed.

The customer cleared his throat.

She looked up just to tell him the shop was closed. But then she froze.

Male. Tall. Wrapped in a travel-worn cloak that didn't match the fine boots beneath it. His eyes bore into her with an intensity that felt both a little unnerving and oddly comforting.

He held out a cloth-wrapped object. She shook her head and motioned for him to set it on the counter instead.

Even through the fabric, the object pulsed — not with heat, but with resonance. Not the kind that whispered memories, but something deeper — a low, shifting hum that made the thread under her skin react like it recognized something it shouldn't. Eira's fingers tingled, her thread-sense prickling like wind against skin. She didn't touch it, not yet. A childhood warning echoed in her memory: "Stone hearts hold echoes of old griefs."

She didn't have to unwrap the bundle to know what it was. The humming energy of the threads was a dead giveaway.

A geode.

Cracked. Glowing faintly. Thread lines etched into the surface like veins.

Not Caelen's. His was sealed safely in a drawer in the cottage workroom, its threads quiet. But this one pulsed like it had stolen its rhythm from a memory she hadn't lived — one that wasn't hers, and yet felt like it might try to *become* hers.

A familiar heat rose behind her left ear.

Not pain - not quite. Just a warning.

The man looked at her with blue eyes like frost after fire and smiled a half crooked smile.

"What do you want me to do with it?" she asked.

"It's broken," he said. "Or maybe just... wrong. I thought you might be able to tell which and fix it."

She glanced briefly out the window, catching a glimpse of Brookwyn settling in for the night. A lantern cart clattered past, firelight catching on damp cobbles and down the road a tired looking laundress haggled for tea at the corner stand.

Eira turned back to the wrapped object. "You want me to fix it?"

He didn't move. "If you can."

She stared at it in silence.

Her hands itched for a needle, the way they always did when a pattern whispered beneath the surface of a thing. But the geode offered no clear thread — only the heavy, humming quiet of something unraveled and waiting.

CHAPTER SIX

She hadn't touched it.
Not yet.

The geode sat between them on the counter, pulsing faintly with something like light — veined with memory or something trying to pass as memory, humming like a thread pulled just a little too tight. Wrong in the way only something familiar-but-not can be.

But she'd felt the resonance the moment it passed through the heavy cedar door of her shop — old wood swollen by generations of rain and wind and lined with iron runes that muffled most enchantments. The magic hadn't so much flared as rippled — quiet and immediate, like a note struck inside her chest. Not a warning. Not quite. But a presence, sharp and sure.

She stood still behind the counter, one hand resting just out of reach of the geode. Watching. Waiting.

"I don't take unsourced magic," she said, her voice even and unmistakably firm — the kind of calm that didn't waver, didn't invite argument, and didn't need to.

The man didn't flinch. "I didn't say it was magic."

Smooth. Polished. Like someone used to being listened to — and not hearing no.

Eira arched a brow, gaze flicking between him and the geode. "You didn't have to."

He offered the faintest smile, but it didn't reach his eyes. "Still, I thought it might interest you."

"Stray magic usually doesn't," she replied, tone cool.

"Even when it hums like this one?" he asked skeptically, almost like he was daring her.

Her fingers twitched at her side. She hadn't touched it, but she felt it. That hum. It was a quiet dissonance, just out of tune — and very much aware of her. The awareness felt strange, memories had never shown awareness of her before.

She finally let her eyes settle back on the man who'd brought it.

He was tall — that much she'd seen right away. Built for distance more than strength, lean and long-limbed, but with a posture that said he didn't rattle easily.

His coat, open to the cold, was stitched at the shoulders with mismatched thread — hand-mended, but recently. The boots below were almost too fine, polished clean of road dust. A contradiction. Like the man himself.

His hair was dark like coal dust in candlelight and wind-tossed, with one stubborn lock falling toward his brow. The kind that would always slip loose no matter how tightly it was bound.

His skin was warm-gold — like late honey, like hearth light — but it was his stillness she felt more than anything. The kind of stillness that wasn't passive, but *listening.*

And his eyes — frosty blue with specks of gold so subtle that she hadn't noticed them at first glance. Those eyes held a steadiness that felt too familiar. Like she was a thread he already knew how to pull.

She hated that she noticed all of it and found the overall package quite appealing.

"You didn't bring this in by accident," she said. "You knew it would resonate."

"I suspected," he replied, voice even. "I've seen magic misbehave before — but not like this."

Eira narrowed her eyes, fingers still resting near the geode but not on it. "Misbehave?"

He didn't answer right away. Just looked down at the stone, his brows drawn slightly as if listening for something.

"It hums when I touch it," he said at last. "Most stones do not. It's not loud, but… deliberate."

"And yet you thought bringing it to a stranger was the best idea?" she asked with a bit of challenge in her tone.

His mouth quirked. Not quite a smile — more like the memory of one. He lifted his gaze back to hers, steady and unreadable, "Let's just say you have a reputation and what I've heard about your work was hard to forget."

Her guard edged higher. "From who?"

"No one you'd know. Just travelers. Traders. People who've passed through."

She didn't move. "And what did they say?"

"That you see things others don't. That your repairs last. That the magic doesn't just behave — it heals."

Eira snorted, a low sound in her throat. "People say a lot of things. Doesn't make it true"

He didn't react. Just watched her like he was trying to decide if she was bluffing — or protecting something worth bluffing for.

"They're not wrong," he said after a pause. "I've seen a lot of threadwork and even other geodecraft. None of it hums like this."

Eira's throat tightened.
She hadn't heard that word — geodecraft — in years.

"I don't do that anymore."

He tilted his head. "Then why does it hum for you?"

The pulse behind her ear flared again. Just once. Just enough. She didn't know.
It didn't feel like memory, not really. More like something buried — a truth twisted beneath layers, trying to rise.

She reached out — not to touch the geode, but to slide it back toward him.
"Take it and go."

"Eira—"

Her eyes snapped up, sharp and unyielding.
"Don't mistake a name for knowing me."

He paused. Studied her. Then, as though conceding the point, he inclined his head.
"Kael," he said. "Since you've been wondering."

And then — infuriatingly — smiled.
"I'll be back," he said simply, reclaiming the geode and wrapping it with the same care one might give an heirloom. "You'll change your mind."

The door chime jingled behind him as he stepped out into the gray light, jangling once like a curse she hadn't cast.

Eira stood perfectly still.
The echo of the geode's hum lingered in the air, a memory not yet gone.
And beneath it, buried deep, the quiet pull of something she didn't want to name.

That night, the North Barrow was slick with rain and half-melted fog. It clung to the air in pale ribbons, rising from the forest floor like breath and catching the glow of lanterns strung haphazardly between crooked posts and woven bramble arches. Smoke from the fire pits tangled with the mist, carrying the scent of woodsmoke, wet earth, and sweetbread.

Folk gathered in loose knots near the flames, trading stories, songs, roasted chestnuts, and rumors.

Eira stood at the edge, half in shadow, scanning the crowd for familiar faces and wishing she'd stayed home.

The place was loud. Not in sound — in feeling. The threads of magic, memory, and emotion pressed in from every side, buzzing like a swarm just beneath her skin. Too many people. Too many lives brushing against hers. She took a step back, preparing to turn around and leave.

A hand found her elbow. Soft. Familiar.

Anwen.

The moment she saw her, Eira felt anchored — more herself. Anwen was always the quiet to her storm.
"You came," Anwen said, not as judgment — just quiet surprise wrapped in warmth.

"Of course she came," Beck cut in as he materialized beside them, juggling two mugs and an impish grin. "Threadmage never misses the good gossip."

"She hates the gossip," Anwen added.

"Exactly. She comes to scowl at it from a distance. It's part of her charm." He held out a mug with a theatrical bow. "Hot cider and bad decisions, freshly acquired."

"Only one of those is appealing," Eira said dryly, but her fingers curled around the warm mug anyway. The spiced cider's steam curled against her chilled face, and she took a sip just to feel the heat spread through her chest.

Beck laughed — a low, familiar rumble that pulled her in like gravity. She followed them toward one of the smaller fire pits tucked just far enough from the music to hear themselves think. The music itself was a slow, lilting tune on fiddle and drum, its beat softened by the fog.

A mossy log served as their usual perch, damp but familiar. When she sat, the moisture seeped through her skirts, grounding her in the here and now. Someone had carved initials into the bark since they'd last been there. Beck squinted at them.

"R.T. loves K.B.," he muttered. "They'll last three weeks at best."

"Two," Anwen said without missing a beat.

Eira raised a brow. "You're both wildly optimistic."

Beck held up a hand like a scholar presenting a scroll. "My list of doomed romances in Brookwyn is very well-researched. I have names, dates, and one dramatic poem about that goat farmer's nephew."

Eira smiled in spite of herself. Around other people, the threads buzzed too loud. Here, with Beck and Anwen, they settled. Wove familiar patterns. This — this was the closest thing to quiet she ever got when out in public.

"So," Beck said, leaning back on one elbow. "What's got your stitches in a twist?"

Eira hesitated.
She hadn't meant to bring it up — hadn't even meant to stay long. But the encounter had lodged itself under her skin, quiet and persistent. She couldn't stop turning it over in her mind, like a thread snagged on something sharp.

And here, with Beck's teasing and Anwen's steady presence, the words found their way out before she could stop them.

She told them. Not everything, but enough. About the man who'd arrived after hours. The geode he carried. The way it hummed.

She didn't mention how it reminded her of Caelen. Or how unsettlingly handsome the stranger was. Or how sure he'd been that she would help.

She expected questions right away.

Instead, silence stretched out across the firelight.
Beck no longer looked amused. He stared into the flames like they held a map he couldn't quite read. Anwen's jaw had gone taut.

"You think it's connected to your past," Beck said at last. "I mean… a geode like that can't just be a coincidence, right?"

"I don't know," she said. "But it felt... too close."

Anwen nodded, eyes still on the firelight. "Feels like it's not a coincidence."

"That's what I'm afraid of," Eira said softly.

None of them spoke for a while after that. The fire cracked and hissed as resin pockets burst. The mist crept closer, curling around their boots and rising up their shins like an uninvited guest.

But the threads between them held her steady.

CHAPTER SEVEN

Eira had hoped that talking to Beck and Anwen about the handsome stranger would settle her thoughts. Not even Beck's dramatic reading of his latest "Spy Suspects of Brookwyn" list had distracted her — despite the fact that she was ranked third, just below the suspicious baker who always wore gloves. Her mind kept returning to the unsettling man with the troubling geode.

The stranger's face lingered behind her eyes - that overconfident smile, the smooth way he said you'll change your mind like it was a prophecy, not a guess. The way the geode hummed for her.

She'd fallen asleep early, curled on her side, the thread still looped through a half-finished stitch ring on her finger.

And now—

The dream crept in quietly, like thread slipping through a loose seam.

Eira stood in her workroom—but it wasn't quite right. The edges were too soft, the lantern light too gold. Threads floated in the air, weightless and slow, as if caught in a breeze she couldn't feel. Her fingers itched for a needle, but her hands were empty.

Across the room, he leaned in the doorway. Kael. Shirt undone at the throat. His eyes shimmered like dark glass catching firelight.

"You dream of me often?" he asked, voice low and velvet-smooth.

She opened her mouth to deny it— but the threads hanging in the air twisted suddenly, pulling toward him. Her breath hitched. He stepped closer, and the temperature changed. Warmer. Brighter. His hand brushed hers, and the scent of smoke and wild honey bloomed around them.

His touch wasn't urgent. It was inevitable.

"You feel it too," he said, quiet but certain.

Before she could answer—

A crack split the room like breaking glass.

She turned—and the light shifted. The door was gone. The shelves had warped. And in the far corner stood Caelen. Tall. Still. Shadowed.

His form flickered like the last breath of a flame, but his gaze burned steady. Threads stirred in the air, drawn to him in quiet recognition. He didn't speak with words—

But she felt him: "You were the reason I stepped into the flame."

Kael turned sharply. "He's not real," he said, voice suddenly brittle.

But her magic reached anyway—unbidden, sure. A single thread looped from her heart toward the shadow.

She didn't choose it. It had already chosen her.

The light flared—white and sharp -- she awoke with a start, the names of both men a tangle on her tongue.

Her hands were shaking. Her mouth dry. The stitch ring around her finger had snapped clean through.

The hearth had burned low. Her breath came shallow and fast, like her lungs were unsure what to hold onto. It wasn't fear, exactly—
It was recognition.

Not of Kael. Not fully. Not even of Caelen. But of something older, deeper, threaded through her magic in a way she didn't understand.

That line—**You were the reason I stepped into the flame.** Had it come from Caelen? From memory? From something buried in her?

She rose without thinking, feet bare on the cold stone floor, and reached for her notebook. Her fingers moved faster than her thoughts, scrawling:

geode markings — humming — resonance
Stepped into the flame - what does this mean?
choice vs magic — does magic choose?

She paused, pen hovering over the page. Why was this man she had just met invading her dreams like she should care about him?

She needed answers.

The back room smelled of paper and time. The kind of dust that settled in places you meant to leave undisturbed. She lit a single candle, pulled down a leather-bound tome, and turned the pages with the quiet hesitation of someone opening a door they had closed for a reason.

Symbols. Stitch patterns. Spellwork diagrams. And in the margins, Caelen's handwriting — slanted, sharp, familiar enough to twist something in her chest.

Threadmancy relies on resonance, she read. *Emotion first. Memory second. Intention third.*

She whispered it aloud, as if the words could steady her. They didn't. They pressed.

Her eyes skimmed downward:

"Magic doesn't begin with will. It begins with feeling. Resonance is not about force — it's about invitation. Thread answers to the emotion it recognizes."

Her breath caught. Emotion first. That's why her magic had reached out in the dream. It hadn't been choice — it had been recognition.

She turned the pages faster now, breath quickening. A sketch caught her eye — a geode split down the center, threaded like veins through crystal. Labels marked the strands:

Binding-thread

Memory-glow

Flame-thread (volatile)

Anchor-stitch (resonance key)

One word circled in faded ink: Revenai

No translation. No margin notes. But there was something about the way it was marked—careful, deliberate.

She checked the page again, scanning for clues.

Threadwork notations nearby, partially smudged. A reference to "resonance pairing."

Revenai.

She whispered it, feeling the pull of something old. Maybe a command. Maybe a name.

She didn't know what it meant—yet.

But she had a feeling it wasn't written there by accident.

She traced the ink, and her fingers tingled faintly — not magic exactly, but awareness. Her thread-sense stirring.

Another note:

"Some threads carry more than power. They carry intent. These are the most dangerous. And the most honest."

She sat back slightly, heart still unsteady. Kael in her dreams. Caelen's voice in her head. A thread she didn't choose, reaching toward something half-remembered.

"What are you trying to tell me?" she whispered to the page. "What am I supposed to remember?"

The candle flickered. A thread curled loose from the spine of the book, weightless and silver.

She watched it twist once in the air—then vanish.

It was why geodes mattered. They didn't just contain magic - they responded to it. Resonated with intent. Anchored it. Threads could live inside them like roots in stone.

She found a sketch - one that looked too much like the stranger's stone. Tri-cut facets, vein-glow scoring, a ripple effect in the memory weave.

She traced the shape with her fingertip.

And suddenly-

Caelen's laugh echoed in her head. Not real. Not magic. Just memory.

"You always overthink your loops," he'd said once, showing her how to soften a tension knot. "Magic listens better when you don't shout."

Her breath caught.

She hadn't thought of that day in years.

The candle flickered. A breeze?

No - footsteps.

The candle flickered again. Not from magic this time.
The footsteps stopped outside the door, followed by the soft clink of a teacup.

Her mother didn't knock. She never did in this room.

"You're up early," she said, voice hushed like she didn't want to wake the books. She nudged the door open with one elbow, a steaming cup in her hand. "I figured you might be."

Eira blinked at her, still caught between the dream's residue and the scratch of Caelen's handwriting. "You made tea?"

"I always make tea." Her mother gave a half-smile and set the cup beside the book. "You're just rarely up to catch it."

Eira wrapped her hands around the mug, letting the heat steady her fingers and the fragrant herbal scent fill her nose. "Thanks."

Her mother's gaze swept the open tome. "Is that... our old notes?"

Eira nodded. "I had a dream. Not like usual. It felt—" She hesitated. "It felt like more."

Her mother's eyes flicked to the circled word. "Revenai," she murmured.

"You know it?"

"Not well." She lowered herself into the chair beside Eira, fingers brushing the faded ink as though it might smudge again. "It's an old word. Older than most of what we studied. Caelen and I had only begun digging into its root before he left."

Eira leaned closer. "What does it mean?"

"It translates, roughly, as 'awakening.' A spell meant to stir what lies dormant. But…" her mother's brow furrowed. "It's ancient magic. Threads that wake can't always be put back to sleep. Best to tread carefully.

Eira whispered the word again, softer this time. Revenai. The syllables felt heavier now.

"Curiosity is good," her mother said gently, "but don't use it lightly. Even the kindest threads can tangle if pulled too hard."

Her mother didn't press. She just moved to the nearby shelf and pulled down a folded shawl. "You get that look when you're holding something heavy. I figured you'd end up in here."

"Didn't mean to wake the house," Eira murmured.

"You didn't. I was up." A pause. "Wind's wrong this morning. Gave me a bad feeling."

Eira glanced down at the book. "I think Caelen's geode is reacting. My magic reached for something in the dream... without me choosing to."

Her mother's eyes sharpened slightly, though her hands stayed calm. "That can happen. Especially with unfinished threads."

"You mean Caelen."

"I mean anything that's still open." She stepped closer, smoothing a hand lightly over Eira's hair — a habit from childhood she hadn't quite broken. "Whatever it was, you don't have to sort the whole world before breakfast."

"Tell that to my notebook."

That earned a quiet huff of amusement. "Bring your tea. Come tell me what work you have planned for the shop today. You can think and eat at the same time."

Eira hesitated — still half tangled in magic and memory — then stood and followed her mother down the narrow hall and into the kitchen.

The early light spilled through the curtains and across the roughhewn counter in pale stripes. A pan was already warming on the woodburning stove, and the smell of herbs lingered faintly from last night's stew.

Her mother moved with the rhythm of someone who'd made the same breakfast a hundred times. "So," she said, cracking two eggs into a bowl without looking up, "what's on the agenda for your mysterious back room today? Any more skirts that turn inside out when the charm wears off?"

"Not if I can help it," Eira muttered, sliding into a chair and sipping her fragrant tea. "Mostly just repairs. That tea kettle is finally coming in — the one that sings off-key?"

"The one that screams in F sharp. Simply delightful. We fixed a similar problem a few years back." Her mother snorted softly and whisked the eggs. "And the traveling cloak? The one with the security lining stitched wrong?"

"Redid the border last night. But I want to rework the invisibility trigger — it keeps going off when the wearer laughs."

"Good thing none of our customers have a sense of humor." Her mother replied winking at her.

Eira laughed, and it surprised her. Her mother smiled but didn't look over as she slid the eggs into the hot pan.

"And the geode?" she asked gently.

"Still humming." Eira paused. "Still... calling. I don't know what it wants."

"You don't always have to know right away. Sometimes listening is enough."

Silence settled for a breath or two as the pan hissed and the first whiff of breakfast filled the air.

"You want toast or the last biscuit?"

Eira blinked. "You saved the biscuit?"

"Don't make it weird. I was tired last night."

"You never save biscuits."

"Well. Maybe I'm growing as a person."

Eira smiled, then looked down at her tea. "Thanks, Mum."

"Eat your breakfast before it goes cold," her mother said, sliding the plate across the well-worn table. "And try not to accidentally unravel the fabric of the world today, would you?"

"No promises."

She spent the rest of the day in the shop, but her mind stayed elsewhere.
Repairs blurred together. A mending stitch unraveled twice before she realized she'd looped it backward. A tea kettle blinked at her in confusion when its charm reset without warning.

She blamed the dream. Or the geode. Or maybe both.

By late afternoon, she had given up on pretending to be productive. The drawer back at the cottage stayed locked — but she kept feeling its weight in her thoughts, as if the geode inside were humming from a distance. It was the one holding Caelen's memories, sealed away seven years before.

She didn't touch it again. She didn't need to.

Something in her chest had already begun to vibrate with its pull — not constant, but waiting. Like breath held between beats. Like it had in the first few months after the sealing spell. Like the grief of him leaving.

When the sun dipped low and the last customer left, she tidied the workbench with slow, deliberate motions. She gathered stray threads into a glass jar, wiped dust from the edges of her charms, turned the wooden sign to Closed. The shop exhaled with her — magic in the walls softening to a faint thrum, the air cooling as if the day itself were pulling away.

She set the kettle on to boil, not because she wanted tea, but because the whistle would keep her company. Outside, clouds bruised purple at the edges. Two young children tossed a ball back and forth in the grass across the road. Inside, she sat on the stool behind the counter, fingers tracing idle patterns into the wood.

For the first time in a long while, she didn't know what she was waiting for.
Only that she was.

The bell above the shop door rang once.

He stood there — same calm posture, same confident air. Kael. The geode, wrapped in silk, rested in his palm. He stepped forward and placed it carefully on the counter.

"I told you I'd be back."

She didn't answer. Not with words.

She reached out — not with anger, not with fear, but with purpose. With resignation.
And touched the rough gray stone.

CHAPTER EIGHT

Just as Eira's hand made contact with the geode, the world shivered.
So did Kael.

His breath hitched — just once — but it was enough for her to notice.

He stared at the geode like it had whispered something only he could hear.

"You felt that too," she said quietly.

He didn't answer at first. Just watched the silk shift slightly under the stone, as if it had moved on its own.

Finally: "That's new."

Eira's hand hovered just above the geode now. "What is it?"

Kael shook his head once, almost imperceptibly. "It's been reacting differently lately. Humming, sometimes. Pulling at me." He looked up. "I thought it was just me. Until you touched it."

"Do you know why it's changing?"

His mouth pressed into a line. "No," he said.
But the pause before the word said otherwise.

He took a slow breath, like measuring what he was willing to reveal. "The magic feels... less anchored. Like something's slipping."

Eira blinked. "Slipping?"

Kael met her gaze for the first time, steady and unreadable. "Whatever's holding the world together... it's not holding as tightly as it used to."

A silence bloomed between them — not awkward, but vast.

Then Eira's fingers brushed the geode once more, the world exhaled.

Not just a shimmer - not a flicker.

A *rupture.*

She staggered backward, heart hammering, vision swimming with light. The stone pulsed like it had a heartbeat, casting a glow that wrapped around her fingers in threads of gold and violet.

Memory-threads.

Her knees hit the wooden floorboards. For a breathless instant, she wasn't in her shop anymore.

She was *inside* something.

A forest. A thread pulled taut through trees that looked like the ones in her dream — but different. Realer. Darker.

A scream rose in the distance — familiar, awful.

Her voice. Not now. Not the woman she was.
The girl she had been.

She reached out — her hands were younger. Her thread ring glowed. A fire lit the horizon. Caelen's voice, faint but sharp, whispered: "Don't forget who you are, Eira. Don't forget—"

She gasped and yanked her hand back from the stone. The vision shattered in a blink — light splintering into nothing. The forest dissolved, leaving only the heavy stillness of her shop.

The dull, honeyed glow of the lanterns swam back into focus. Rain ticked against the warped glass of the window, a slow, deliberate rhythm. The familiar scent of beeswax and steeped ashroot tea wrapped around her like an old blanket, grounding her in the now. On the counter, the geode lay motionless, its inner light snuffed to a cold, unremarkable shell.

Magic shattered inside her like a clay bowl dropped from a height — sharp, silent, irretrievable.

Eira sagged against the worn floorboards, breath shallow and ragged. Her fingertips still tingled where they'd grazed the stone, the echo of power threading along her skin in faint silver shimmer before fading back into her pulse.

Kael knelt beside her, his movements deliberate, as though sudden motion might cause her to break. He didn't speak right away.

"That was… more than I expected," he said at last, his voice low and even. He offered her his own.

She ignored it, forcing herself upright on her own. "I told you it was dangerous," she muttered.

He didn't argue.

He shifted, the crate beneath him creaking under his weight as he sat on its edge. The lanternlight caught in the dark planes of his face, softening nothing. He kept his distance, but not far enough to disappear — a space that felt intentional.

It wasn't just caution. It was watchfulness.

"That geode… it's part of something bigger," he said, unwrapping it with the careful precision of someone handling an unpinned trap. "There are others. I found this one in the ruins near Fellmere."

Her eyes narrowed. "No one goes to Fellmere."

"I do," he said simply. "Or did. For answers."

"And?"

"I think there's something stirring. And that we're both being watched."

"By who."

The air in the shop thinned. Silence stretched between them like a thread pulled so tight it might snap with a single breath.

He didn't smirk this time. "The council," he admitted finally.

She digested that and didn't reply. He waited.

And somehow, that was worse — like he already knew what she was capable of and was only waiting for her to decide if she'd prove him right.

"I'll do what I can," she said finally. realizing that the past wasn't going to stay in the past no matter how much she tried to forget.

Later, after he left, Eira sat on the workshop floor with the geode resting in her lap like a burden too long ignored. Her hands still trembled. The ache in her chest hadn't faded.

The vision hadn't just been a memory.

It had been Caelen inside of Kael's geode, where it shouldn't be.

She stood slowly, joints stiff, and crossed to the washbasin in the corner. The splash of cold water against her face hit like a slap — grounding her, but not soothing.

She braced her hands on either side of the sink and stared into the mirror above it. Her reflection stared back — pale, hollow-eyed, thread scars glowing faintly under the skin of her wrists.

"You're fine," she whispered.

But she wasn't.

She dried her face with a towel and moved through her shop like a ghost, touching familiar things without really feeling them. Her fingers ran over thread spools, over the stone counter, over the basket where Caelen had once left a note folded with the kind of precision that meant he'd rewritten it three times.

She should have burned that note. But it was still in her journal, tucked between pages like a pressed leaf.

She drew her cloak tighter and lit a small candle, needing something alive in the quiet.

Outside, the wind was picking up — not stormy, just unsettled. It scraped across the shutters like fingers looking for a way in.

The geode still sat on the table. Quiet. Innocent.

Eira didn't trust it.

But she didn't trust her heart, either.

She crossed the room one last time and reached for the cloth to cover the geode. Her hand hovered.

It didn't glow. Didn't hum.

But it didn't need to.

She felt it anyway — the pull.

A memory half-remembered. A name barely spoken.

Caelen.

And beneath it, quieter still:

Kael.

She wrapped the stone, tucked it into the warded drawer, and turned the key. Her fingers lingered on the lock as if expecting it to vanish.

She blew out the candle and left the room in darkness.

She entered her bedroom and did her nightly rituals. Removing her skirt and top and hanging them on the hook behind her door and slipping into a worn nightdress. Washing her face with the green tea soap Anwen had gifted her on her last birthday, more out of habit than need. She laid down on her soft, single bed and slid under the handmade quilt. But she couldn't sleep.

Because when she closed her eyes, she saw him — not Kael, not the stranger.

Caelen.

Smiling like he still remembered.

And whispering like he knew she still did too even with seven years standing between them.

Somewhere deep in the Archive's sealed halls, a dragon stirred.

And the walls shook.

CHAPTER NINE

Sunlight in Brookwyn was a rare, golden coin. Most days it hid behind the mist that crept in from the coast, softening the stone streets and cloaking the crooked gables. But this morning the mist had burned away, leaving the market square bright and warm enough that shutters hung open and laundry flapped from second-story windows.

The square itself was ringed with squat, weather-dark buildings, their stone walls patched in places where frost had worked them loose over the years. Market stalls leaned against the edges like friendly gossipers, their canopies of dyed linen shifting in the breeze.

Eira wove through the early crowd, skirts brushing damp cobblestones. She favored plain wool in shades that hid dirt and ink alike, a habit of her trade, and she blended easily among the farmers in coarse homespun, the fishwives in rolled-up sleeves, and the hawkers with their mismatched waistcoats and bright sashes.

The air carried a lively braid of smells: fresh bread from the baker's stone oven, damp wool from a shepherd's cart, and rosemary crushed underfoot. Somewhere, a pair of fiddles tried to outplay the chatter.

She told herself she came for supplies, but truthfully, she came for the news. Ordinarily she despised gossip, but memories of the council watching years before had her searching for the threads of truth that came woven inside of the stories. The traveling vendors were often the best source of what was happening around the country, and something sure seemed to be happening.

Today, it was impossible to miss. The voices around her pulled tight like a loom strung for weaving, every conversation a different-colored thread.

"...three nights in a row, they've kept the council hall lit past midnight—"
"...about time someone challenged their overreach—"
"...challenged? You mean undermined! That opposition group are nothing but a cult of troublemakers—"

Eira slowed near a table of clay lamps. The seller, a sharp-faced woman with sleeves rolled high, was speaking in low, clipped tones.

"You'll see—they're dangerous. Stirring people up just when we need to be united. The council's the only thing holding the country together."

Her customer lifted a lamp to the sunlight, squinting at its carved spirals. "Or holding it back. They may be zealots, but perhaps they're the only ones willing to do what's needed. If the council's hiding something, don't we have the right to know?"

The word *zealot* seemed to stick to the air, gathering a few nods and more than one scowl.

A few stalls down, a man cursed as the twine on his crate snapped. "Jona, give me a binding twist, would you?"

Jona, a thin boy in a green tunic, laughed. "You know I've got no coil magic. Ask Marli—her knots will hold against a gale."

Marli, two stalls over, didn't look up from her pile of radishes. "Not until I'm paid for the last three. My threads don't run free."

The man grumbled and tried again, muttering about "magic-snobs." The insult was unusual — most folk in the country didn't treat magic as a mark of status one way or the other.

Eira drifted on, passing a cheese monger's stall where the conversation was sharper still:
"...heard they sent for more ward-mages—"
"...means the council's serious about keeping us safe—"
"...means they're scared of losing control, more like—"

She left the square with her basket no heavier than when she'd arrived, but her mind weighted with the knot of rumors, politics, and small-town grudges that seemed to be pulling tighter with each passing week.

The bell over the haberdasher's door gave a cheerful jingle as Eira stepped inside, following the faint, honeyed scent of beeswax polish and the warm, slightly dusty fragrance of cloth bolts stacked in tidy towers. The light through the front window fell in buttery stripes across the counter, catching the gleam of glass jars filled with buttons, clasps, and thimbles. She hadn't planned to stop, but a voice she recognized made her pause.

"…I only need a few lengths of thread," Kael was saying, his tone polite but stretched taut like a fraying cord.

From behind the counter, Madra—Brookwyn's most exuberant shopkeeper—was already lining up an entire parade of spools in vivid jewel tones, her bangles chiming like tiny bells with every movement. "Nonsense, dear. You'll want at least three colors, and this here—feel that—this is spunlight, soft as morning mist and strong as a ship's mooring. Worth every copper."

Kael looked down at the shimmering thread as though it might bite him. "I don't—"

Madra had already turned to fetch more, her crimson skirts swishing and the air around her humming with the certainty of someone who always won the sale.

Eira's lips curved despite herself. She'd seen that look on plenty of travelers' faces—overwhelmed and outmaneuvered before they even knew the rules.

Stepping forward, she leaned a casual elbow on the scarred wooden counter. "Madra, if you load him down with half your stock, he'll be back before the week's out asking how to use it."

The shopkeeper straightened with mock indignation. "And what's wrong with that?"

"Only that you'll scare him off before he realizes Brookwyn's worth lingering in," Eira said, her tone light and teasing.

That earned a quick, surprised chuckle from Kael, as though he hadn't expected her to come to his defense.

Madra gave an exaggerated sigh and began putting away the excess, the bangles at her wrists clinking in playful protest. "Fine, fine. But don't say I didn't offer the best."

When they stepped back into the rare mid-morning sunshine, Kael shifted the small paper parcel in his hands. The air was fresh with the mingled scents of baking bread from the nearby bakery and the faint tang of the sea drifting in from beyond the fields. "You didn't have to do that."

"I know," Eira said, glancing at him sidelong. "But you looked like you might agree to buy a loom if she brought one out."

His mouth curved faintly. "I might have. If only to escape."

She found herself smiling back, a small concession she didn't bother to hide. "Then it's a good thing I came along when I did."

They strolled down the cobblestone lane together, stepping around shallow puddles from the night's mist and pausing once to let a hay cart creak and rumble past. The air was warm for once, the pale stone buildings catching the sun and casting long, soft-edged shadows.

"It's nice to see you out of the shop," Kael said after a moment. "I was beginning to wonder if you ever left it."

"I do," she replied with faint amusement. "The sun just has to put in a proper appearance first."

He tilted his face toward the sky, squinting. "Then I should count myself lucky that you were out and came to my rescue."

She pretended to study him from the corner of her eye. "Careful, Kael. That almost sounded like a compliment."

"It was," he said simply.

Her step faltered for just an instant before she covered it with a small shrug. "Well, don't get used to it. I'm meeting friends."

"And I should make for the library," he said. "I've been meaning to see if it's as charming as the rest of the town."

They paused at a fork in the lane where one road wound toward the village green and the other toward the bustling square.

"Enjoy your rare day out," he said.

"And you enjoy your dusty shelves," she replied, but her tone was light, almost playful.

He dipped his head in farewell, and they went their separate ways—each carrying, perhaps without realizing it, the faintest trace of a smile.

The pond lay like a sheet of polished glass under the rare, generous sun, it's surface only broken by the lazy ripples of water bugs skating along. Children darted along its edge, skipping stones and daring one another to dip their toes in the still-chilly water. The air smelled faintly of damp earth and cattails, with the occasional whiff of woodsmoke drifting from the chimneys of houses that ringed the far side of town.

Eira had claimed her favorite spot on the grassy bank, knees drawn up, skirts tucked neatly to the side. A light breeze teased strands of hair from her braid. She'd been there only a few minutes before Anwen's voice carried across the water.

"There you are! I thought maybe the pond had swallowed you whole." Beck proclaimed loudly.

Anwen appeared with a picnic basket in hand, her cheeks pink from the walk, a sprig of lavender tucked carelessly into her hair. Beck trailed behind her, balancing a large pie tin on one palm with exaggerated care.

"You know," Beck said, his grin crooked, "if I drop this pie in the pond, you're both going in after it."

"It's your mother's pie," Anwen scolded. "You'd better not drop it at all."

Eira smirked. "It might be worth being wet and cold for your mum's pie. She makes the best pie crust in town—better than the bakery's."

Beck's grin widened. "Finally, someone with taste."

They settled on the grass, unpacking bread rolls, cheese, and slices of berry pie so purple they could stain a person's smile for the rest of the day.

"How'd you manage to beat us here for once," Anwen teased.

"I was at the market finding out the latest gossip and then rescuing someone from a shopkeeper," Eira said, settling herself on the blanket. "There wasn't enough time to head back to the cottage so I headed this way early."

"Rescuing? I bet it was more like meddling," Beck teased, but his grin was warm.

Anwen shook her head. "Ignore him. He's only bitter because I told him he couldn't go swimming until after we ate. I'm not sitting here in wet clothes because someone can't wait ten minutes."

Eira laughed, the easy rhythm of old friendship settling in as comfortably as the sun on their shoulders.

Beck leaned against a large rock, midway through a story about a council decree that would, according to him, require everyone to wear matching socks on Tuesdays.

"You're making that up," Anwen said with a lighthearted glint in her eyes.

"Prove me wrong," Beck challenged, his grin infuriatingly confident.

Before she could reply, a child's wail carried over the water. Near an old oak a small boy pointed up into its tangled branches. An enchanted toy bird flapped helplessly high above, its charm sputtering with every wingbeat.

Without hesitation, Beck rose, brushing crumbs from his trousers. "On it."

"You don't even know them," Anwen called after him.

"Don't have to," Beck replied, striding off. A moment later, he'd scrambled halfway up the oak, his boots braced against the bark as he freed the fluttering bird.

"Here you go, mate," he said, crouching to offer it back. The boy's tears dried instantly and his mother mouthed a grateful thank-you. Beck ruffled the boy's hair and gave a quick nod to the mother before returning to sitt by the rock.

"Show-off," Anwen muttered, but there was affection in it and her gaze stayed on him for a heartbeat longer than necessary. Eira noticed, but kept it to herself.

They passed the remainder of the afternoon sprawled out in the grass, the day's warmth sinking into their bones. The pond lapped gently at the shore, and for a little while, the world felt small and safe.

They lingered by the pond as the sun sank low, the water catching streaks of molten orange and rose-gold. Eira was midway through a teasing remark about Beck's "matching socks" decree when a ripple split the mirrored surface.

It wasn't wind. The air remained still, heavy with the warm scent of grass and faint woodsmoke, while the disturbance spread in widening rings. Magic often moved like that—quiet, deliberate—when it was listening for something.

Near the far bank, a cluster of water lilies burst into bloom all at once. The petals unfurled too quickly, shivering as if an unseen current passed through them.

Eira's thread-sense prickled sharp against her skin. She crouched at the water's edge, slipping her fingers into a simple stabilizing loop, coaxing the wild charm back into balance. The frantic flutter of petals eased, their movement slowing until they lay still on the water's glassy skin. But beneath that calm, she felt it—a faint, discordant hum. Wrong, like a note played just off-key.

She reached for it, trying to follow the thread, but it slipped away before she could catch hold.

When she straightened, Beck and Anwen were watching her with quiet expectation. She forced a smile.
"Just a hiccup," she said, dusting her hands on her skirts.

But as they turned toward the path home, the last light fading behind them, the wrongness lingered—an echo she couldn't shake.

CHAPTER TEN

The door to Anwen's family apothecary stuck just a bit, the way it always did when it rained. Eira leaned into it with a practiced shoulder nudge, and the frame gave with a soft groan. Inside, the scent of rosemary and clove wrapped around her like a familiar shawl. The shop had always smelled like memory - warm herbs, dry scrolls, ink, and sun-warmed glass.

Eira stepped inside, brushing her fingers along the worn oak counter - a ritual more than a need. Shelves towered around her, heavy with labeled jars and dried bundles of flora - some magical, most just honest plants with honest uses. In the corner, a small loom clicked steadily, powered by a delicate threadwork charm that had been running quietly since Anwen set it years ago.

From behind it, Anwen looked up. Her blue eyes caught the light and sparkled when she smiled - not with teeth, but with the kind of warmth that needed no explaining.

"You came early," she said, moving to the counter.

"I figured I'd beat the storm," Eira said, unwinding her scarf and shaking the mist from her sleeves. Her cheeks were pink from the cold, and a lock of copper-brown hair clung damply to her temple. "I need more emberroot and silverfloss. I've been working late and am going to need it. I'd also like to look through your fathers old scrolls if that's okay.."

Anwen rose from her stool with a quiet nod, moving between shelves in that graceful, quiet way she always had. Her braid - almost white, like sun-bleached flax - swung like a metronome as she walked.

"The usual blend?"

"Add dawnleaf," Eira said, rubbing her thumb along a scar on her palm. "The geode resonance burned through some of my stabilization threads."

That earned a pause.

Anwen didn't turn around, but her hands stopped moving - hovering just above the row of labeled jars.

"You touched it?" Her voice was quiet. Not scolding. Not afraid. Just... aware.

Eira hesitated. "It felt more like it touched me."

Anwen's jaw ticked but she said nothing as she resumed her work, but when she handed over the jar a moment later, her fingers lingered - and her blue eyes searched Eira's for something unspoken.

Eira turned the bottle in her hands, watching the way the amber liquid caught the light.

"How's your father's shoulder?" she asked.

Anwen snorted softly. "Better than his patience. He tried to chop wood again yesterday. Claimed he was 'only testing it.'"

"And the verdict?"

"He got as far as lifting the axe before Mother yelled loud enough to shake the rafters. He's been banished from the shed."

Eira smiled. "Some people never learn."

"You're one to talk," Anwen said lightly, casting her a look. "I heard about your late-night geode incident. Beck said you nearly fried your hands again."

"I didn't *fry* anything," Eira muttered.

"That's not how Beck tells it."

"Beck's version always includes unnecessary drama and snack metaphors."

They both laughed, the sound bright in the quiet shop. It lingered a moment, softened the edges.

Eira hesitated, then leaned her elbow on the counter, studying her friend's face. "Can I ask you something?"

"Of course."

"You've been giving Beck that look," she said, a little too casually. "The one people give someone when they think no one's watching."

Anwen's eyes widened. "What look?"

"The look," Eira said, grinning. "The one with the soft eyes and the tiny smile and the I-might-love-you-but-I'd-rather-die-than-say-it-out-loud energy."

Anwen flushed and turned away, busying herself with the herb jars. "That obvious?"

"Only to someone who knows you."

A long pause. Then: "I do," Anwen admitted. "I have feelings for him."

Eira waited.

"But I don't know if it could work," Anwen said softly. "Beck has this way of turning everything into a joke. Like if he laughs first, nothing can hurt him. He's reckless—not just with magic, but with his heart, with time, with everything that matters. Charming, yes. Kind, always. But I live in the real world, Eira. I have responsibilities. I see the way things fall apart when people don't show up, when they don't follow through. And Beck… he dances just outside of all that. Like he's afraid to land too close to anything real. I don't want to become something else he sidesteps when it stops being fun."

"You think he wouldn't show up for the serious parts?"

"I don't know if he knows how," she said softly. "And I don't want to become another thing he turns into a joke when it gets too real."

Eira let the words settle between them for a long moment before speaking. "You're right—he hides behind the laughter. He always has."

She looked up, voice gentler now. "But I've seen the way he looks at you, Anwen. When he thinks no one's watching? It's not a game. There's no smirk, no joke—just... *quiet.* Like you're the one thing in his life that feels real enough to still him."

Anwen didn't turn, but her hands stilled on the jars.

"You should tell him," Eira said gently. "Before the world shifts again."

They were quiet for a beat longer. Then Anwen reached into the drawer and pulled out a small wrapped bundle of dried petals, tied with green string.

"Tea blend. For grounding," Anwen said, her voice light again but her hands still careful. "You'll ignore it, but I'm giving it to you anyway."

Eira took it with a huff of gratitude. "Thanks."

"Now we can be quiet," Anwen said. "Unless you want to hear Beck's theory that threadwitches are just magical puppets controlled by ancient sentient scarves."

Eira snorted. "I would read that book."

"I think he's trying to write it."

A long, companionable silence followed — not heavy, not awkward. Just full. Like a braid woven tight enough to hold, but soft enough to breathe.

They fell into familiar rhythms after that - the kind born not of instruction, but of years side by side. Eira sorted bundles of wax-sealed scrolls by touch, checking for faint enchantment traces, while Anwen crushed dried herbs with the quiet confidence of someone who no longer needed to measure.

The silence between them wasn't empty. It was full - with memory, with trust, with the kind of comfort that made words optional.

"Remember when we tried to dye thistle thread with berry juice and ruined your mother's linens?" Eira said finally, a crooked smile tugging at her mouth.

Anwen's lips twitched. "She still has the stains. Says it's a lesson in impatience."

"She's not wrong."

They didn't laugh out loud, but the warmth sat between them anyway - a thread of connection stitched in long ago that has never come unspooled.

Eira reached for a fresh scroll, her fingers brushing parchment edges softened by time. She was about to speak again when Anwen glanced at her sideways, one pale brow lifted.

"I saw him, you know."

Eira blinked. "Who?"

"The stranger. Yesterday morning." Anwen dropped a pinch of crushed dawnleaf into a small vial like it meant nothing. "Tall. Dark. Brooding. He has that... feral edge. Like a storybook rogue or a cursed prince."

Eira groaned and bumped her shoulder lightly against Anwen's. "You're ridiculous."

"Am I wrong?"

"No," she muttered, feeling her cheeks grow warm.. "But still."

Anwen's eyes sparkled again. "You didn't say he was that handsome."

"I didn't say anything."

"You're saying plenty now." she said with a soft, knowing smile.

The door slammed open.

"Did someone say thread crimes?" Beck called out, entirely too pleased with himself. He pulled out his journal with a flourish. "Crime number one: using glow-in-the-dark thread for stealth spells. Rookie mistake."

His curls were wind-tossed, his scarf misbuttoned, and his grin... dangerous.

Eira rolled her eyes. "We were being nostalgic."

"Ah, nostalgia. Nothing like reliving magical misfires to warm the heart."

He leaned dramatically against the counter, nearly knocking over a display of scented oils.

"Beck," Anwen said dryly, steadying the bottles with one hand and shooting Eira a look that said *this is what I mean* . "Touch nothing."

"I'd never," he said, already reaching for a cinnamon stick.

At that moment, the door creaked open again - a slower, more deliberate entrance this time. An older man stepped in, hunched in a heavy green cloak and dripping from the rain. His brows were knit tightly over deep-set eyes, and he said nothing as he approached the counter.

Anwen straightened. "Good morning, Mr. Yarrow. Your usual?"

The man gave a curt nod, his eyes flicking toward Beck with open disapproval.

Beck shrank half an inch, trying not to look guilty.

Eira raised an eyebrow.

"Wasn't me that transfigured his boots," Beck whispered. "Just... supervised."

As Anwen handed over his parcel, Mr. Yarrow grumbled, "You ought to fix that blasted door. Sticks every time the weather turns."

"We're working on it," Anwen said with practiced patience.

"Hmph."

He dropped a few coins on the counter and muttered something about "the youth these days" before vanishing back into the mist.

The door thunked shut behind him.

Beck let out a low whistle. "That man hasn't smiled since he walked in on the knitting circle calling him a dropped stitch."

Anwen hid a smile and handed him a mug of tea. "Then maybe don't transfigure his footwear next time."

"Lesson learned. Probably." Beck said with his trademark grin.

They settled at the back table, the one worn smooth by years of elbows, mugs, and spellwork planning. Anwen refilled the kettle without asking; Beck peeled off his coat and draped it over the back of his chair like it had personally wronged him.

Steam curled between them as cinnamon tea filled their cups. The scent was grounding, but it couldn’t soften the shift in Beck’s posture. His grin slipped — not gone, but resting. His hands curled around the mug like a shield, though he didn’t drink.

"So," he said at last, "the stranger."

Eira didn't respond at first. Then, quietly: "Kael."

Beck raised a brow. "So he does have a name."

She looked down into her tea using the rim to hide the flush that rose in her cheeks.

"He's still in town," Beck continued, though his tone had softened. "Asking questions. About you."

"I figured," Eira said quietly. The words came out too calm for the storm inside her. Part of her wished he’d just take the geode and disappear. The other part was relieved he hadn’t.

He met her eyes - unusually direct. "Eira, if someone's stirring Archive magic again - really stirring it – we can't just wait for the threads to settle."

She traced the grain of the table with one finger, her brow tight with thoughts she didn't speak.

Anwen said nothing, but her gaze didn't waver. Steady. Present.

Eira felt it - that flicker in her chest. That pull behind her navel.

It wasn't fear. Not quite. But it wasn't peace either.

She didn't nod. Didn't speak. But the decision settled in her like stone.

Tomorrow, she would leave Brookwyn and seek out the leylines. Problems with old magic might need old solutions.

The threads were calling

CHAPTER ELEVEN

The morning air bit sharper outside of Brookwyn's gates. Mist hugged the frost-hardened grasses and swirled around Eira's boots as she walked, the sound of each step softened by dew. The town's stone walls vanished behind the trees, swallowed by the hush of the waking woods.

She adjusted the strap across her chest, the weight of her satchel pressing against her hip – heavier now, packed with her weaving kit, spellbound threads, a weathered map folded six times,and Kael's geode carefully wrapped in protective cloth. It pulsed faintly against her side, like a second heartbeat.

She hadn't told anyone where she was going. Not Anwen. Not even her mother.

It wasn't that she didn't trust them.

It was that she didn't want to hear herself say it out loud. The words would feel too final and she wasn't sure she could, or should, do this. Besides her mother would know anyways, she always seemed to know.

The forest path narrowed the farther she walked. Pines pressed close, their needles dusted white with frost, and the hush grew deeper -- no birdsong, no wind, only the occasional creak of boughs and her own breath.

A twig snapped behind her.

Eira stopped cold.

The silence rushed in around her.

She turned, slowly, scanning the trees. Nothing but trunks and shadow. Her fingers slipped to the pocket where she kept a defense charm, her pulse suddenly louder than the forest.

Probably a fox. Or a deer. Maybe even just your nerves, she told herself.

Still, she didn't put the charm away until she was well past the bend.

The next mile was steeper, climbing into the hills. Mud slicked the stones beneath her boots, and her breath steamed in the morning chill. She was beginning to relax again when a hidden rock caught her boot mid-step and sent her stumbling.

Her hands hit the ground hard.

Mud spattered her skirt. Her knees ached.

She sat back on her heels, shoulders slumping for half a breath as her satchel swung forward, jostling the wrapped geode.

Eira stared down at the ground, scattered with gold and red leaves that cracked beneath her palms, letting herself breathe before trying to rise.

You could go home. Say it was a false thread. Pretend it doesn't matter.

But it did matter. She knew it did.

She wiped her palms on her cloak, rose stiffly, and brushed the moss from her skirt as though brushing away the thoughts about turning back.

Resolve settled into her bones, steady and cold.

She kept walking.

The woods grew quieter as she climbed higher. The trail had long since vanished, replaced by instinct and memory. Years ago, her mother had shown her the path to a weaver's retreat -- a forgotten place once used for meditation, thread alignment, and tapping into leyline flows. It wasn't marked on any map. It didn't need to be.

Eira walked by feel now, not sight—watching for the way trees leaned, for the soft rise of moss and lichen, for pale fungi gathered in hollows, and most importantly, for the occasional glimmer of thread-residue in the air like dust motes caught in sunlight.

By the time she reached the clearing, the sun was high and pale. Light filtered through skeletal branches, casting stitch-like shadows across the mossy floor. In the center, the ruins of the old spinner's cottage slumped in upon themselves, only a single crumbling wall still standing.

She stepped into the glen and exhaled.

It felt thin here because of the leylines -- not empty, exactly, but stretched. Like the veil between memory and reality had frayed just enough to let a whisper through.

She knelt by the flat stone that once served as a focus altar and opened her satchel. The geode emerged slowly, wrapped in layers of enchantment-thread and linen. When she peeled them back, the stone was cool and still -- just as it had been since the stranger left it in her shop.

And yet... it felt awake.

She reached for a prepared strand -- moonwoven thread braided with a sliver of her own memory – and whispered, "Revenai."

The thread sparked.

Magic answered.

A faint blue glow flickered along the strand's length, then jerked taut, pulling north by northeast -- not the direction she'd expected. Not the usual pull of geodes reacting to collective memory sites or archivist traces.

This path was... skewed.

And personal.

She followed.

Down through briar-laced underbrush, across a narrow stream so clear it mirrored her flushed face. The scent of half-decayed leaves filling her nose.

Up a slope marked by frost-scarred birch trees that leaned toward one another like old gossiping women.

As she crested the hill, the thread slackened -- and then stilled completely. There was a small clearing devoid of any living creatures. Not a single bird chirped.

Before her, half-sunk in moss, was a ring of stones. Faint etchings traced their surface – weather-worn but still visible.

A stitch-circle.

Older than anything she'd seen in her research.

She dropped to her knees and brushed a layer of debris away. The pattern wasn't common and it wasn’t recent.

But it was familiar.

The curve of the binding mark. The overlapping spiral at the northmost edge. She'd traced it once before -- years ago, under a canopy of stars, her fingers entwined with Caelen's as he taught her to feel the way thread sang through stone.

Her chest tightened with sadness.

She reached out, fingertips brushing the center of the circle.

A hum answered.

Low. Resonant. Thrumming with long-sleeping power.

From behind her, the geode still in her satchel, the one she had been protecting for seven long years -- warmed as if in warning..

She turned.

The trees were still quiet.

Too quiet.

Then -- a flicker of movement.

A figure at the edge of the clearing, just inside the tree line. Tall. Still. Watching.

Eira didn't move and tried to calm her breath.

Inwardly her pulse surged. Her fingers tightened around the protection thread still looped in her palm.

The figure didn't step forward.

Didn't speak.

Just... stood.

She didn't call out.

Didn't run.

But every fiber of her being pulled taut like a loom set to snap.

Whoever -- or whatever -- it was, they weren't there by accident.

And neither was she.

CHAPTER TWELVE

The clearing felt too still.

Eira remained crouched by the stitch-circle, one hand half-raised and the other clutching a thread still faintly glowing. The figure at the tree line hadn't moved. Nor had she.

The unbearable stillness left Eira feeling exposed.

And then he stepped forward from the shadows just a bit. She recognized him immediately. Tall. Calm. A shade too still to trust. Kael.

He stepped forward slowly, but didn't leave the protection of the pattern.

"Didn't expect you so soon," he said.

"Did you expect me at all?" Eira's voice was sharper than she meant it to be.
She didn't lower her hand from the geode.

"Eventually," he said. "You were always going to follow the thread."

"And you were always going to be here waiting?" She studied his face, but it gave nothing back. "How did you know where I'd go?"

He didn't answer. His eyes flicked to the stitch-lines between them.

"This circle," she pressed, stepping closer to the edge, "is old magic. Not something you just stumble across. Did you make it?"

"No. Absolutely not. It's not my thread affinity"

"But you knew it was here."

"I did."

"That's not much of an answer."

He shrugged, the motion lazy, but his shoulders were too tense. "I don't have the right ones yet."

"Try anyway," she said. "You can use thread magic. You know things you shouldn't. And you keep showing up even in places you shouldn't be."

Kael was silent for a moment, then said quietly, "I'm not your enemy, Eira."

"You don't get to say that," she snapped. "Not when you've been spying on me from the shadows and answering my questions with vague half truths."

He didn't argue. Just watched her with that same unreadable calm that made her want to throw a rock through it.

"You should go home. You've seen enough here," he said eventually.

"Why?" she asked. "Because of what's coming?"

His jaw tightened. "Because of what might already be happening and who might already be watching."

Eira's hand clenched around the geode at her chest. The threads here were too still. Like they were waiting. Or listening.

Eira didn't look away. Not right away.
She wanted to press further, to demand real answers, to pull the truth out of the tight weave Kael kept so carefully stitched around himself.

But the clearing was too still. Too quiet in a way that didn't feel empty — it still felt watched.

The geode gave a faint pulse against her chest. Not urgent. Not warning. Just… waiting.

She rose slowly, fingers loosening around the glowing thread. "Fine," she said, mostly to herself.

There would be other chances. There had to be.
Kael was hiding something — something big — and she meant to find out what. But not here. Not now.

Not with the trees listening.

She turned and started the walk back to Brookwyn.

By the time she returned to town, the sun had crested and begun its descent. Her boots were caked with mud, and pine-needled mist clung to the hem of her cloak. She didn't go to her shop.

She went home. She needed the comfort of home and the wisdom of her mother.

The cottage garden welcomed her with the gentle rustle of silverleaf, the heady scent of threadmint, and the faint shimmer of floating pollen motes — some magical, some not. The warding chimes on the porch spun lazily in the breeze, their soft clinks harmonizing with the threads buried in the soil.

Her mother was in the garden, knees tucked beneath her skirt, coaxing new shoots from the earth with practiced ease. A vine curled obediently around her wrist, its leaves glossy with spell-kissed dew.

She didn't look up. "You've been walking the ley edges."

"How do you always know?"

Her mother tapped the base of a glowing seed pod. It released a faint hum. "The thread at the garden gate sang louder than usual when you passed. And you smell like pine ghosts."

Eira stepped closer, watching as her mother guided the threadvine up a trellis. The twine followed her hand as if charmed — and it was. Her magic pulsed soft and steady, green-gold and grounded in things that lasted.

It was different than Eira's magic. Quieter. More settled. Like deep roots rather than quick flame.

"I found an old stitch-circle," Eira said.

Her mother's hand paused. "Where?"

"In the northern woods. Beyond the ley bend."

That made her mother look up. Her eyes were sharper than Eira remembered — not with anger, but memory.

"There's nothing up there now," she said.

"There was."

Her mother nodded slowly, rising to her feet. She dusted off her hands and brushed a few specks of soil from her apron.

"I suppose that thread was always going to call you."

Eira studied her. "You knew about it."

"I know many things I don't speak of," her mother replied. "You don't learn to shape thread without learning when to hold it still."

They stood in silence for a moment, surrounded by the garden. A hummingbird flicked between blossoms. The air smelled of sun-warmed basil and magic.

Eira hesitated. "There was someone else there. Kael."

Her mother didn't flinch. "The stranger."

"You've seen him?"

"I've felt the ripple in the threads." Her mother's gaze softened. "He carries something… sharp. And old. Something that doesn't want to be forgotten. He also carries heavy emotions, be careful."

Eira's throat tightened. "He said magic is acting strangely and that people are watching. He brought a geode that almost seems to be waking."

"Watching? The council." At Eira's nod her mother looked toward the horizon. "Then the Archive won't sleep much longer."

A breeze stirred the chimes again. Eira turned away, eyes stinging.

"I miss him," she said softly. "Caelen."

Her mother didn't respond right away. Instead, she crouched beside a cluster of wilted feverblossoms. She pulled a silver thread from her satchel, knotted it once around the base of the stem, and whispered a simple weave.

The flower straightened.

Her magic didn't blaze. It mended.

When she stood, she looked Eira in the eye. "You have his fire. But you have my hands."

Eira swallowed the ache in her chest.

“I don’t know who to trust,” she whispered.

“Then start with yourself,” her mother said. “And when that fails, come home to all of us who love you. The threads here will always recognize you.”

The sun dipped lower, casting gold across the garden.

And for the first time in days, Eira let herself rest.

Just for a little while.

CHAPTER THIRTEEN

The geode lay on the worktable like a dare.

Eira hadn't touched it since the strange unraveling yesterday, but it pulled at her now—quiet as breath, heavy as memory. Threads hummed in the air around it, brittle and silvered like frost on a spider's web.

She wasn't even channeling, yet they shimmered—taut and trembling—as if the geode had spun its own spell and was waiting for her to complete it. That alone should have made her pause.

Instead, she reached out.

Her fingers hovered just above the stone.
"This time," she whispered, "I'll anchor myself."

But she didn't thread herself in. Not properly.
No grounding rune. No tether. Just the memory of a promise and a scrap of intention.

It wasn't enough.

She pressed her palm to the cool, dappled surface.

The workshop vanished like a flame snuffed in wind.

She was standing in a forest.
Or no—*someone* was.

Eira could feel the weight of their thoughts pressing into her ribs, aching with regret and something darker—an edge of desperation that made her breath catch.

Half-light clung to the trees. Damp bark steamed in the air, the scent of moss and distant fire curling around her senses. Somewhere behind her, footsteps echoed—his footsteps—but the figure ahead didn't turn.

A memory, she realized. Not hers.

That certainty chilled her more than the forest air.

Her magic never looked like this—so clean, so raw.

She was always part of it: threads responding to her presence, emotions tinting every color. But this was flat. Fixed. Like walking through a painting someone else had made of pain.

She couldn't shape it.
Couldn't touch it.
And it was pulling her under anyway.

Her pulse stuttered. What if she hadn't stayed shallow enough to escape? What if the anchoring—

No. She hadn't gone deep. She'd been careful enough.
Hadn't she?

This wasn't how her threads worked. Her magic filtered emotion like stained glass, luminous and shifting. But this… this was something older. Sharper. The edges of the memory cut. Like glass—not thread.

She had no control here. Only the helpless clarity of witnessing.

"Run," a voice gasped—disembodied and close, like it had been pulled forward in time and stitched into the air beside her.

The forest lurched. The trees blurred. Eira felt panic surge like a rising tide—heart thundering, lungs burning, air thin and too far away. A clearing opened ahead. Stone ruins slouched in the overgrowth, half-swallowed by vines, but the figure sprinted past without hesitation.

No time to stop.
No time to breathe.
Something was chasing them.

A shadow peeled itself from the trees.

It had no source, no weight, no shape—just the suggestion of form, like ink bleeding through parchment. Where it passed, threads in the memory *snapped.* Not unraveled—shattered. Fragments of color and thought drifted like ash.

Her own magic recoiled—untethered, exposed. She wasn't deep enough to shape it, not shallow enough to escape clean.

The figure stumbled. Fell. Reached for something in their cloak—

And the vision tore.
Split down the center.
Gone.

Eira gasped and yanked her hand back from the geode. Her chair scraped loudly as she staggered to her feet.

Her mother burst through the workshop door, skirts hitched in one hand, eyes wide. "Eira?"

"I'm okay," she lied, blinking hard. Her hands trembled. "I just... I went too deep."

Her mother was already at her side, brushing damp hair from Eira's face. "You're burning."

Eira flinched at the word, and her mother's lips thinned. "Threadburn?"

"Not bad. Just... strange. It wasn't my memory." She turned toward the geode, which now lay dull and inert on the worktable. "But it was someone's. And something corrupted it."

Her mother's eyes flicked to the stone. "You shouldn't use it again until we know who it came from. Were you properly anchored?"

Eira grimaced guiltily and then shook her head slowly, her gaze still focused on the geode. It felt different now -- heavier. Like it knew she'd seen something she wasn't meant to.

Her mother didn't move away. Instead, she reached past the table and pulled a small tin from the shelf -- one of the old salves she kept for burns, infused with juniper and valerian. She unscrewed the lid and dipped her fingers in without asking.

Eira winced as the cool balm met her wrist. The skin there pulsed, faintly silvered and sore.

"You always run hot when you burn," her mother murmured, voice gentle as she worked. "This will help. But you'll feel the chill after."

Eira nodded, and her mother took a shawl from the back of her chair and wrapped it gently around her shoulders.

For a moment, they sat in silence, the salve's scent mingling with old wood and singed thread. Then Ysolde said, "You're not the first in our line to yield so much thread magic, you know."

Eira looked up. "You mean—?"

"My aunt Brenna," her mother said. "She was brilliant. Talented. Stubborn as all flame. Thought she could weave through anything if she just held tight enough."

"What happened?"

"She anchored to nothing," Ysolde said softly. "Reached too far, too fast. Got threadburn so bad… she couldn't weave anymore. Every time she tried, the threads recoiled. Said it felt like the magic remembered what she'd done—and resented her for it."

Eira swallowed hard. "It remembers?"

"Not like people do," her mother said. "But it has… resonance. Threadwork isn't just about power. It's relationship. Trust. If you snap that, it takes a long time to mend. If it mends at all."

"She stopped weaving?" Eira asked, her voice small.

"She taught theory. Techniques. But she couldn't even braid her own hair without gloves, in the end."

Eira sat very still, her gaze drifting to the geode. "What if I already broke something?"

Her mother's hand found hers. "Then you take care. And you listen. And next time, you anchor yourself well."

"I won't press any further," her mother said gently. "But if you don't want to talk to me, talk to someone. Beck or Anwen. Or both. Don't let these emotions knot up inside you."

"I know," Eira whispered.

Her mother stood, gathering the unused cloths and carefully capping the balm. "Sleep, then. You've pulled more than enough thread for one day."

Eira nodded, still wrapped in the shawl. She didn't move until her mother had left the workshop, her soft footsteps retreating down the hallway.

Only then did Eira glance once more at the geode.

It sat quiet and dull.

But in the silence of the room, she felt the faintest hum beneath her ribs -- like a thread still tugging.

Waiting.

CHAPTER FOURTEEN

Eira found them in the usual spot, tucked behind the bakery's alley where Anwen preferred to wait out the morning rush. The scent of fresh bread clung to the air, warm and sweet, but Eira's stomach was too knotted to enjoy it.

Beck spotted her first, leaning back against the chipped brick wall like he'd been waiting hours. "There she is," he called, spreading his arms dramatically. "Our resident thread witch returns from the abyss."

"I didn't go to the abyss," Eira muttered, though her voice lacked conviction. "Just... further than I should've."

Anwen rose, brushing flour dust from her skirts. "You look tired."

"She *is* tired," Beck said. "And probably hungry. You didn't bring her anything, did you?"

Anwen reached into her satchel and handed over a still-warm crescent bun. "Of course I did."

Eira smiled weakly and took it, letting the silence settle between them a moment before she spoke again.

"Something's wrong with the geode."

Beck's easy grin dimmed. "Yeah, I thought it might be."

Anwen's brow furrowed. "What do you mean?"

Beck hesitated, then sighed and pulled a slip of parchment from his coat. "Because I've been following our charming stranger. Lightly. Casually. Spy-list-style."

Eira raised an eyebrow. "Seriously?"

"What? He showed up with a memory-stone, a tragic backstory aura, and cheekbones that could cut thread. You *both* got distracted."

Anwen snorted. "And you didn't?"

"Not the point," Beck muttered, then tapped the parchment. "The point is I trailed him this morning when he left the inn. Thought maybe he'd lead me to whoever he's working for — or at least buy a suspicious pastry."

"And?" Eira asked, worried about what Beck might have discovered..

"And he didn't buy anything. But someone *else* did – no council badge, but not local, one of those brisk types with a bad coat and worse manners. Asked the seamstress stall if anyone around here was working with charged geodes. Called them thread-triggered cores. That's not a phrase ordinary folk use."

Anwen's arms folded. "So someone's looking."

Beck nodded. "Didn't name Kael. But his eyes flicked toward him twice, then he left. Fast. Like the question was more warning than curiosity."

He handed Eira the parchment. The paper was thin, creased and faintly burned at the edges. A symbol was scrawled across it — a circle interwoven with sharp, angular lines. Not a language she recognized. But the threads around it prickled.

"It's warded," she said, softly.

"Badly," Beck added. "And not for keeping people out. For tracking."

Eira's heart thudded.

"So someone knows," Anwen whispered. "Someone's trying to find it."

Beck didn't respond. He just looked at Anwen.

And for a breath, she looked back — no words exchanged, just a flicker of shared unease that passed between them like a thread pulled tight.

Eira returned to her workshop with the parchment sealed in a lead-lined pouch -- a trick her mother had taught her for containing thread-charged objects. She didn't touch the geode again until the sun had dipped past the windowpanes and the shadows grew long and sharp.

This time, she prepared.

She layered the floor with grounding thread -- wool soaked in lavender and ash, wrapped three times around the old iron nail in the floorboard. She braided a second cord and tied it to her wrist, its matching end looped around a bronze ring set into the worktable.

She lit a single candle and let the rest of the room fall into shadow.

"This time," she whispered, "we do it on my terms."

Her fingers brushed the geode.

The shift was immediate -- not the jarring tumble of yesterday, but a gentler slide. The threads shimmered, thinner now, not showing her a full memory but pieces -- disjointed and fluttering.

A bootprint in mud.

A torn sleeve.

A voice, distant: "We were never meant to hold this."

She focused. Pulled at the threads gently, trying to stitch them into place.

But something resisted.

It fought the shape she tried to give it -- not like a memory but like will. And then, just as she was about to pull free, a strand lashed toward her -- a hair-thin thread of silvery black, faster than thought.

Eira ripped her hand back with a gasp.

She staggered, nearly knocking over the candle, and clutched at the cord wrapped around her wrist. Her braid had held. Barely.

She looked down.

A single thread clung to her sleeve -- black and fine and humming faintly.

Not one of her threads.

She plucked it free and dropped it into a dish of salt to neutralize it. It writhed before going still.

Eira stared at the black thread in the salt dish, her breath still unsteady.

It shouldn't have been able to reach her. She'd anchored herself, worked with care, made sure her intent was clear. She had followed every protective technique she'd learned and a few she'd invented. But the thing in the geode hadn't unraveled like a memory – it had lunged like a trap.

She touched her sleeve again where it had clung. The fabric felt normal, but her skin buzzed beneath it, as if the thread had left something behind.

"I'm fine," she said aloud, to no one. Then again, quieter, "I'm fine."

She wasn't. This made no sense and it was dangerous.

Her wards had held -- barely. If she'd gone in without precautions, would she even still be here? Would she be lost inside someone else's twisted recollection, threads of her own memory pulled loose and fraying? Could she have lost her ability to wield threads?

She sat down heavily at the workbench and pressed her hands to the scarred surface.

This wasn't just a corrupted stone. Someone had shaped this. Altered its memory weave intentionally. For what, she couldn't tell -- but the precision of the trap meant it wasn't accidental. And if someone wanted it back badly enough to trace it... they'd come looking.

It wasn't the first time since this geode arrived that she wished Caelen were here.

She closed her eyes, surprised by the sharpness of the ache. He would've known what kind of weave this was.

Would've walked her through the theory and the danger. Would've warned her before she got burned.

But Caelen wasn't here. He hadn't been for years.

And Kael -- gods help her -- was far too charming and way too much of a mystery to trust.

She didn't trust him, not really, but he made her want to. He made her feel something -- a flutter in her chest she hadn't felt in years, warm and unexpected. He stirred butterflies in her belly and a tension beneath her skin, the kind that made her acutely aware of how close he stood, how his icy blue eyes had started to soften when he looked at her.

No, she didn't trust him -- but he was hard to walk away from although a not so small part of her told her she probably should.

She looked again at the blackened thread in the dish. It had gone still, its energy faded, but she didn't believe it was truly inert.

She would find out who had made it. Why they had hidden it. And what it meant that she was the one who found it.

Even if the answers burned.

The scent of stew drifted down the hallway as Eira emerged from her workshop. The warmth of the kitchen beckoned, a contrast to the cold hum still clinging to her skin.

Her mother was at the hearth, ladling soup into two bowls. "Whatever you tried just now," she said without turning, "it reached the wards. I felt them hum."

Eira sank into the seat across from her. "It wasn't a memory. Or if it was, it didn't want to be seen."

Her mother set the bowls down, her movements slower than usual. "Some memories bite back."

Eira wrapped her hands around the clay bowl, letting its heat seep into her fingers. "Did anyone ever come through asking about geodes before? Ones like this?"

Her mother sat across from her, stirring her soup without eating. "Not in years. But there was a traveler once – right before Caelen left."

Eira's spoon paused. "What kind of traveler?"

"Quiet. Tired. Carried herself like someone who'd forgotten how to rest." Her mother's gaze went distant, as if she could still see her standing in their doorway. "She had a blade at her hip -- silver-threaded. And her eyes...they remembered too much."

Eira swallowed. "Silver threaded? Did she say what she was looking for?"

"She didn't have to. She was drawn to the stones. Spent a whole afternoon just holding one and staring into it like it would speak. Then she left. Didn't buy a thing."

Her mother finally took a bite. "She reminded me of Caelen. Not physically, but magically and emotionally. Like the whole world was pressing down on her"

Eira didn't respond. Her chest felt too tight.

A long silence followed, filled only by the soft clink of spoons against bowls. Her mother didn't press, and Eira didn't explain the thread in the salt dish or the way her own memory had felt fractured earlier.

But the mention of Caelen -- of a woman like him. Here and seeking something lost – made thoughts of him curl around her thoughts like smoke.

Later, after the dishes were washed and her mother had gone to bed, Eira sat alone at her desk, candlelight dancing in the warped windowpane. Her journal lay open beside her -- she hadn't written anything yet, hadn't dared try.

She only meant to turn the page.

But there, near the spine, nestled between two blank sheets, was a single strand of black thread -- no longer humming, but present.

Eira froze.

It wasn't from her braid. It wasn't from her mother's weaving. It was too fine, too dark, and it pulsed faintly at her touch, like a heartbeat.

She carried it with tongs to the hearth, laid it atop the coals, and waited.

The thread curled... but did not burn.

It darkened slightly. Glowed faintly red. But it never turned to ash.

Eira watched it for a long time, lips pressed in a tight line.

When she finally turned away, she didn't look back.

Some threads don't want to be cut.

CHAPTER FIFTEEN

The morning light spilled through the shop's old glass windows in softened bands, catching on the dust motes that danced like golden snow. Eira unlatched the shutters, their worn hinges creaking faintly as she pushed them open to the quiet street beyond.

The shop was still — shelves of thread wound crystals glinting faintly, spools of thread arranged by hue, the weaving loom in the middle of the back room waiting like a silent sentinel.

She moved through the familiar rituals of opening: unlocking cabinets, setting out her tools, checking the thread-infused crystals for shifts or signs of wear. It should've been soothing.

But she hadn't slept well.

Her dreams had been jumbled knots of half-seen faces and threads that pulled too tight when she tried to look at them. Still, it was better than silence. Silence left room for the memory of the thread that hadn't burned.

A brisk knock interrupted her thoughts — quick, like a rhythm tapped out on a tabletop.

"Delivery for the Threadwitch!" came a too-loud voice through the door.

Eira opened it to find Finn, the parchment shop's apprentice, no more than fourteen, grinning beneath an unruly mop of sun-bleached curls. He held a wrapped parcel in one hand and a sweet bun in the other.

“You’re early,” she said.

“I’m efficient,” he replied with a wink. “Also, I wanted to be first in line at the baker’s and figured you’d be up.”

He handed over the package. “From Master Wren. Said you’d want it before noon.”

“Thanks, Finn.”

“Tell your mother that her pickled beets ruined me for anyone else’s,” he added, already backing away with a wave.

“I’ll do that and fix your boot laces before you trip again!” she called.

“Style hazard,” he called over his shoulder. “You wouldn’t understand.”

The door swung shut behind him, leaving Eira in the stillness once more. She set the parcel down and glanced toward the workshop door, her smile from the cheeky lad’s antics fading.

Her fingers tingled faintly — the same low-level hum she’d felt since the thread had refused to burn.

Not painful. Not magic. Just prickling awareness that didn’t let her mind settle.

The bell above the door gave a soft chime — not the usual cheerful trill, but something lower, like the sound had thickened in the air.

Eira didn't look up. She felt it first — the threads had shifted. Pressed inward.

"Does the bell always sound like that," Kael asked, voice quiet but dry, "or is it just warning you about me?"

His tone held a familiar curl of humor, but not the performance behind it. No practiced grin, no flippant tilt of the head — just stillness, like he wasn't sure what he'd walked into.

Eira glanced up. "It complains about everyone," she said with a faint smirk. "But I think it likes you slightly less than most."

A pause.

"Good to know," Kael said, and stepped into the light his boots nearly silent on the wooden floor.

He looked… different this morning. Less polished, maybe. His shirt was rumpled beneath his coat, and a single curl had escaped its usual styling to fall across his brow.

Kael nodded toward the wrapped bundle on the counter. "That from the parchment shop?"

Eira gave him a sidelong glance. "Is that you being observant or nosy?"

"Observant," he said easily. "Finn was waving a sweet bun like a victory flag. Hard to miss."

She let a small smile tug at the corner of her mouth.

"But it's not the delivery I'm curious about," Kael added.

The smile vanished.

He stepped closer — not crowding, but present. "Yesterday… when you touched the geode. Your hands shook."

Eira turned away, reached for the shelf like it mattered. "Long day. Happens."

"You weren't afraid," Kael said. "But something hit you. I saw it."

"You see a lot," she murmured. "For someone who keeps so much to himself."

"Maybe that's why I notice it in other people."

Eira stilled. For a second, the threads near her wrist shimmered — just once, like they'd caught their breath.

Eira turned back to face him, arms crossed loosely — not defensive, just grounded. "You ask a lot of questions for someone who only answers half of mine."

Kael's smile curled faintly, more rueful than amused. "Only the ones I'm sure you actually want answers to."

"You assume a lot."

"I observe a lot," he said. "I haven't decided what to assume yet."

The silence between them shifted. Not sharp — not hostile — but dense with something unspoken.

Kael stepped a little closer. Not enough to press, just enough for her to notice the faint scent of smoke and cedar, like a memory waiting to catch fire.

"May I see it?" he asked. "Not the geode. The thread you used yesterday."

Eira hesitated, then reached below the counter — not for the geode-thread, but for something older. More honest.

"Here," she said, laying the folded weave gently between them. "It belonged to my mother. Woven when she was still an apprentice."

Kael didn't reach for it immediately. He leaned forward, hands resting lightly on the counter's edge, studying the fabric like it might speak to him first.

"It remembers something," he murmured.

"Of course it does," Eira said. "Everything she made remembers."

His gaze flicked up. "It doesn't want me touching it."

"It doesn't know you."

A pause.

"Neither do you," he said — not accusing, just quietly true.

Eira held his gaze. "Maybe I'm trying."

He smiled — just a little. "Then I'll try not to offend the thread."

"Good luck," she said, and for once, it didn't sound like a warning.

"I don't want to be a stranger to you," Kael said softly. "And I'm not going to hurt you."

Eira held still. Not frozen — listening. There was weight in his voice, not just promise but memory, like he was trying to mean it more than he ever had before.

"You keep saying that," she said. "Like words are stronger than fear."

"They're not," he admitted. "But they're where I start."

She didn't reply. Her fingers brushed the edge of the weave. The air shifted — not temperature, but pressure — and the thread began to hum.

Not loudly. Not dangerously. Just enough to be felt.

Kael's gaze snapped to it. "That wasn't me."

"It wasn't me either," she said, her voice lower now. "It was the thread."

"Responding to emotion?" he asked.

"To connection," she corrected. Then immediately regretted how honest it sounded.

The hum faded. But the tension did not.

The thread hummed again and Kael stepped back — not startled, not afraid. Just... reverent. Like he'd edged too close to something sacred.

Eira gathered the thread slowly, folding it with care before returning it to its place. Her fingers lingered on the woven edge, then drew back as if it burned.

She'd said too much and something in her heart had opened. Shifted.

He made her honest without even trying, and she didn't know if it was because of the magic between them or something in *him* — that steady way he watched, not with hunger, but with understanding. Like he was trying to see all of her.

That unnerved her more than charm or cleverness ever could.

Kael glanced toward the rear door. "That where the loom is?"

Eira nodded.

"Would you show me?"

She hesitated — not because she didn't want him to see, but because part of her *did*. And that was the problem. Why did she want him to stay around so much when she wasn't interested in getting hurt again?

"Don't touch anything without asking."

"Noted." He offered a faint smile. "Though I think the thread already got its say."

The workshop was cooler than the front of the store, the stone walls thick enough to keep the summer heat at bay. Light filtered in through narrow slats above, striking the dust in long gold lines.

Her loom stood at the center of the room, worn smooth by generations of hands. The shelves around it were lined with jars of memory crystals, bowls of bone and salt, and spools of thread in every color — each one labeled in her mother's steady hand.

Kael moved with quiet attention, not browsing — *cataloging.* Noticing the order in the chaos, the care in the clutter. But his gaze kept drifting back to Eira.

She caught him watching her as she brushed loose threads from the bench beside the loom. He didn't look away quickly enough to pretend.

"What?" she asked, a little sharper than intended.

"You're…" He hesitated, then smiled faintly. "Different than I thought you'd be."

"Disappointed?"

"Not remotely."

Eira looked away, her cheeks heating and the corners of her mouth twitching before she could stop them.

Kael's eyes moved to the loom. "Your work… feels old. Not just skilled — *ancient.*"

"It is," she said, voice smoothing into something calmer. "I learned from my mother. She from hers. We don't keep records in books."

"You keep them in thread," he murmured.

"Every line," she said. "Woven, knotted, preserved."

He walked a slow circle around the loom. "How far back does it go?"

"Farther than I can name. We used to say there was always a threadwitch in the bloodline, even when there wasn't a name for it."

Kael looked at her — not startled, just quietly impressed. "So this magic isn't just something you *use.* It's something you *are.*"

Eira's hands stilled on the loom's frame. "Yes. And that's why it matters when something feels wrong."

Kael's brows furrowed, but it wasn't confusion — it was curiosity. A rare kind.

Kael circled slowly back toward the loom, his eyes tracking the shape of it — not just its construction, but its weight in the room.

"That thread you showed me," he said quietly, "it didn't feel like memory. Not exactly."

Eira leaned against the table's edge, arms crossed, one hand brushing the wood as if for reassurance. "What did it feel like?"

"Twisted," he said. "Like someone tried to reshape the memory mid-stitch — but the weave resisted."

Her brow furrowed. "That's not possible."

"Isn't it?"

"Magic remembers," Eira said, firmer now. "You can dull it. Burn it. Unravel it if you're willing to pay the price. But it doesn't lie. It doesn't change."

Kael met her eyes. "It lies if the memory is a lie. Someone tried to make it change."

Her fingers curled against her sleeve, holding back something sharp. "That would take precision. Intent. It's not something done by accident."

"No," Kael said. "It's not."

A long pause stretched between them. The air in the workshop felt still — not empty, but bracing.

"You'd have to splice emotion mid-flow," Eira said, slower now, like speaking the words made them heavier. "Break the thread, but keep the resonance from shattering."

"You'd have to substitute truth with something that *feels* true," Kael said. His hand hovered just above the loom's edge but didn't touch it. "A lie that wears a memory's skin."

Eira exhaled — not in fear, but like something sacred had just cracked underfoot. She laid her hand on the loom again, grounding herself against its familiar grain.

"That's not just forbidden," she whispered. "It's desecration."

Kael didn't speak at first. He looked at her — really looked — and something shifted in his stance. His shoulders set, like someone remembering the shape of a burden they'd hoped was gone.

"It's erasure," he said quietly. "And I think someone's been doing it for a long time."

Eira's hand tightened slightly on the loom. "But who would do that? And why? What would they gain by rewriting someone else's past?"

"Control," Kael said. "Influence. If you can alter a memory—make someone question their own truth—you can shape how they act, what they believe, even who they are."

Eira stepped back, crossing her arms again. "But that's not how thread magic works. Memory isn't just a spell. It's lived. It's… anchored."

"It was," he said softly. "Until someone found a way to *lift the anchor.*"

Her gaze flicked to the shelf of woven records — family work, preserved history. "There'd be traces," she said. "Even subtle tampering would leave resonance scars. Shifts in tone, breaks in emotional logic—"

"I think there *are* scars," Kael said, voice low. "We just haven't learned how to read them yet."

Her chest tightened. Eira didn't answer right away. Her gaze swept over the threads hanging behind the loom — projects unfinished, records untouched. Each one carried echoes. Some were hers. Others had been passed down, generation after generation.

"If that's true…" she said slowly, "then we don't just have to find what's been changed." She turned back toward Kael. "We have to understand why."

He nodded. "And who."

She looked at him for a long beat, searching his expression like there might be more answers there than he was giving. "You've seen something like this before."

His jaw tightened. "Not exactly. But I've followed enough threads to know when one's been tied off too cleanly. When a story doesn't end where it should."

"So where does this one lead?"

"That's what I came here to find out. I think you will be the one to help me find the answer."

The silence that followed wasn't cold — it was full. Heavy with unspoken questions and the slow stitching of trust.

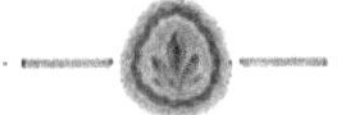

Eira let the words settle, a thread of shared purpose weaving itself between them.

Eira glanced over, her voice quieter now. "You talk like someone who's worked with thread magic before."

Kael gave a short, dry laugh. "I have. But not like you."

She tilted her head, studying him. "How, then?"

"My magic was taught differently. Structured. Restrained. Meant to reinforce what already existed — not to pull the truth from the weave like you do."

"Still sounds like threadwork."

"It is," he admitted. "But I was trained to contain threads. Knot them down. Stabilize." His voice lowered slightly. "Not to listen to what they wanted to say."

Eira tilted her head, watching him. There was a tension behind his words — not fear, but memory. Something hard-earned and heavy.

"You've seen it go wrong," she said softly.

Kael nodded, slow and grim. "I've seen what happens when someone tries to bend thread magic to their will instead of working with it. And I've been part of that, once. Long enough to know the difference."

She felt the ripple of truth beneath his words. He didn't elaborate — didn't need to. Magic that bound too tightly could suffocate whatever it was meant to preserve.

"But geodes," Kael added, nodding toward the one on her worktable, "don't usually respond to me. That's why I brought this one to you."

Eira frowned slightly. "You said it hummed when you touched it."

"It did," Kael said. "Not like it does for you — not with that kind of resonance — but enough to know something's wrong. It shouldn't respond to me at all."

She looked at him, startled by the admission — and by the honesty in his voice. "Then it's already unraveling."

He nodded once. "Or already been tampered with."

Eira's pulse fluttered in her throat, a quiet, familiar warning. Something in the threads was shifting. Not just in the geode — in the space between them.

Kael held her gaze. "And it's unraveling for you."

"And you think my threads can stop it?"

"Maybe. But I think your work is the first thing I've encountered that doesn't lie."

The compliment startled her more than it should have. Not because it was unexpected — but because it sounded like he meant it.

She let her fingers drift towards the stone. The geode pulsed faintly beneath her hand — not with light, but with presence. Memory and emotion wrapped tightly around a core that resisted unraveling.

"I don't know what it is yet," she said. "But it's old. Older than either of us. And something about it's been….fundamentally changed."

Kael watched her, not the geode. "Can you help me find out how?"

She looked up, her copper-brown hair falling across her cheek as she met his gaze. He was closer now — not enough to touch, but enough to feel the warmth of him. Enough to feel her own heartbeat reacting.

"I'll try," she said.

Something like relief passed over his features — chased by something gentler.

"Thank you," he said. And for once, it wasn't laced with charm or bravado. Just quiet sincerity and genuine warmth.

Eira guided Kael toward the loom, the rhythm of her steps slower now, deliberate. Something had shifted — not just in the thread, but in her.

She wasn't sure if it was the geode's echo still pulsing through her chest or the way Kael moved beside her, steady and open, but she felt it. The awareness. The possibility.

She pulled out a box of spools, each one wound with thread spun from a different fiber — memory-thread dyed with emotion, stasis-thread that preserved, and one nearly black with grief.

Kael glanced at the dark one. "That's heavy."

"Because it remembers too much," Eira murmured, brushing her fingers over it.

He didn't ask which memory it held, and she didn't offer. That earned him a point in her mind.

Instead, she selected a pale violet spool and seated herself at the loom, beckoning him with a tilt of her head. "Watch closely."

Kael leaned in — a little too close — and she pretended not to notice the way her skin warmed under the attention.

She threaded the loom, her fingers moving with unconscious grace. This was her language, older than words. As she wove, the threads began to vibrate — faintly at first, then with more insistence.

Kael leaned closer. "That vibration… it's like it's alive."

"It's not the thread," she said. "It's the story inside it."

The tension built with each motion — threads pulled taut, magic singing between them like a harp string strung too tight. The air itself shifted, warped around them.

Then it snapped.

A single strand frayed mid-stitch, recoiling as if burned. Eira flinched back, her palm stinging.

Kael stepped forward immediately. "Are you alright?"

She nodded, already examining the broken thread. "It wasn't me. It was the memory I was chasing — it unraveled before I could catch it."

He hesitated. "Is that normal?"

"No." She looked up at him. "It means someone doesn't want it found."

Their eyes locked again. This time, there was no pretense. Not even curiosity. Just understanding — sharp and sudden.

Kael reached forward but stopped himself just before his hand touched hers.

"I won't push," he said.

"I know," she replied.

But gods, part of her wanted him to and she wasn't sure how she felt about that.

Eira set the shuttle down, cradling the broken strand in her fingers. The silence that followed felt sacred — like disturbing it would unravel something more fragile than the thread itself.

Kael stood beside her, gaze lingering on the loom. "You said memories can hide… but can they fight back?"

Eira exhaled slowly. "They can resist. Especially if they were never meant to be unraveled."

His brow furrowed. "Then how do you ever find anything true?"

She looked at him — really looked at him — and for a moment, forgot to be wary.

"You follow the threads anyway," she said softly. "Even if it hurts. Even if it leads somewhere you didn't expect."

Kael studied her in return. Not just her face, but the exhaustion hiding behind her eyes, the way her shoulders held more weight than one person should carry alone.

"I meant what I said earlier," he told her. "I don't want to be a stranger to you. And I'm not going to hurt you, Eira."

The sound of her name on his lips did something dangerous to her chest.

"I'll do that," she murmured, not quite looking at him.

He blinked. "Do what?"

"Make sure you're not a stranger."

A quiet beat passed between them — something unspoken but alive.

The thread on the counter began to hum again. So did Eira's heart.

CHAPTER SIXTEEN

The market square came alive beneath the thinning mist, bright awnings flapping in the early breeze. Eira stepped between stalls with practiced ease, Anwen at her side. The scent of spices and baked bread mingled with the faintest glimmer of spell-thread — wards stitched into satchels, tokens braided with blessings, ribbons dyed in memory-ink.

"You were quiet last night," Anwen said.

Eira gave a small nod. "Just… thinking."

They paused at a table draped in shimmering scarves, its vendor nodding in greeting. Eira let her fingers drift over the fabrics, not really seeing them.

"About him?"

Eira didn't answer.

The square had always been a comfort — familiar, noisy, alive. But today, something in her chest felt tangled. Off-kilter. As if the threads she usually sensed in the world around her had shifted.

"You don't have to talk about it," Anwen said, more gently this time. "But I'm here if you do."

Eira met her friend's eyes and managed a grateful smile. The breeze lifted a lock of her hair, cool against her cheek. The world hadn't changed. Not really. But something inside her had.

And the day had only just begun.

Just as Eira opened her mouth to speak, a sharp clatter rang out from farther down the lane. A young boy sprinted through the square, his boots slick from the damp stones, knocking over a stack of wooden crates in his hurry. A leather satchel skidded across the ground, its contents spilling in a colorful, chaotic mess: enchanted baubles, delicate glass charms, a tangle of thread-bound scrolls, and a single rune-carved talisman that pulsed faintly.

"Thief!" someone shouted from behind a nearby cart.

The boy didn't even look back. He darted down a narrow alley and vanished like mist.

Eira and Anwen rushed to the scene, finding an older woman in a pale blue shawl bracing herself against her overturned stall. Her knees trembled as she bent to gather the fallen goods, her breath coming in quick bursts.

"Easy," Eira said, crouching to help. "You're alright."

The scroll closest to her still sizzled faintly with residual charm-light, the threads around it shimmering like it had been freshly cast.

“Careful,” Anwen warned, stooping beside her. “It might be triggered.”

“Or worse,” Eira muttered, eyes narrowing as she reached for it.

Before either of them could act, a familiar voice rang out — light, amused, and far too casual.

“Every time I sleep in, you two go looking for trouble.”

Beck strolled toward them, shirt untucked and hair just barely tamed, with that maddeningly unbothered grin tugging at the corner of his mouth.

“We weren’t looking,” Eira said. “It found us.”

“Same difference.” Beck crouched beside them, inspecting the humming scroll like it was a particularly fussy frog. He tapped the glowing rune with the blunt edge of his ring, then tilted his head as if listening.

The scroll gave a soft pop and the charm-light blinked out.

“Was set to vanish if anyone but the owner touched it,” he said, handing it carefully to the wide-eyed vendor. “I just asked it nicely not to.”

The woman blinked, then gave a baffled nod of thanks before shuffling back behind her cart.

Anwen let out a soft laugh. “You’re ridiculous.”

“And yet,” Beck said, rising with a flourish, “effective.”

The three of them fell into step as they continued past the vendor stalls. The pace was easy, the chatter of the square returning to normal behind them.

Beck ambled between the two friends, hands tucked in his pockets. "So, what's got you both wandering North Barrow before breakfast? Thread trouble?"

Eira hesitated, then glanced at Anwen, who gave a barely perceptible nod of encouragement.

"I tried weaving with Kael yesterday," she said, voice low.

Beck gave a low whistle. "That explains the squint in your eyes."

"It wasn't like that," she said. "It was—strange. The threads reacted. They shimmered, they pulled. It was almost like the geode had something to say."

"Sounds romantic," Beck quipped, but there was a subtle edge of concern in his voice.

Eira didn't smile. "I don't trust him. But he... stirs something. Not safety. Not danger, either. Just—" She paused, searching for the right word. "Restlessness. Like I'm being drawn toward something I'm not ready for."

Beck grew quiet at that. Anwen, beside her, gently touched her arm. The gesture said more than words.

After a few beats, Beck exhaled. "You want me to poke around? Ask some quiet questions?"

"No." Eira shook her head. "I think I need to figure this one out myself."

They walked in companionable silence for a moment. The weight of the conversation softened as the square opened up before them.

Then Beck bumped Anwen lightly with his shoulder. "You still owe me tea for that scroll save, you know."

"I never agreed to that," Anwen said, cheeks turning a delicate pink.

"You did now," he replied, the corners of his mouth tugging into a teasing grin.

Eira caught the way Anwen's eyes lingered on him. There was something gentle and quiet blooming there — a warmth Eira could appreciate, even envy. Beck was handsome, kind, effortlessly charming. He was safe. Familiar. And yet... he didn't ignite the butterflies Kael stirred or echo the ache left by Caelen.

That was the difference.

They reached the edge of the square where the morning sun began to filter through the treetops beyond the stone arch. A breeze stirred the edges of Eira's cloak, and with it came the faintest hum from her satchel — soft, steady, like a heartbeat.

She paused, hand brushing the flap. The threads inside were quiet now, but not dormant. Waiting, perhaps. Always listening.

"You okay?" Anwen asked.

Eira nodded, then looked between her two oldest friends. "Thanks. For being here."

Beck gave her a small smile — one of the rare, serious ones that softened his whole face.

"Always."

Anwen simply squeezed her hand.

For a moment, Eira felt anchored. The strange new threads in her life were weaving in unpredictable patterns, but this — this was still strong. Still whole.

She turned to go, but just as she stepped away, the threads in her satchel gave the faintest spark beneath her fingertips. Not painful — just a flicker. Like a whisper she almost heard.

She paused, breath catching.

"I'll see you later," she said, voice gentler than she meant it to be.

As she walked away, the weight of Kael's presence returned to her mind — not as a danger, but a mystery. One that called to something deep in her magic. And in her heart.

Eira didn't head straight back to the shop. Instead, she slipped through the gate at the far end of the square, boots crunching softly along the overgrown path that led to Brookwyn's little garden grove. It wasn't much — just a cluster of benches and crumbling stone planters half-swallowed by ivy — but it was quiet. Familiar.

She sat near the old sundial and let the silence settle. Her fingers brushed the edge of her satchel, feeling for the geode tucked within — not weaving, not stirring it. Just… listening. It hadn't spoken, not really. But something in it pulsed with the weight of memories she hadn't dared unwrap.

She'd nearly spoken back in the square. The words had risen, unbidden. But then the boy had run past and the moment had scattered like seeds on the wind.

A few minutes passed before Anwen appeared. She didn't speak right away — just sat beside her on the bench like she'd always belonged there.

"You were about to say something earlier," Anwen said gently. "Then you didn't."

Eira gave a small nod.

"I thought maybe you needed to be heard."

Silence stretched, long and quiet.

"I thought I was past this," Eira finally spoke. "But something about the geodes… and Kael… it's like they've stirred up everything I've tried to bury."

Anwen said nothing, only waited.

"We trained together," Eira said softly. "He was my first thread partner — before either of us really knew what we were doing. I was eight when he first came. He was older. Steady. Patient. My mother always said he helped keep my magic from pulling itself apart."

A ghost of a smile touched her lips. "He used to braid protective knots into my sleeves when I was anxious. Said it helped the threads listen."

"Did it?"

Eira nodded. "Always."

Then Eira whispered, "Then I helped him leave."

Anwen didn't respond, didn't push — just waited, calm and steady.

"He asked me to preserve his memories. In the geode. Said it had to be me." Her voice cracked. "He trusted me with everything, but he's been gone so long."

Her hands clenched around the satchel's edge. "I thought I understood. That there was some noble reason, something bigger than both of us. But he didn't tell me what it was. He just disappeared. And I've spent years wondering if I was just convenient."

Anwen shook her head. "You were never that to him."

Eira's throat tightened. "You saw us. You *knew.* Toward the end… it was more than friendship. We never said it until right before he left, but it was there. And now I don't know if he'll ever be back and how he'll feel if he ever comes back."

The pain in her chest rose like a tide. "Kael stirs everything up. I get butterflies when he's around. The geode hums when he's near. My magic *aches.* And I keep thinking… if Caelen were here, he'd know what it meant. I wouldn't feel this pull towards Kael. He always knew how to steady the thread."

"But he's not here," Anwen said softly.

"No. Just the part of him I helped hide."

Anwen reached over and gently took her hand. "You don't have to untangle it all right now. Whatever Caelen's reasons were — they don't erase what he meant to you. Or how much it hurt. You are allowed to move forward though."

Eira nodded once, but the motion felt fragile.

"You won't unravel," Anwen said. "And if you do, I'll be here. We'll stitch through it together."

CHAPTER SEVENTEEN

Eira shut the door to her workshop with a soft thud, the worn wood clicking into place behind her. The quiet felt heavier than usual — not peaceful, but watchful. She crossed the room and set her satchel down on the central worktable, her fingertips lingering on the flap.

The geode inside pulsed faintly beneath the leather. Not with light or heat, but presence — like the way a thunderstorm sometimes made the air feel too full, too expectant.

She drew it out carefully, cradling it in both hands. Its gray outer shell caught the lamplight in rough flecks, but the interior glimmered softly: pale blue and violet veins, like frozen lightning beneath glass.

This was the stone that had started it all — and for the first time, she wasn't entirely sure it belonged to her and to Caelen.

"Let's see what you're hiding," she whispered.

She placed the geode on a circle of woven thread at the center of her table — the weaving disk she'd used hundreds of times before. It should have welcomed her magic easily, absorbing her intent and offering stability.

Instead, as she reached for the nearest memory-thread — a silver strand with a faded violet tinge — it quivered beneath her fingers and then recoiled. The pulse inside the geode flared slightly in response.

"Don't play coy now," she muttered, her voice tight.

The thread twitched again, not violently, but like a cat flicking its tail in irritation. Something was off.

She took a deep breath and reached farther into her woven memory collection, settling on a thread that once held a joyful childhood moment — a safe one. A tether to her younger self.

As she tried to anchor it into the geode's magic, her vision blurred — and the joy that came wasn't hers. It was his.

A different hand. A different warmth. A quiet laugh in a deeper, older voice.
Caelen.

And not just his memory — his feeling. A moment soaked in affection.
She felt it too clearly, too intimately. Her magic wasn't just reading it. It was resonating.

She pulled back with a gasp, heart thudding. Maybe this had been a bad idea.

Eira paced.

Back and forth between her worktable and the shelves that lined the east wall, where stacks of parchment, ink-smudged journals, and folded woven samples leaned in chaotic companionship. She pulled out one of the older journals — a leather-bound one with a frayed tassel bookmark and a long-dried ink stain across the cover.

Her mentor's handwriting danced across the pages in familiar, looping script. Caelen had always written like he spoke: elegantly, with the occasional impatient scratch where he couldn't get the thought out fast enough.

She flipped to the bookmarked section.

"Resonant imprinting appears stronger when the weaver has experienced intense emotion. Threads may hold echoes — not just of memory, but of intent. Caution: improperly anchored geodework risks entanglement with past energy."

Eira swallowed hard. "Thread-echoes…"

She turned the page slowly, careful not to smudge the fading ink. An entry from years later, marked with a thin slash of red wax along the margin, caught her attention.

"Binding through grief leaves a stronger echo than joy." Of course it does, she thought numbly. Grief never did let go. She continued reading. "Some threads are never meant to be rewoven. Still, I try."

The room tilted for a second. Her knees buckled slightly, and she caught herself on the edge of the desk. Her heart pounded, not with fear exactly, but recognition — the kind that lived in the bones, the kind that said: you've touched this pain before.

This wasn't about Kael's geode at all.

This was about hers. The one she'd hidden deep in the cottage drawer, tucked away under fabric swatches and scent-infused pouches. She'd pulled it out instinctively when Kael arrived, not even realizing why. It was like it had called it her silently.

Now she did.

The geode didn't just contain fragments of her work — it contained fragments of Caelen. Of them. And of something else that she just couldn't name, something that didn't belong there.

Her fingers brushed over a line of thread coiled near her wrist, and a memory uncoiled so vividly she forgot to breathe.

Laughter, warm and low. A hand brushing hers across a candlelit table. The scent of rosemary tea and waxed wool. Caelen, smiling. His thumb tracing a thread between them like it was sacred. Like it meant everything.

It had. But did it still?

The knock on the door was brisk — polite, but certain.

Eira startled, her heart still tangled in echoes of the past. She stood, brushing her palms against her skirt as if she could erase the memory of Caelen's touch.

Kael stood on the other side of the door when she opened it, windblown and flushed from the cold, his dark hair tousled and the edges of his coat damp. He offered her a crooked smile that nearly masked the tension in his jaw.

"Thought I'd check in," he said. "See how the... resonant gem's behaving."

"Geode," she corrected automatically, stepping aside. "Come in."

He did, shoulders brushing past hers with a warmth that lingered too long in the narrow space. She closed the door gently behind him.

Kael's gaze swept the room. "You've been working."

"Trying to." She moved toward the table and gestured at the still-glowing geode. "It's... resistant."

He walked closer, his boots silent on the worn floorboards. "I noticed it acted strange when you touched it yesterday. Like it knew you."

"I've had it a long time," she said, watching him carefully. "I used it years ago for some spellwork, but it's been tucked away safely for years.

Kael turned toward her. "Then why did it hum for me?"

That stopped her.

"I don't know," she admitted, her voice low. "But the threads are acting like they've been touched before — like someone's already tried to weave with them."

"Could be the geode's history. Or yours." He paused. "Or... someone you used to know."

The words landed too precisely. Eira crossed her arms, not to seem guarded, but because she suddenly felt exposed. She quickly changed the subject.

"Do you know any of the history of the one you brought in." she asked.

"I've asked around, but don't always get polite answers when I ask questions," he said, but there was no bite to it.

That, at least, rang true.

Eira reached toward the geode again. As her fingers neared, Kael mirrored her without meaning to. Their hands stopped a hair's breadth from the surface, breath syncing in the shared space.

This time, the threads didn't hum. They stilled — entirely silent.

Kael drew back first. "That's not normal, is it?"

"No," she said. "It's worse."

Kael didn't move right away.

They both stood there, side by side at the table, hands hovering near the threads. The silence between them stretched long — not uncomfortable, but uncertain. A breath held too long.

Eira broke first, stepping back and rubbing her arms. "It's not like this with anyone else," she said quietly. "Not with Anwen, or Beck, or... anyone."

Kael watched her. "And that bothers you?"

"It confuses me," she admitted. "Everything about you feels like an unsolved puzzle. I don't like puzzles. I like predictability."

That earned a soft laugh from him — a genuine one, low and a little rough. "I don't blame you. I've been told I'm frustrating."

She looked up at him then, just as his expression softened.

"I meant what I said," he added. "I'm not here to hurt you, Eira."

"Maybe not," she murmured. "But you still might break something."

Their eyes met — and something in the air shifted. The tension between them wasn't sharp now, but soft, almost magnetic.

Kael cleared his throat and stepped away, rubbing the back of his neck. "I'll give you space. You'll want quiet to work."

She nodded, but didn't look away.

At the door, he paused. "If anything changes — with the threads, with the geode — I want to know."

"Why?" she asked.

His answer came slowly, as if it cost him something. "Because I think you're the only one who might be able to understand what's really inside them."

Then he left, and Eira stood alone with far more questions than answers.

Eira barely moved, only stared at the geode sitting in the center of her table like a stone heart refusing to beat. The threads around it had fallen still, limp in the quiet, but they didn't feel dormant — they felt... watchful.

She lit a second lamp, bathing the room in amber glow, and took up a fresh weaving circle. She wasn't done. Not yet.

Her fingers moved with practiced ease, threading emotion into motion, weaving strands of calm, curiosity, longing. The spell was subtle — a memory-pull — designed to coax any lingering imprint from the stone. It was old magic. Dangerous, if misused.

But Eira didn't flinch.

The geode warmed. A soft hum vibrated through the table and into her hands, like a heartbeat she hadn't realized she was missing. The threads shimmered—faint, then brighter—until the workshop faded around her and something else took its place.

Firelight.

Stone walls.

A man's voice.

Not Kael's. And not hers.

"She doesn't know. She can't."

The image flared, half-formed. A man stood at the edge of a cliffside camp, cloaked in deep green. His eyes burned gold in the shadows. He was speaking to someone out of sight — urgently, as if time were slipping through his fingers.

Eira tried to focus on his face. It was Caelen's face but the dragon's eyes.

Before she could call his name, the scene shattered like glass. The thread in her hands jerked taut, then seared her palm with a flash of heat so sharp she cried out.

The memory snapped back into silence.

She looked down.

A name hovered on the threads in faint light, as if burned there: Elander.

A new piece to the puzzle. A new thread to follow.

Eira sank to the floor, heart racing, breath shallow. Her hand trembled where the burn had faded into a silvery shimmer. A mark. Temporary, but real.

Something was unraveling.

She thought it had started the moment Kael had walked through her door, but perhaps he had just brought it back to the surface.

CHAPTER EIGHTEEN

Eira stared at the weave she'd just unraveled.
The threads, pale and limp, still hummed faintly with residual magic — like the echo of a song she no longer remembered. But nothing had taken. No vision. No memory. Just silence.

She reached for another strand of emotion-thread — one spun in the quiet hours of worry and isolation — and tried again. Her hands moved precisely, muscle memory guiding her as she coaxed the geode for any sliver of what she'd seen before.

Still, nothing.

The name still echoed in her mind: Elander.

She pulled her ledger toward her — the thread-bound book that held every notable experiment and thread attempt she'd ever crafted. The cover twitched faintly at her touch, threads responding to her magic. With a charmed quill, she jotted down her notes:

"Memory thread triggered name: Elander — appears tied to Caelen, or a memory involving him. Immediate burn sensation, temporary marking. Attempted reweave unsuccessful. Residual hum in thread and stone persists."

Her hand hovered.

She hesitated. Then wrote the next line more slowly:

"Emotional impact = significant. Felt… watched. Not by Kael. Something older. Bigger."

A chill traced her spine just remembering it.

She shut the book a little harder than intended, and the threads on the cover stiffened, then curled protectively inward. She laid her hand gently upon it as if asking forgiveness. They didn't like being startled. Neither did she.

She sat in the silence a moment longer, listening. The geode rested in its warded drawer beneath the heavily worn worktable, and though she couldn't see it, she felt the faint pull of its presence. Always there. Always waiting.

She couldn't force the memory back. Not like this.

But she could find the name.

And she knew exactly where to look.

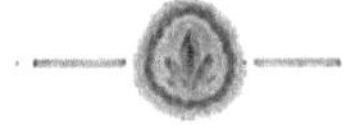

The heavy oak doors of the Brookwyn Library closed behind her with a deep, resonant thud. Carvings of mythical beasts lined the panels — owlbears and stags with threaded antlers, dragons coiled in flight — each worn smooth where generations of hands had brushed against them. The sound echoed through the stone chamber like punctuation.

Inside, the air was dry and scented with parchment and old ink — less magic than memory. A soft hush clung to the walls, not imposed but inherited. Here, even silence had ancestry.

A few elderly scholars were tucked into corners, heads bowed over scrolls and ledgers, their fingers whispering across time-worn pages. A threadwitch in one alcove coaxed ink from parchment with the tip of her nail, unraveling a secret one loop at a time.

Eira moved toward the back desk where a clerk was cataloging returns. He was an older man with a quill behind his ear and an expression like someone who had once smiled and regretted it.

"I'm looking for name records — regional," she said softly.

The clerk glanced up. "Specific period?"

"Roughly… fifty to a hundred years ago. Military or noble registry, if possible."

He raised a brow but didn't comment, turning to a wall of binders behind him. After a moment, he returned with a thick ledger wrapped in faded green twine.

"Start with this one. Registry ledgers for that time span are sorted by family origin, noble standing, and district. If the name's sensitive, don't expect a complete record."

Eira paused mid-reach. "Sensitive?"

The man's eyes flicked up. "Some names vanish. Nothing to be done about it. Paper forgets quicker than memory… especially when asked to."

The quill behind his ear twitched as if in agreement.

She said nothing, accepting the book with a nod and retreating to a quiet table in the back.

She worked quickly, skimming the alphabetized entries with the ease of someone who'd done this too many times before. A few names sparked glimmers of familiarity but none matched what she was looking for.

Her finger paused over one page — a torn fragment where a name had clearly been removed.

Clean. Intentional. Like surgery.

"Ela—"

The rest was missing.

Eira sat back in her chair, the stillness around her heavy and watchful. This wasn't erasure by time. Someone had wanted this name gone — carefully, completely.

And that meant someone else had remembered it.

The chair across from her creaked as someone dropped a coat and scarf over the back of it and then sank into it uninvited.

"You know you make that face when you're either reading about something truly horrific or planning to set someone's eyebrows on fire."

Eira didn't need to look up. "Hello, Beck."

He grinned and reached across the table, plucking a blank scrap of paper and folding it with quiet precision. "It's the 'eyebrow-on-fire' one, isn't it? Please tell me it's that. I could really use some excitement."

She sighed, leaning back in her chair. "It's just research. Boring, infuriating, missing-pages kind of research."

Beck held up the now-folded scrap — a crude paper raven. "That's the worst kind. Except maybe the kind with footnotes. Or academic rivalry. Once had a historian throw a scroll at me."

He puffed out his chest. "I dodged. It hit Anwen. She didn't even flinch."

Eira let herself smile, just a little. Beck had that effect. He could walk into a thunderstorm and leave it sunlit in his wake.

The library stretched quiet around them, heavy with thought. The scent of old paper and dust pressed at the edges of her focus, grounding and intimate. Lanterns above cast warm, shifting halos over their table, as if even the light was trying to soften the day.

"You're not usually in the library," she said.

"Correct. This place smells like mothballs and disappointment." He tapped the paper bird against her knuckles. "But Anwen mentioned you were brooding again, and she thought maybe I could lighten the mood before you turned into a historical footnote yourself."

Eira gave him a look. "That sounds more like your idea than hers."

He winked. "She might've rolled her eyes. Once."

There was a pause between them. Not awkward — familiar. Companionable.

Beck leaned in a little, voice softer now. "Want to talk about it?"

Eira hesitated, finger brushing the spine of the green-tied ledger. "It's a name. One I saw during a… magical experiment. The record was removed."

Beck didn't laugh. Didn't joke. He only nodded. "Want help?"

And for a moment, she remembered all the reasons he was one of her best friends. He had a way of standing beside her without pushing, like gravity that didn't pull too hard. He knew when she needed his humor, but also when she needed his kindness.

But as his fingers brushed hers on the table — just slightly — she felt nothing stir.

Not like Kael.

Not like Caelen.

Still… when Beck smiled, the lines around his eyes deepened, and warmth settled in her chest. Something simpler. Something safe.

She could see it now and then — quiet looks of longing he sent Anwen's way when he thought nobody was looking. And Eira hoped — deeply, quietly — that Anwen would take a chance on him someday.

Beck glanced down at the raven, turning it over in his fingers. "You know," he said lightly, "if you find out who erased the name, you should let me punch them. For dramatic flair, of course."

A scholar two tables over cleared her throat — sharp, disapproving.

Beck froze mid-flourish.

Eira arched a brow.

He leaned closer and whispered, “Apparently even hypothetical violence violates the sacred quiet.”

Then he smirked. Unapologetic. Entirely himself.

Later that evening, the wind had picked up, scattering early leaves through the streets like restless thoughts. They scraped along stone and brick, catching in doorways, slipping through fences. Eira pulled her cloak tighter as she neared her workshop — not because of the chill, but because of the man leaning casually against her doorframe.

Kael.

He looked almost bored, arms crossed, his cloak shifting in the breeze. The soft glow of the lantern above him painted gold along the line of his cheekbones, lit the shadow beneath his jaw.

“I knocked,” he said without preamble. “Three times. Thought perhaps you’d enchanted the door to ignore me.”

Eira arched a brow and smiled as she reached the door. “That’s a good idea. Don’t tempt me.”

The lock responded to her touch with a soft click, and Kael followed her inside without invitation.

Her shop was quiet in the way sacred spaces often were. The scent of oil and dusted herbs lingered beneath the sharp tang of threadwork. The work counters had been tidied from the day's tasks, but faint strands still shimmered in the air — not yet claimed or bound. They drifted lazily, like spider silk caught in hesitation.

Kael's eyes swept the room with that same calm intensity he always carried — the kind that cataloged everything but gave little away.

Eira moved with quiet purpose, hanging her cloak, pushing a stool back beneath the counter. She could feel the weight of his gaze, not leering, just *there*. Watching. Waiting.

"I need to see the geode again," he said finally.

"No," she replied without turning.

He didn't move. "You don't even want to hear my reason?"

"You're not ready." She turned then, arms crossed. "You don't understand what it holds. I barely do. Until I do… I'm not putting it at risk. Or myself."

Kael exhaled, sharp and quiet. "This isn't just about what you understand."

That pulled a bitter smile from her. "No? Then tell me what *you* know. Stop asking me to risk everything while you guard your secrets like precious coin."

He looked away for a moment — just long enough to feel intentional. "There are eyes on you, Eira. Ones you haven't seen yet."

Her arms dropped slightly. "What does that mean?"

"It means you don't have the luxury of waiting until you feel ready. The choice might be taken from you." His gaze returned to hers, steady. "Soon."

"And you think giving you the geode will fix that?"

"I think understanding it might give you a chance."

"And you'll just… hand that understanding over?"

"If I can," he said quietly. "If I think it will help you."

She turned away again, pretending to rearrange a tray of thread spools just to give her hands something to do. "I'm protecting memory," she said at last. "Not just mine. Not just yours."

There was a long pause before he spoke again, his voice softened but no less firm.

"I know you don't trust me. I've earned that. But I'm not your enemy, Eira."

She didn't respond. He was simultaneously infuriating and appealing.

When she turned back, he was closer than she expected. Not enough to startle — just enough to feel it. The shift in air pressure. The quiet gravity of him.

"I'm not your enemy," he repeated, gentler now.

"I know," she said finally. "That doesn't mean you're safe."

For a breath, neither moved.

Then — his fingers brushed hers. Light. Tentative.

The threads on the counter stirred — a soft shimmer of golden magic rising like dust motes, catching in the lamplight.

So did her heart.

Kael's expression shifted, something unspoken trying to surface — but he let it fall back beneath the surface.

"I don't want it to hurt you," he murmured. And then he was gone.

CHAPTER NINETEEN

A week later and time had run out. The envelope was thick — the kind used for tax disputes, legal warnings, or inheritance claims. The kind that made your name look more like a sentence than an address.

Eira stood in the doorway of her workshop, staring at it. Her name, written in elegant looping script, looked oddly foreign now.

Eira Wynfell
Brookwyn, Western Reach

The wax seal was already broken — her mother must've brought it in with the early post. But she hadn't said a word over breakfast. Maybe she hadn't recognized the sigil pressed into the red wax. Or maybe she had… and hadn't wanted to say it aloud.

Inside were several neatly folded pages:

A list of Council-approved inns within Virelda's southern quarter

A code of conduct for visitors to the Hall of Threads

And, atop the rest, a single sheet of heavy parchment — laced with faint traces of threadwork, its surface shimmering just enough to make Eira's skin prickle

To Eira Wynfell, daughter of Ysolde,
You are requested to appear before the Council of Threads at the Hall of Records in Virelda within seven days of receipt of this notice.

Recent disturbances in the magical registry have raised concerns regarding resonance weaving and memory-bound threadwork. Your expertise has been noted as critical in clarifying these anomalies for the Council's ongoing inquiry.

Please observe proper conduct during your journey. Magical manifestations while in transit are discouraged and may be subject to inquiry.

Approved accommodations and travel guidelines are enclosed. Travel expenses will be compensated.

Your cooperation is expected and appreciated.

With due respect,
High Registrar Maren Rellor
For the Council of Threads, Virelda

Eira read it twice.
Then a third time, hoping the words might soften.
They didn't.

Her stomach twisted as she slowly folded the letter again, pressing the crease like it might hold her world together.

The Council. The one body powerful enough to name a person gifted… or cursed.

They weren't summoning her to tea. They knew something. Maybe not everything — but enough. Kael had been right. She was being watched. She hadn't felt this sick since the day Caelen disappeared.

Eira found her mother in the garden behind the cottage, knees deep in the mint beds, coaxing stubborn weeds from around the roots. The scent of damp earth and crushed leaves swirled on the breeze, sharp and grounding.

"I take it you saw the letter," Eira said.

Ysolde didn't glance up. "I did."

"This is worse than I could have imagined," Eira murmured, stepping onto the stone path that wove through the herbs. "They want me in the capital in seven days."

Ysolde straightened, wiping her hands on her apron. "Then we start preparing."

Eira blinked. "Just like that?"

"You thought I'd chain you to the porch?"

"No," Eira said, "but I expected a lecture."

"You have no choice, so I'll save it for after you come home."

A noise behind them made Eira turn. Beck and Anwen stood at the edge of the garden — Beck with his usual grin, Anwen with her hands folded neatly, eyes calm and clear.

"What are they doing here?" Eira asked, heart already beginning to sink. "Please don't say you told them—"

"I didn't just tell them," Ysolde said. "I invited them."

Eira stared. "Why?"

Ysolde arched a brow. "Because they're not going to let you walk into this alone, and you know it."

"You should've asked me first."

"I did. You just didn't answer." She winked then turned to Beck and Anwen, giving them a small nod of welcome. "Come sit. I imagine we have a lot to discuss."

Anwen stepped forward first, silent but resolute, her near-white braid catching the last slant of sunlight. Beck followed more casually, tossing a pebble off the garden path as if this were any other day.

"I told you she'd be grumpy," Beck said to Ysolde, not unkindly. "It's part of her charm."

Eira gave him a withering look. "You're not helping."

"We know," Beck said, with that maddening grin. "But we're still coming."

They settled around the low stone bench, still warm from the day's heat. For a long moment, no one spoke.

"I don't want to drag either of you into this," Eira finally said. "The Council isn't just a few stuffy old mages — they can ruin lives."

"And you think we'd just stay home and knit socks?" Beck asked, incredulous.

Anwen's voice was soft but firm. "You'd do the same for us."

Eira opened her mouth to argue, but Ysolde cut in gently, "There's strength in being chosen. Let them choose to help you."

Eira's shoulders dropped. "I still think it's a bad idea."

Ysolde looked at the three of them together and exhaled slowly. "I hoped you'd have more time before they noticed your work again. I agreed seven years ago to keep them updated on your progress as a thread mage, and I have, to a point."

"I was working from my own research. Quietly." Eira said, bitterness creeping into her voice. "It wasn't even meant to be public,"

"Apparently not quietly enough."

"They're interested in resonance weaving," Eira continued. "They say they want to observe, but who knows what their true intentions are. I doubt they are calling me to the capital for something they've clearly already been observing."

Ysolde folded her arms. "They've drawn a line around what magic should be," she said. "And you crossed it. Now they're coming to pull you back if it suits them— or twist what you can do into something they can use."

Eira blinked, her stomach twisting. "What do you mean, I crossed it? I've barely shown anyone my work."

Ysolde's gaze dropped to her hands. "Once. Years ago. You weren't as skilled as you are now, but… even then, they saw the shape of what you might become."

"And?"

"And I made sure they left you alone. It wasn't easy." Her voice was quiet now, laced with something that sounded almost like regret. "But they agreed to keep their distance, and you stayed here. With me. Where it was safer."

"You always said I wasn't ready."

"I said that because you weren't," Ysolde replied gently, "because if they'd seen the full truth of what you can do, they'd have taken you away before you could choose who to be. I needed to know you would have the strength to resist if they asked you to use your magic in ways that would only suit their purposes."

Silence settled over the garden, heavy and still.

Beck shifted beside her and fiddled with the edge of his scarf, his easy grin long gone. Anwen's expression didn't change, but her hands had curled into the edges of her coat, eyes sharper than before.

Eira's mouth felt dry. "You should have told me."

"I didn't want you to grow up afraid of your own magic." Ysolde's voice stayed steady, but there was something tight underneath. "I wanted you to understand it first. To build something with it, before they told you what it was allowed to be."

Beck stepped a little closer — not touching Eira, but close enough she could feel the quiet heat of his support.

"Wait," he said slowly. "What is it exactly that she does?"

Ysolde looked at him, then back to Eira. "Threadwitches read memory. They interpret it, shape it, preserve it. But Eira…" She took a slow breath. "Eira feels it. Resonates with it. She draws out not just what was remembered — but what was *meant.* Even the pieces the thread's owner never meant to share. It's why she has an affinity for so many forms of thread magic. She and the threads have a deeper tie than most of us."

"I've only ever followed what the threads show me," Eira said faintly.

"No," Ysolde said. "You've followed what they *feel.* You don't just recall — you reveal. You draw out what was felt, not just what was recorded. Even if it contradicts the thread."

Eira stared down at her hands, palms faintly tinged green from the mint beds. They looked ordinary. But they didn't feel ordinary anymore. Maybe they never had.

"I thought I was just… good with resonance," she whispered.

"You are," Ysolde said. "But your magic doesn't just echo — it *cuts through.* And the Council has spent generations curating what magic is allowed to remember."

Anwen finally spoke, her voice as steady as her gaze. "So that's why they're afraid."

Ysolde nodded. "And why they'll be very careful about what they show her in return."

Eira pressed a hand to her satchel, where the geode nestled inside still pulsed — quiet, steady, insistent. Like a heartbeat trying to match her own.

"Then I guess we have to be careful, too." She said with resolve.

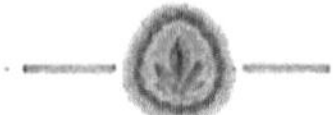

Kael showed up just before sunset.

Eira heard the low crunch of boots on gravel and the soft click of the garden gate before she saw him.

He stood just outside the fence, backlit by the golden haze of late-day sun, his coat slung over one shoulder like he hadn't a care in the world.

He looked different here — not in her shop, not in the Archives, not tangled in the wilds of memory. Softer, somehow. Less guarded. More real.

"Thought I might find you here," he said as she approached.

"You're becoming predictable," she replied, though her voice held more amusement than irritation.

Kael's grin tugged at the edge of his mouth. "Or maybe I'm just persistent."

She didn't argue. Instead, she let the silence stretch, long enough for the tension to settle between them like thread waiting to be pulled.

"I heard," he said finally, his gaze flicking toward the folded letter in her hand. "The Council."

Eira nodded. "It's not a request."

"No," he said quietly. "It never is."

He stepped inside the fence now, close enough that she could see the faint mark on his jaw — a scar, maybe, or just a memory the light hadn't yet faded.

"I want to come with you."

The words hit like a dropped needle — small but sharp.

Eira blinked. "Why?"

"Because I know what the Council does to people they don't understand."
He hesitated, then added more softly, "And because you shouldn't have to face that alone."

She opened her mouth — almost reminded him that she wouldn't be. Beck and Anwen were already packed. Already stubborn. Already with her.

But this wasn't about company.

They'd never stood in the Hall of Threads. They'd never had their magic questioned, dissected, cataloged like something dangerous.

Kael had.

She looked at him again — really looked. And for a moment, she saw something beneath the calm: the weight of it, the years, the regret. Something worn into him like creases in well-loved fabric.

Her heart fluttered — soft, unwilling.

"I don't even know what they want from me," she said.

"Then let's find out together."

She hesitated. Then, with a sigh, she stepped aside and opened the gate.

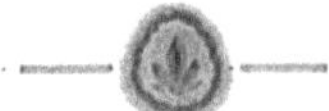

The cottage felt smaller with Kael inside it. Not because of his height — though he was tall — but because he moved with that quiet, self-assured grace that filled space without effort.

Ysolde noticed it, too. She offered him tea with a politeness Eira recognized as her mother's version of a note to proceed carefully.

They sat at the table, the letter from the Council spread between them. Kael traced a finger along the edge of the parchment — not touching the words, just thinking.

"So," he said. "They're finally paying attention to resonance weaving."

"They've paid attention before," Ysolde said, voice crisp. "They've just never been allowed to see as much as they have now."

Kael looked at Eira. "Did you sense they were watching your work?"

"I didn't, not until you cautioned someone was watching. They must be hiding better than the last time" she said. "Most of my research has been personal. Quiet. Not the kind that draws official interest."

"Unless someone mentioned your name," he said, eyes narrowing slightly.

Eira thought of the stone in her satchel — the one she still hadn't shown him. It pulsed sometimes, like it was trying to speak. Like it remembered something she didn't.
She didn't trust what the Council might read into that. So she said nothing.

"Have you ever faced them?" she asked Kael.

"Yes." His voice cooled. "They don't forget. Or forgive."

Ysolde stood and turned to the counter, her back to them. "Then we'll make sure they don't get the chance to decide either."

She wasn't looking at Kael when she said it, but Eira felt the message all the same.

Kael looked back at her. "You're going either way, aren't you?"

"Yes," she said. "I don't have a choice."

"Then I'm still coming."

Ysolde sighed. Not in resistance — just weariness. "At least take the night to rest. It's a three day journey and they've given you seven. The road south doesn't show mercy to the tired."

Kael smiled faintly. "I'm used to long roads."

The cottage was still, wrapped in the hush that came just before sunrise. Eira moved through the familiar space with practiced hands, checking her satchel for the third time. She didn't trust herself to remember everything — not today.

She tucked in a packet of dried ginger bark, a spool of thread that shimmered faintly blue, and a small velvet pouch Anwen had pressed into her hands the night before. "Something for steadiness," her friend had murmured. "In case the road shakes you."

Last of all, she added the geode — wrapped in linen, but still warm to the touch. It pulsed faintly when her fingers brushed the surface, like it knew she was leaving.

A knock sounded at the back door.

Beck, already saddled with a second satchel, and extra long scarf, and a mismatched pair of gloves, grinned as he pushed the door open. "Ready for a terrible breakfast and a long walk?"

Eira rolled her eyes. "You could try pretending to be helpful."

"I *am* helpful. I brought the rolls for breakfast." He held up a slightly crumpled paper bag. "And Anwen."

Anwen appeared behind him, braid coiled tightly against her pale neck, boots laced with quiet determination.

"Didn't think we were letting you sneak off," she said softly.

Eira's throat tightened. "I still think it's a bad idea."

"We know," Beck said. "But we're still coming."

Kael arrived a few minutes later, leaning against the post outside as if he'd been there all along. His coat was freshly brushed, his satchel slung over one shoulder, and his expression unreadable.

CHAPTER TWENTY

The road out of Brookwyn was little more than a worn footpath, the kind used more by foragers and wandering deer than regular travelers. As the village disappeared behind them, the last signs of civilization faded too — fences gave way to low stone walls crumbling with moss, and carefully tended orchards surrendered to wild thickets of hazel and ash.

Eira adjusted the strap of her bag and exhaled slowly. Her boots already carried the wear of recent miles — the stitch circle hadn't been far, but it had reminded her how much the world could shift just outside town limits. Now, with the capital three days ahead, that shift felt heavier. The path narrowed between tangled trees, a slow descent into older woods where the light filtered green and gold through the canopy above.

Behind her, Beck whistled a meandering tune that wandered as much as the trail. Anwen kept pace silently at her side, ever-watchful, her gaze scanning the trees with the same careful rhythm she used to sort herbs in the apothecary. Kael walked a few paces behind them all, his presence quiet but unmistakable — like a shadow that knew your name.

They'd only been walking a few hours, but the mood was already taut. Eira felt it in the silence more than anything — the unsaid things strung like thread between them.

Beck cleared his throat dramatically. "I don't mean to alarm anyone, but I think we've already passed at least three perfect picnic spots. If we keep this up, I may be forced to start ranking them aloud."

Anwen didn't look at him. "You do that anyway."

"I do *not,*" Beck said, mock-offended. "I rank for educational purposes. So that future travelers may benefit from my tireless devotion to scenic seating."

Eira snorted. "You just want to sit down."

"I *do* want to sit down," Beck admitted cheerfully. "But also — don't we have, like, three whole days of this ahead of us? Seems rude not to pace ourselves."

"No one's stopping you," Kael said evenly, the faintest edge of wryness in his tone.

Beck looked over his shoulder with a grin. "Careful, Kael. That almost sounded like camaraderie."

Kael didn't respond. But he didn't deny it, either.

By late afternoon, the trail had thinned into little more than a suggestion between roots and stones. The forest had grown denser, quieter — the kind of quiet that made your ears strain and your thoughts wander. Eira felt the shift in the air like a thread being pulled — away from home and toward something she couldn't name.

They made camp in a small clearing nestled among moss-covered stones and wind-fallen trees. The last rays of sunlight filtered through the branches in lazy slants, gilding everything in soft gold.

Beck started gathering firewood with theatrical purpose, declaring himself the "flame whisperer." Anwen, unfazed, silently helped him gather kindling with the efficiency of someone who was used to turning Beck's chaos into order. Kael said nothing, but unslung the packs and began arranging the bedrolls around a central log.

Eira stepped away from the bustle, her fingers trailing along the bark of a gnarled beech. The forest here smelled older — not in decay, but in memory. She closed her eyes and breathed deep.

It felt like the beginning of something.

"Fire's ready!" Beck called, his voice breaking the hush. "And — surprise — I didn't burn my eyebrows off."

Eira smiled, stepping back into the ring of light. They passed food between them — dried meat, soft rolls wrapped in cloth, and an herbal tea Anwen brewed from her travel pouch. The warmth seeped through the chill that had settled in her bones.

Laughter came more easily than expected. Even Kael, when pressed into the conversation, offered a wry observation about Beck's obsession with ranking wild mushrooms by personality. It was ridiculous, and oddly charming.

As night deepened and the flames danced lower, the group sat in the flickering hush of embers. Beck stretched and sighed dramatically.

"Do you remember the first time we met?" he asked, voice soft.

Anwen raised a brow. "You tried to steal Eira's satchel."

"It was a *misunderstanding*," Beck said, hands raised in defense. "I was young. Impulsive. Bold. Also, I really liked that satchel."

"Mine was green. Yours was blue," Eira said with a smirk.

"See? Practically identical." He nudged her with his foot. "Anyway, if I hadn't tried to swipe it, we wouldn't all be here. I'm a walking destiny catalyst."

"You're a walking cautionary tale," Anwen muttered, but there was a smile on her lips.

Kael tilted his head slightly. "So… you three have known each other since childhood?"

"Brookwyn isn't big," Anwen said. "We've known *everyone* since childhood. But somewhere along the way… these two stuck."

Eira met Beck's gaze, her voice quiet. "They became my people."

Beck's teasing smile faded into something gentler. "You're ours too, you know."

The fire crackled between them. The words settled soft as wool — and warmer.

Kael didn't speak right away. But his gaze had gone distant, shadowed by something unspoken.

"I didn't think I'd ever feel that again," he said eventually, his voice low.

Eira looked at him. "Feel what?"

He hesitated in a way that was rare for him. “Belonging.”

No one replied.

But no one dismissed it, either.

Later, as the fire burned low and shadows stretched long across the forest floor, the group settled into a soft hush. Anwen sat beside Beck near the edge of the firelight, her head eventually tipping against his shoulder. He didn’t move — just let her rest, his posture relaxed but alert, gaze fixed somewhere beyond the glow.

Eira and Kael were the only ones still speaking.

She sat cross-legged, arms wrapped tightly around her knees, her cloak drawn close. The fire cast soft light on her face, painting her expression in gold and ember-red. Her gaze was fixed on the flames, unmoving — as if they might answer a question she didn’t want to say aloud.

Kael stirred the fire absently with a stick, sending a small spray of sparks into the night. “You know,” he said quietly, “I didn’t lie about why I came. But there’s more to it than the geode.”

Eira didn’t look at him. Her voice was calm, but distant. “I assumed there was.”

A silence settled between them — not cold, just cautious.

"I knew about your threads," Kael continued, his tone soft, not quite confessing, not quite defending. "What you could do. What your family had guarded. But I wasn't sent to take it."

She finally turned, eyes reflecting the firelight like candlelit glass. "Then why come?"

Kael hesitated, rubbing his hands together as if unsure whether to speak or warm them. "Because I needed to understand it. And because I needed to meet the person who carried it."

Eira's breath caught in her throat.

"Why?"

He looked at her then — not the sidelong glance of someone testing the water, but a full gaze, open and steady.

"Because you matter," he said, "and truth matters. Before I ever even met you, you mattered."

The fire cracked softly. Eira didn't speak. She didn't move. But something behind her eyes flickered.

Kael dropped his gaze again, as if suddenly unsure of the moment. "I thought I could stay detached. Just gather information. Keep my distance. But…" He trailed off, the words failing him for once.

"You can't," Eira said quietly.

He gave a small, dry laugh. "No. Turns out I'm not as good at distance as I thought."

They sat in silence after that, the hush between them thick with unspoken things. Something was being woven there in the dark — something fragile, and real.

After a bit, Kael pulled out a notebook and soft charcoals and began sketching the scene around him. For the first time, Kael looked less like a spy or a soldier and more like a man who had lost more than he let on.

Eventually, Anwen stirred and sat up, rubbing her eyes. Without a word, she uncurled from Beck's side and slipped into her bedroll nearby. Beck watched her for a moment, then stood, brushing off his coat and beginning a quiet loop around the edge of camp.

The fire had burned down to low embers, and the stars stretched sharp and silver overhead. The night was quiet — not heavy, just still — as if the forest had decided to listen instead of speak.

Eira sat wrapped in her blanket with her back against a tree, knees pulled close. Kael sat a few paces away, his notebook resting on his lap, though his pencil hadn't moved in a while.

"You're different out here," he said quietly.

Eira turned her head toward him. "Out where?"

"Outside the shop. Outside the village. You seem… lighter. You smile more."

She shrugged, a small motion beneath the blanket. "The past few years have changed me a lot. I have a lot more responsibilities. I forget how much the walls press in until I'm not surrounded by them."

Kael nodded, his gaze tilted toward the stars. "I always felt that way in cities. Like the buildings are holding their breath, waiting to close in."

A pause settled between them, soft-edged. Then Kael glanced her way again. "So tell me something not magical."

Eira raised a brow. "Not magical?"

"Not magical. Not world-ending. Not stitched into ancient thread conspiracies. Just… something about you."

She was quiet for a moment, then said, "When I was seven, I tried to dye my hair with beetroot paste because I thought it would make me look more mysterious."

Kael smiled. "Did it work?"

"No. My hair dried into clumps so stiff I looked like a scarecrow that had lost the fight with the rain. It took three days and half the town's herbal rinse stock to get it out."

He laughed — a real one this time, low and surprised. "Why mysterious?"

"I'd just read a story about a sorceress with plum-colored hair and a tragic past. I didn't know what a tragic past was yet, but I figured I could at least do the hair."

He shook his head, still grinning. "You're dangerous. The kind of girl who takes the narrative into her own hands."

"I was a handful as a child." Eira smiled, brushing a bit of leaf from her blanket. "Your turn."

Kael tilted his head, considering. "When I was nine, I tried to build a glider out of barn wood and linen scraps. I was determined to fly off the ridge behind our house."

She blinked. "Did you survive?"

"Barely. I broke two toes and dented our neighbor's goat pen."

"That explains so much."

He grinned. "Hey, you never know unless you try."

They sat there a while longer, the conversation meandering from one story to another — tiny, harmless truths traded like charms around a fire. It made Eira's heart relax in a way it hadn't around him before.

Eventually, the air cooled and the quiet stretched long again. Eira drew her blanket tighter and exhaled slowly.

Kael's voice came again, softer this time. "I meant what I said earlier. I'm not going to hurt you, Eira."

"I believe you," she said, surprised by how much she meant it.

He looked at her then — really looked — and she felt it again: that slow, steady pull that had nothing to do with thread or geodes.

"I should try to sleep," she said, eyes dipping to the fire.

Kael nodded. "Good night."

"Good night."

Even as she closed her eyes, warmth lingered beneath her skin — not just from the fire, but from the way laughter had made the night feel less haunted.

CHAPTER TWENTY-ONE

The first light of morning filtered through the trees, brushing the clearing with gold. Mist still clung to the low ground, softening the world into blurred edges and chilled breath. The fire had burned low overnight, reduced to a cradle of coals that cast little warmth.

Eira woke to the scent of ashroot tea and something sharper—dawnleaf, maybe. Her limbs were stiff, the ground beneath her sleeping roll stubbornly uneven. She sat up slowly, tugging her cloak tighter, and scanned the camp.

Beck crouched beside the fire pit, coaxing it back to life with exaggerated determination. "Witness the miracle of flame," he intoned solemnly. "May it toast our toes and spare our breakfast."

Anwen handed him a tin mug without comment, her hair already braided and her sleeves rolled. "Try not to set yourself on fire," she said, though her voice held no urgency. She was already sorting supplies with the practiced calm of someone who had traveled often and packed wisely. It made sense since she often went with her mother to forage wild grown plants for the apothecary.

Eira rubbed at her eyes and stretched. A bird called once, somewhere high in the trees. Otherwise, the world was still.

Kael sat apart from the others, perched on a flat stone just beyond the ring of mist. He wasn't watching them.

He was sketching.

His coat was folded beside him, and his journal rested on one knee. The charcoal in his hand moved with easy familiarity—not rushed, not idle. He glanced up occasionally, gaze flicking between the trees, the embers, the tilt of Beck's mug.

He sketched the world the way it was when no one was looking.

Eira didn't speak. Didn't move. But something about it struck her—not the act itself, but the quiet care of it. Kael, the ever-unreadable stranger, was drawing while the world still yawned around them.

And no one else seemed to notice.

By the time she stood and rolled her blanket, he had closed the journal and tucked it away. His expression was unreadable, his posture easy.

"Trail looks steeper today," he said as if nothing had happened.

"Of course it does," Beck muttered, stuffing a half-burnt crust of bread into his mouth. "Nature is a cruel and vengeful mistress."

"Eat faster," Anwen said. "We've got miles to cover and not enough daylight."

Eira took the mug Anwen passed her and drank the warm tea slowly, letting the heat unknot her muscles. No one rushed the moment. They each ate what they could—some dried fruit, a bit of bread, jerky softened near the fire.

Only when the food was gone did Anwen begin lacing up her pack again.

Eira shouldered her own, her gaze drifting once more toward Kael's coat pocket, where the journal now rested.

She didn't know what he'd drawn.

But she knew it made him feel more real.

Beck stood last, brushing crumbs from his fingers. He gave a quick glance around the camp, then looked at the others—his expression still light, but quieter.

"Whatever today throws at us," he said, "you won't face it alone."

He didn't elaborate.

He didn't need to.

Anwen tightened the straps on her satchel and nodded toward the east. "Trail picks up past the ridge. We'll want to get through the switchbacks before the mist thickens."

Beck groaned. "Switchbacks? Again? I miss flat terrain. I miss roads. I miss chairs."

"You slept in a chair last time and complained for three days," Anwen said.

"Exactly," Beck replied, adjusting his scarf. "Chairs keep me humble."

Kael rose without a word, already scanning the tree line. He moved with a fluid sort of alertness, like someone always listening for the next shift in the wind.

Eira tightened her cloak and followed the others onto the narrow path that wound up through the trees, damp and leaf-strewn, the air thick with morning chill.

Day two had begun.

And the threads were pulling tighter.

The trail narrowed beneath their feet, winding up a steep hill where tree roots curled like knotted veins across the dirt. By midday, the morning mist had begun to lift, but the dampness lingered—clinging to cloaks and turning dry leaves into slick hazards underfoot.

Eira focused on her footing, but her mind wandered—drifting between the memory of Caelen's steady gaze and the spark of Kael's teasing smirk. Both unsettled her in different ways. She didn't have room in her thoughts for more complications. She should be focusing on her upcoming meeting with the council.

"Watch the slope," Anwen called softly from ahead.

Too late.

Behind Eira, the crunch of gravel gave way to a muffled curse. She spun just in time to see Kael's boot slide on the slick incline. He tried to catch himself, hand reaching for a tree—but momentum carried him backward. He twisted as he fell, one knee slamming into a jagged outcrop before he hit the brush below with a grunt and a rustle of leaves.

"Kael!" Eira rushed down the slope, heart pounding.

Anwen and Beck turned at the sound, but she was already kneeling beside him, hands hovering.

He winced, but his grin still surfaced—crooked, familiar. "Don't worry. Just testing the ground's sturdiness. Thoroughly."

"Idiot," Beck muttered, but the concern behind the word softened it.

"You're bleeding," Eira said, fingers brushing the tear in his pant leg. The gash wasn't deep, but blood was already soaking through the fabric. "Didn't you hear Anwen's warning?"

Kael shrugged with one shoulder. "Thought I could manage. Usually can."

Her hands hesitated. She wasn't used to touching him—had tried not to, in fact—but now that she was this close, she couldn't ignore how warm he was. How solid. How his grin faded just slightly the longer she stayed.

"Let me see it," she murmured, voice softer than she meant.

She reached into her pouch and tore a strip of cloth from the lining. As she worked, a faint shimmer pulsed through the threads woven into it—responding to her focus, humming softly against her skin.

Kael noticed. His gaze flicked from the cloth to her hands, then back up to her face.

"Fancy stitches," he said.

She didn't answer. Couldn't. Because as she tied the makeshift bandage around his leg, her fingers brushed his skin—and the threads hummed louder. As if they, too, recognized something shifting.

He looked at her then, really looked. No grin this time. Just stillness, and something searching behind his eyes.

"Thanks," he said quietly.

Eira swallowed. "Don't be stupid again."

"I'll try," he said. But there was warmth in it now. Real warmth. Something deeper than amusement.

From farther up the trail, Anwen called, "We'll rest at the next clearing!"

"Come on," Beck added. "Before Kael finds another way to test gravity."

Eira stood and offered Kael her arm. He took it—just for balance, just for a moment.

But neither of them let go right away.

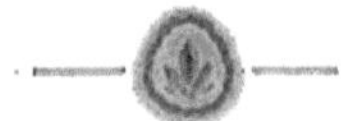

The clearing was small, nestled in a quiet dip between moss-covered boulders and the trunks of old pine. Dappled light filtered through the trees, casting golden flecks on the damp earth. Anwen laid out a woven mat while Beck gathered kindling, his brow furrowed in rare silence.

Eira sat beside Kael on a smooth stone, inspecting the makeshift bandage. She gently unwrapped it, fingers practiced and careful.

"You could've done worse," she said, cleaning the wound with a small vial of herbal tincture from her satchel. The scent of witchhazel and rosemary rose between them, sharp and grounding.

"I've had worse," Kael murmured. The humor from earlier was gone now, replaced by something quieter. Warier. "But I appreciate the concern."

Eira glanced at him, unsure how to respond. His tone had shifted again—less smug, less guarded.

Vulnerable, almost.

"It's not about concern," she said. "It's about keeping us all moving."

But the words felt thinner than she intended.

Kael studied her for a long moment. "You're not very good at pretending you don't care."

She didn't meet his gaze. "That's not fair."

"No," he agreed softly. "It's not."

Silence stretched between them, not heavy—just wide enough for truths to echo if they let them.

Eira focused on the bandage, weaving faint threads of healing into the cloth before wrapping it snugly around his leg. The magic pulsed once, barely visible in the shifting light. Kael's eyes tracked the movement like someone watching the first hint of fire in a cold hearth.

"Does it hurt?" she asked, more to fill the space than out of necessity.

"Not as much as you ignoring me."

She turned to glare at him—but found herself smiling, despite everything. "You're insufferable, I'm right here clearly not ignoring you."

He leaned just slightly closer, the angles of his expression softened into something almost shy. "I suppose you haven't run off screaming yet. I'm taking it as a good sign."

The tension between them hummed—quiet and real. A thread pulled taut in her heart. She looked away first, rising to her feet.

"I should check in with Anwen."

Before she could step away, Kael caught her hand. Gently. No pressure. Just contact.

"You don't have to be afraid of me."

She stilled. Looked down at their joined hands. Her threads stirred again—warm and uncertain.

"I'm not afraid of you," she whispered. "I'm afraid of what I don't know yet."

Then she slipped her hand free and turned toward Anwen—heart thudding far too fast for someone who claimed she wasn't afraid.

They walked in silence for a time, the rhythm of boots over damp forest floor steadying Eira's thoughts. Beck led now, humming something half-remembered under his breath, while Anwen followed just behind him, eyes always scanning the trees.

Kael walked beside Eira again, his limp slight but undeniable. She kept glancing at his bandage.

"You should've let me reinforce it," she said quietly.

"I'm fine," he replied. "You did enough."

"That's not what I meant."

Kael slowed just enough for their shoulders to brush. "I know."

Up ahead, Beck ducked beneath a low-hanging branch and called back over his shoulder, "If you two need a moment to whisper sweet nothings, I'll wait."

Eira flushed. "We're not—"

Anwen cut her off with a glance. "Let him be Beck. You're just jealous no one's walking beside you."

"Incorrect," Beck said, grinning. "I'm waiting for someone with better taste."

"Then I suggest a long wait," Kael muttered.

Beck's laughter bounced off the trees. It felt good. Familiar. For a moment, the tension in Eira's chest loosened.

But then a sharp crack echoed in the distance — too crisp, too deliberate to be wind or wildlife.

Eira froze. "Did anyone else—"

"I heard it," Anwen said immediately, her hand already moving to the blade at her hip.

Beck turned, eyes narrowing. "Could be an animal."

Kael's fingers hovered near his knife. "Or not."

The forest went still. Not silent, exactly — but listening.

Watching.

Eira's magic stirred. Threads she couldn't name prickled at her fingertips like static before a storm.

"We move," she said, steadying her voice. "Fast, and quiet."

They slipped into the trees like water finding the cracks — low, quiet, practiced. The hush of their steps barely disturbed the underbrush, but still, Eira couldn't shake the sensation of something trailing them.

Not close.

But near enough to unsettle.

Only when the woods gave way to a rocky outcrop did they slow, breath fogging faintly in the cooler air, every one of them listening.

Kael spoke first. "Whatever that was… it was watching us."

"I hate being watched," Beck muttered.

"You like being admired," Anwen said.

"That's completely different."

Eira didn't smile. Not this time. Her pulse hadn't slowed. She moved to the edge of the clearing, eyes scanning the woods behind them.

Nothing.

And yet—

Her magic pulsed. Threads twitched.

Something was coming.

She could feel it.

Not in her body.

Not in her mind.

But in the threads.

By the time the sun dipped below the forest canopy, shadows stretched long across the path, and the unease of the earlier disturbance still clung to them like mist. They made camp in a sheltered alcove between several large pines, their small fire carefully shielded with stones and a low line of woven brush to hide the glow.

Eira chewed a strip of dried meat slowly, barely tasting it. Her back ached, but she didn't complain. No one did. The tension hadn't vanished. The idea that someone might be following or watching didn't sit well.

"We'll take first watch," Beck said, tossing a twig into the flames. He glanced at Anwen with a tired grin. "Try not to fall asleep mid-sentence this time."

Anwen didn't look up. "One of us has to stay awake."

Kael shifted slightly, eyes flicking to Eira before he spoke. "That puts you with me on second watch."

He raised a brow—not a challenge, not a tease. Just a quiet question.

Eira met his gaze across the fire. "Fine by me."

They took over when the fire had dwindled to embers, and Beck's snoring punctuated the quiet like an overly confident drumbeat. Eira sat cross-legged, hands tucked into her sleeves for warmth. Kael settled beside her — a little closer than necessary.

"I didn't mean to scare you earlier," he said.

"You didn't," she replied too quickly. Then, after a breath: "Maybe a little."

He tilted his head. "Was it the fall? Or just me?"

She glanced sideways at him. "You want the honest answer?"

"I'll take whatever you give me."

Eira exhaled, long and soft. "It's both." She hesitated. "You walk through my world like you belong here, but you don't. And yet, I keep wanting to trust you even though I feel like you're not telling me everything."

Kael watched her, expression unreadable. "I never expected to find someone like you."

"That's vague."

"It's honest." He plucked a leaf from the ground, rolling it between his fingers. "You care deeply. But you hide it well. I think it's a defense."

"Everyone has defenses."

"True. But not everyone builds theirs with such precision."

Eira was quiet for a long moment, then said, "My mother had another student when I was younger. He was a few years older and always looked out for me. He was more than a friend, more than a mentor. He left before we had really defined our relationship and we'd thought he would be back within a year or two. He wasn't."

Kael didn't speak. He just waited.

"When he vanished," she said softly, "I buried every thread tied to that part of me. If I seem hard to know, it's because… I'm still stitched together with the memory of someone who never said goodbye."

The fire cracked softly.

Kael's voice was low as he reached his hand out and gently brushed her cheek with his fingers. "I'm not him. But I'll stay. As long as you'll let me."

She didn't answer immediately. Instead, she tucked a stray copper strand behind her ear and met his eyes.

The glow beneath her skin caught the moonlight — faint, but unmistakable.

Kael noticed. But like before, he said nothing.

He offered her silence.

And understanding.

And somehow, that felt like the beginning of something important.

CHAPTER TWENTY-TWO

The wind off the high ridge tugged at Eira's braid, threading through her cloak like curious fingers. Below them, the city of Virelda shimmered—its domed Archive gleaming in the afternoon light, ringed by narrow towers and crowded rooftops. From here, it looked still and perfect, like something stitched in glass.

But Eira's thoughts were anything but still.

Caelen was down there. Somewhere.

Whether in human form or as the dragon that had once sheltered her, she didn't know. He'd left her with memories folded into stone, promises stitched into silence, and not even a proper goodbye. Her stomach twisted.

She was torn—caught between the past and present, between the echo of Caelen's warmth and the unfamiliar pull of Kael.

Anwen stood quietly a few steps away, eyes scanning the city. Kael lingered behind them just out of hearing range, arms crossed, face unreadable. But it was Beck who stepped closer.

"You look like you're about to jump off this cliff just to avoid a conversation," he said softly.

Eira blinked. "Is it that obvious?"

He shrugged. "Only to someone who's spent enough time hiding behind jokes."

She turned to look at him. "You don't hide."

Beck grinned, but it didn't quite reach his eyes. "Sure I do. Just... louder than most."

The wind shifted, carrying the scent of hearth smoke from the valley below. For a long moment, they both stood in silence.

"Want some advice?" Beck asked finally.

"From you?" she teased, trying to find her footing.

He elbowed her lightly. "I'm full of surprises."

Eira gave a faint laugh. "Alright. Let's hear it."

Beck's voice lowered. "When it comes to feelings—the big, messy, heart-splintering kind—you've got to stop treating them like thread."

She frowned. "What do you mean?"

"You can't untangle them cleanly," he said. "Can't sort them by color or stitch them into neat rows. They're wild. They overlap. Sometimes they fray."

He glanced at Kael, then back at her. "And sometimes... you care about two people at once, and it doesn't make you a villain."

Eira's throat tightened. "I never meant to—"

"I know," Beck said. "You've got a good heart, Eira. Just don't tie it so tight trying to protect everyone else that you forget to let it feel."

She looked at him then—really looked—and for once, the grin was gone. What she saw instead was someone *steadfast beneath the chaos.*

"I'll try," she said.

He smiled and clapped her shoulder. "Good. Now let's go dazzle a bunch of power-hungry thread-snobs with our charm."

"Subtlety," Anwen said, dryly.

"Oh right. That too."

The path down from the ridge grew narrower, then widened again as it curved toward the capital, where the trees fell away and the full sweep of Virelda revealed itself.

It glittered in the afternoon light, all tiered rooftops and gleaming domes, stitched across the hills like a tapestry woven of copper and stone. The Archive's great dome rose near the city's heart, its glass panes catching the sun like a beacon.

But what struck Eira wasn't the view — it was the *energy.*

Magic pulsed in the air here, thick with threads. Thousands of threads. So many that they buzzed faintly against her skin, like static before a storm. Emotions clung to the streets ahead like fabric hung out to dry — fear, hope, memory, weariness — and the constant hum of motion beneath it all.

She pressed her palm briefly to the satchel at her side, grounding herself.

"Is it supposed to feel like this?" she murmured.

"It's like walking into a spell mid-weave," Beck said, voice pitched low. "There's beauty in it. But get tangled, and it'll eat you alive."

Kael said nothing, but Eira felt his awareness sharpen beside her.

Anwen exhaled slowly. "Let's not linger."

The city gates loomed ahead — carved archways with spiral inlays and thin columns etched with threadscript too fine to read at a distance. People filtered in and out beneath them: merchants in travel-worn cloaks, a courier balancing scroll cases, a cluster of children trailing glowing thread charms that danced like minnows.

As they passed through, no guards stopped them. No checkpoints. But Eira still felt eyes on them.

Inside the walls, the city unfolded in layers — streets braided like ribbon, lanes twisting upward into terraced marketplaces and downward into narrow shadows. Color spilled from every corner: banners strung between buildings, shutters painted fern green or sun-bright gold.

But not all the marks on the city were so bright.

Here and there, clusters of figures loitered at corners and archways, their cloaks plain but each marked with a band of dark orange tied around the arm. The cloth was rough, unevenly dyed, yet unmistakable in its defiance. Some leaned against walls with idle confidence, others pressed pamphlets into passersby's hands.

Eira frowned. "Those armbands—?"

"Veilbreakers," Kael said, his tone like a blade sheathed in cloth. The name was enough to make a few heads turn as they walked past.

"They believe truth itself can be broken," he continued, low enough for only their group to hear. "Not just veiled, not just hidden. Changed. Rewritten. They want to tear down the veil between what is, and what they wish it to be."

One of the orange-banded zealots caught Eira's gaze and smirked, as if daring her to challenge the idea. A ripple of unease ran through her.

And always, the *magic*. Too much, too fast. Not hostile, but heady. Thrumming through the bones of the city.

A thread-glass spinner demonstrated her art in a corner stall, coaxing flame-thread into a sculpture of a bird mid-flight. Just down the street, a boy offered "weather-thread weaves" for travelers — little woven charms said to shift temperature around your collar.

But for every marvel, there was a mirror.

In the shadowed spaces between alleys, Eira glimpsed patched cloaks and worn shoes. A woman selling cut flowers leaned heavily on a cane wrapped in frayed velvet. A man knelt outside a closed door with a sign that read *Back rents due*. Even in a city of thread, not every stitch held.

After what felt like a dozen turns and twice as many stairways, they arrived at the inn.

It stood at the corner of a quiet square, nestled beneath an arched walkway with lanterns hung from wrought iron hooks. The sign read **The Tether's End**, painted in a curling script above a symbol of a threaded needle.

Inside, it was dim and warm. Woven tapestries hung along the walls — abstract pieces of sunbursts, braided rivers, and a phoenix stitched in gold. The scent of tea and wood polish lingered in the air, threaded through with something floral and sharp.

The innkeeper greeted them from behind a carved reception desk. He was older, with silver-threaded hair and ink-stained fingertips, and he didn't ask questions — just passed over four old-fashioned brass keys.

"You're lucky," he said, not unkindly. "One small room each. Cancellations this morning."

Each room had its own narrow door off a rounded hallway, the keys marked only with thread-colored tags.

Eira stepped into hers and let the door shut with a soft *click*.

The room was small but clean, with a round window overlooking a flower-strewn rooftop garden, a narrow bed, a washstand, and a writing desk scarred by decades of use. A vase of fresh sprigs — lavender, mint, and something bitter — sat by the window.

The city's hum was quieter here. Not gone, just... softened. Muted by stone and space.

She sat on the edge of the bed and let herself breathe.

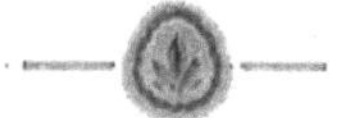

The knock was soft. Hesitant.
Not the kind of knock Kael usually gave.

Eira sat up on the edge of the bed, where she'd been half-lost in the shimmer of magic still buzzing through her senses. The hum of the capital hadn't faded since they arrived — threads brushing her awareness like murmurs she couldn't quite translate.

"Eira?"
A pause. Then his voice again. "Can we talk?"

She opened the door without answering.

Kael stood in the hall with his hands shoved deep into his pockets. He didn't flash his usual grin or offer some offhand quip.

"I know it's been a long day and dinner is in about an hour," he said, avoiding her gaze, "but I could use a little air. And I'd rather not be alone with my thoughts."

She stared at him a beat too long, then gave a small nod and stepped into the hallway, following him silently up the back stairs to the rooftop terrace.

The city stretched out below them in glimmering layers — lamplit balconies, domed towers, a dozen shades of slate and stone. The sky was deepening to blue-violet, stars barely visible through the glow. The Archive's dome glowed faintly, like a lantern beneath thick glass.

For a while, neither of them spoke. The quiet between them was full of things unsaid.

Finally, Kael said, "You've been quiet since we got here."

Eira kept her eyes on the glow of the Archive dome in the distance. "There's someone I knew, the mentor I mentioned earlier" she said slowly. "He's supposed to be there. At the Archive."

Kael didn't speak, but she could feel his attention shift toward her.

"I haven't seen him in seven years," she continued. "He left, and I... never really understood why. I thought I did, at first. But lately, I've started to wonder if I was just telling myself stories so I didn't have to feel how much it hurt."

Her voice had gone too soft, too exposed. She looked away.

"I thought I'd moved on," she said. "But just being here—just *knowing* he might be nearby—it's…" She shook her head. "It's more than I expected."

Kael exhaled, slow and steady. "You cared for him."

"I still do," she admitted, her voice barely audible."It's like... I kept that part of myself tucked away for so long, I forgot I hadn't let it go."

She turned to him. "Does that change things?"

He met her gaze then, and for the first time, there was no teasing glint behind his eyes — just something raw. "Only if you want it to. Everyone has their own ghosts in this place."

She turned to look at him, really look, and for the first time since they'd met, he looked truly uncertain. Like the city had scraped the polish off his confidence, leaving something raw underneath.

"Is that what this is for you?" she asked. "Coming back here?"

He didn't answer right away. "I could tell you," he said, then stopped. His jaw tightened like he was reeling the words back in. "But if I do... I don't know if you'll still look at me the same."

She nodded a look of concern flickering across her expression. "I figured you weren't sharing everything."

He finally looked at her. "We all have parts of ourselves we're not ready to share."

There was no accusation in it — just a quiet truth that settled between them.

They stood in silence for a while, both pretending to watch the city. But neither was really looking at the lights.

After awhile Kael left leaving her to her thoughts. Eira lingered on the rooftop.

The wind had picked up, tugging gently at the hem of her cloak, brushing cool fingers through her hair. Below, the city still pulsed with life — lamps flickering, footsteps echoing in narrow alleys, voices carrying like distant waves.

But up here, it felt suspended. Still.

She wrapped her arms around herself, not from cold, but from something harder to name.

It wasn't just the city. It wasn't just the Archive or the strange hum of magic in the air.

It was the feeling of being pulled in too many directions. Of remembering someone who had once made her feel safe, and standing beside someone who made her feel… seen.

Caelen had left without a word. Seven years, and she still didn't understand it. Kael had arrived full of charm and secrets, and she still didn't understand *him*, either.

But the past couple days — just in small moments — she'd seen a crack in his armor. And it had reminded her that she wasn't the only one haunted by uncertainty.

She closed her eyes, letting the threads brush against her senses. They shimmered and shifted in the air around her — rich with emotion, woven through the city like veins of light. But where they used to feel like extensions of herself, now they felt tangled. Thicker. Complicated.

Maybe that's just who I am now, she thought. Tangled, too.

She stayed there until the wind grew stronger and the rooftop felt less like a sanctuary and more like a question she wasn't ready to answer.

Then she turned, quietly, and went inside to join her friends for dinner.

The sound of a small voice saying, "excuse me Miss." Snapped Eira out of her thoughts.

Eira looked up from her uneaten dinner to find a young courier offering a sealed envelope. She thanked him and offered him a coin before breaking the wax.

"They want to see me," she said, voice steady. "Tomorrow. First light."

Beck groaned. "Don't they believe in breakfast?" But even as he joked, his eyes flicked toward Eira — the way they had earlier on the cliff. Watching. Steady

"How do they already know you're here?" Anwen asked.

Kael's voice was laced with dry humor. "The Council has ears in every corridor and shadows on every street. They always seem to know things they shouldn't." That twig that snapped near the river? I'd bet it wasn't a deer."

Eira looked at her friends. "We need a strategy."

"We won't let you go alone," Anwen said.

Kael nodded. "They'll test you—your magic, your past, your loyalty."

"Then we don't tell them everything," Eira said. "Just what we need to."

Beck gave a two-fingered salute. "Now you're talking."

Kael leaned forward. "Like it or not, we're in this together now."

Eira looked at them all—her chosen family and the man she didn't yet understand.

"Then let's not give them any reason to tear us apart."

CHAPTER TWENTY-THREE

The sky beyond the window was still deep with shadow, the first hints of dawn just beginning to blue the edges of the rooftops. Virelda was quiet at this hour, the capital city barely stirring from its slumber. A cart rattled distantly, the sound muffled by the damp, cobbled streets. No bells yet. Just the breath of a city on the cusp of waking.

Inside the small room at the inn, a single oil lamp flickered low. Eira stood near the window, hands working a grounding charm. Soft threads twisted around her fingers—pale blues and greys, anchored with a loop of copper. She wove with care, her breath in rhythm with the pattern. The charm wasn't complicated, but it steadied her.

Outside the window she spied a few deep orange armbands among those moving about. The Veilbreakers.

Kael's warning from yesterday pricked at her memory, but what struck her now was how openly they moved. They weren't lurking in shadows or whispering in alleyways; they were out in force, their colors plain, gathering on corners, pressing folded sheets of paper into unwilling hands. They didn't want to just change how truth was remembered but to rewrite the truth itself. Her hands wove just a little faster.

Across the room, Anwen adjusted the drape of her shawl in the mirror, her pale hair braided into a neat crown. Her expression was unreadable, but her eyes flicked toward Eira's hands. "You won't have time to finish it."

"I don't need to," Eira murmured. "Just needed to start."

A quiet knock sounded. Before either of them could answer, Beck pushed the door open with his hip, balancing a tray heavy with steaming mugs and a plate of slightly squished breakfast rolls.

"Look what I bribed out of the kitchen," he said, grinning as he set the tray down. "Nothing like tea and yesterday's bread to fuel us for impending doom."

Anwen arched an eyebrow. "They didn't throw you out?"

"Turns out I have an honest face," Beck said, then glanced at Eira. "You alright?"

"I'm braiding calm into my spine," she said dryly, not quite looking at him.

Kael entered a heartbeat later, the door creaking faintly behind him. He was already dressed, his coat sharp and dark, hair tied back. He didn't say anything at first, just leaned against the wall, watching Eira. The flickering lamplight caught on the golden flecks in his eyes, quiet and unreadable.

"You're sure you want to go in first?" he asked after a long moment.

Eira let the unfinished charm rest in her palm. "I don't want them to think we're hiding behind you."

"They already do," Kael said with a faint smile, but there was no bite in it. "They'll see what they want."

"And I'll give them what they don't expect," she replied.

They all fell quiet. Four figures in the half-light, cloaked in uncertainty, but bound—threadwoven—by something more than chance.

The grand hall of the Council Tower loomed in the still morning light, its pale stone walls catching the rising sun like bone polished smooth. Outside, the capital stirred—vendors calling greetings, hooves clattering on cobbles—but within, everything was silent. Controlled.

Eira's boots echoed too loudly on the marble floor as she followed the attendant down the corridor. Anwen walked on her right, Beck on her left, Kael a few steps behind. It felt like a procession.

Or a trial.

The great doors at the end of the corridor were carved with sigils of old threadlore—winding glyphs that pulsed faintly with woven light. The attendant stopped before them, avoiding her eyes.

"They are assembled," he said, then bowed and walked away without a backward glance.

Eira drew a slow breath. Her hands itched. Threads she wasn't trying to summon stirred restlessly across her skin like they sensed what lay ahead.

Beck leaned in and muttered, "Slow, deep breaths. Don't punch anyone."
"Only if they deserve it," she whispered back, only half kidding.

The doors creaked open on their own.

The chamber inside yawned open like a trap disguised as sanctuary. A great dome of polished stone arched overhead, carved into the swirl of a spindle. Magic pulsed through the seams in the walls, humming faintly against her skin like breath beneath stone.

All eight councilors sat in a crescent arc atop a raised platform. Their robes shimmered with ancient sigils, each bearing the colors of their lineage and craft—bronze, obsidian, pearl. Old power, woven deep.

At the center sat Mirelle, her silver hair coiled like thread around a spindle, her gaze sharp as a seam ripper. Eira immediately recognized her as one of the council members that visited just before Caelen left.

"Eira of Brookwyn. You've come."

"I was summoned," Eira said, voice steady.

"And wisely, you obeyed," said Varric, seated beside her. His smile was too smooth, almost rehearsed. "Not all would have."

No chair was offered. No welcome extended.

"We are aware of your connection to Caelen Marrowind," said Thorne, his narrow eyes fixed on her like she was a flawed blade. His voice carried the same edge he'd once used on Caelen himself—though no one named it. "The geode he left is no ordinary relic."

"Is this the resonance you mentioned in your summons? If so, I believe he left something inside it," Eira replied carefully. "A memory. A message. Maybe more."

"We know," Mirelle said simply.

Eira's stomach turned. Of course they knew.

"There has been a shift in the Archive's resonance," said Brannoc, his deep voice a slow drumbeat. "A vibration through the deeper threads. It began shortly after the geode activated."

"I didn't mean to disturb anything," Eira said.

"No one said you did," Mirelle replied. "But you did. And now you are entangled. As is your… company."

Anwen stiffened beside her. Beck's mouth twitched—anger restrained by inches.

Brannoc leaned back, fingers drumming once. "This is not the first time ancient forces have stirred beneath the Archive. But this pattern is older. More volatile."

Eira lifted her chin. "And yet you summoned me—not the one who lives within your Archive walls."

A beat of stillness. Controlled. Darek's gaze flicked between them, calculating, while Ines's quiet eyes held a weight that felt older than any of their words.

"Caelen Marrowind is under observation," Mirelle said. "His role is contained. Yours, however, is still unfolding."

"What role is that?" Eira asked, sharp.

"We were hoping you could tell us that," said Varric, all teeth and charm. Too eager to reassure. "But we do have our theories."

"I'm sure you have your secrets, too."

"Careful," Thorne said. "We are not your enemy."

"I didn't say you were," she replied, "but you've not shown that you are my ally either. Not yet."

The silence that followed cracked like a split seam.

Halden shifted nervously, voice blurting out before he seemed to think better of it. "There are… other forces at work. Agitators—" He caught himself, paling, as Mirelle's fingers stilled on the armrest.

"Enough," Mirelle said softly, smoothing the words like silk. "Rumors are beneath this chamber."

But the flicker of Kael's glance toward Eira told her enough. Veilbreakers. Zealots. They weren't speaking the full truth.

Halden swallowed hard, shrinking back, and Darek's gaze cut across the chamber, redirecting the silence like a blade.

"We don't seek conflict—" Halden tried again.

"No," Kael said quietly from behind her. "You just seek control."

All eyes turned.

Kael's expression was calm. Cold. No grin. Just truth, laid bare. A ripple of recognition—too quick, too subtle—crossed a few of their faces before it vanished.

Brannoc's voice followed, steady but sharp. "Control, in its proper place, keeps chaos from swallowing the weave. We maintain order so the rest of the realm doesn't unravel."

"But there's a difference," Kael said, meeting his gaze. "Between safeguarding the weave and strangling it. The realm is people, not just magic."

A silence rippled through the room. Not broken. Tightened.

Lysari shifted slightly, silver-threaded knife glinting at her belt. When Eira stood firm, Lysari's mouth curved—barely—a flicker of approval, almost a smile. "None of us wish for war. Least of all between those still loyal to the weave."

Eira stepped forward. "I didn't come to threaten you. But I won't be used. If the weave is fraying, I'll help—because I must. But I won't be your pawn."

Her voice steadied, stronger. "And I won't leave my allies behind."

She met each of their gazes in turn. Darek's eyes narrowed, weighing. Ines inclined her head slightly, as though committing the moment to memory. Halden avoided her gaze altogether.

"The threads don't lie to me," she said, quiet but unshakable. "And they're moving again. It's dangerous whether you choose to acknowledge it or not."

A long pause.

Mirelle inclined her head the barest fraction. "Then let us hope your presence proves... illuminating."

Beck stepped up beside her, close but not touching. A show of unity. Of warning.

The tension hovered like a live current, but no command came to detain them.

After a beat too long, Mirelle said, "You will be granted limited access to the Archive. Specific sections. Under supervision."

"For what purpose?" Eira asked.

"To determine whether your instincts might help us stabilize the weave. You will conduct research. Our observations have shown you have an affinity for finding information that others have not," Brannoc said. "Assuming you're willing."

Eira gave a single nod. "I am."

"Then go carefully," Lysari said, her voice carrying further than expected. "And remember—every thread has its watchers."

The doors creaked open once more.

But Eira didn't look back.
Not this time.

Outside the Council Tower, morning light stretched long and golden, but it didn't feel warm.

Eira descended the tower steps with deliberate care, each bootfall a tether to the waking city below. Her thoughts lagged behind, still tangled in the cold hush of the council chamber. The words they'd spoken hadn't echoed — they had sunk. Quiet. Heavy. Intentional.

Kael walked beside her, closer than before. "You did well," he said quietly, his voice pitched just for her. "You didn't flinch."

"I wanted to," she muttered.

She had wanted to scream. To demand why they watched her like a flame on the edge of catching. Why they spoke in riddles wrapped in silk and steel. Every part of her had felt like a thread stretched too tight — ready to snap if pulled wrong.

Beck exhaled sharply through his nose. "I wanted to throw a spool of enchanted thread at them, so you're leagues ahead of me."

A dry laugh almost escaped her lips. Almost.

Anwen didn't speak. She walked on Eira's other side, her hand brushing lightly against Eira's arm—a silent anchor in the soft chaos of her mind.

"They were expecting something," Eira said at last. "But not real answers. Not really. Just... obedience."

Kael's jaw ticked. "They like to hold the blade and call it balance."

His words landed sharp. Too true. Too close.

Beck let out a low whistle. "Poetic. Grim. Are you sure you're not secretly a brooding prince?"

Kael didn't respond, which only made Beck grin wider.

They reached the cobbled market road. Stalls opened around them like sleepy flowers, children darted through with baskets and laughter, the smell of fresh bread floated from stone ovens.

It all felt wrong.

Eira's body moved, but her thoughts snagged and circled.
What do they really want?
Why now?
And why me?

"They didn't say what I'm looking for," she said softly. "Only that I begin tomorrow."

A mission with no map. A test with no rules.

"They want you off balance," Anwen murmured. "And watched."

Kael nodded. "They'll keep her on a leash, but they're counting on her finding something useful. Just without telling her the real reasons it will be used."

"So I'm a tool." Eira's voice was flat.

Beck gave a one-shouldered shrug. "A tool doesn't usually talk back. Or plot."

Plotting sounded like the only power she had left. She clung to the thought like a stitch in fraying cloth.

Eira blinked at that, then managed a small, wry smile.

"Then let them watch. We've got our own work to do."

Later that afternoon, back at the inn…

The four of them had claimed a quiet corner in the dim common room, tucked beneath the stairwell where the innkeeper promised they'd be left alone. A fire crackled nearby—more comfort than heat—its flickering glow casting soft shadows on the walls. The mood was subdued, the weight of the council's veiled warnings still pressing in.

Eira cradled a steaming mug of herbal tea, her fingers tracing slow, distracted circles along the rim. Her thoughts felt like thread pulled too tight—delicate, fraying at the edges.

"They want something," Anwen said, breaking the silence. "They didn't say it outright, but it's clear. That whole performance today… they expect you to prove something."

"They mentioned the geode, barely," Beck muttered, letting his chair tip back on two legs until it hit the wall with a soft thud. "Which means they already know more than they want to admit."

Eira nodded slowly. "They know everything. Or close enough. About the threads, the Archive… Caelen. They danced around it all. But the message was clear. They're watching."

Kael hadn't spoken. He stood near the hearth, arms crossed, eyes fixed on the fire. Finally, he said, "The council in Virelda rarely speaks plainly. What they show you is never the whole story. But today wasn't business as usual. Summoning you with that much ceremony? That wasn't for show. They're nervous."

"Afraid," Anwen corrected, her brow furrowed.

Kael gave a single, slow nod. "Yes. And fear makes people dangerous."

Beck leaned forward. "Afraid of what exactly? Do you know?"

Kael hesitated—just long enough to matter. "Years ago, they lost control of something. A project, a person, a thread of magic too old to contain. I don't know the shape of it… just the shadow. But it's waking again. And there are anti-council factions within the city. We've all seen signs that there are zealots like the Veilbreakers at work."

Eira's voice was quiet but firm. "And you didn't tell me because you weren't sure who to trust."

Kael met her gaze across the fire. "I still don't know. But I trust you."

Silence settled in the space between them—not cold, but thoughtful.

Beck tapped his fingers against his mug. "So what now?"

"We move forward," Eira said, steadier than she felt. "If they want to keep us guessing, fine. We'll play along. But on our terms. We'll watch them as closely as they watch us."

Anwen reached across the table, her fingers warm where they brushed Eira's wrist. "You don't have to carry it all alone."

"I know," Eira said. And for the first time that day, she truly meant it.

Kael finally pulled up a chair beside her. He didn't speak again—but the look he gave her was quiet, steady. And for now, that was enough.

CHAPTER TWENTY-FOUR

The common room of the inn was quiet in the early hours, save for the soft clink of crockery and the hush of distant foot traffic echoing through the high-windowed halls. Pale morning light slanted across the floor, catching motes of dust and the fringe of Beck's scarf as he waved a flaky pastry toward Eira.

"You're late," he said cheerfully, though his plate was nearly empty. "I was starting to think the council kidnapped you overnight for extra scolding."

Eira raised a brow and slid into the chair across from him. "I'd like to see them try."

Anwen glanced up from her travel satchel beside the hearth, fingers deftly checking and rechecking the fastenings. "You look rested," she offered, though her eyes lingered on Eira's face a moment longer. "Or at least… not worse."

"I slept," Eira lied. She hadn't. Not really. The threads in this part of the city never stilled — always humming, always pressing just at the edge of her awareness. Not hostile, exactly. Just… watching. But that wasn't the only reason. Her thoughts had circled one truth again and again: if Caelen was truly here — if she might see him again today. The possibility made her chest feel too tight.

Kael sat in the corner, his chair angled slightly away from the others, one boot braced on the rung. He hadn't touched the tea in front of him. His gaze was distant, fixed on nothing, and his jaw tight enough to suggest he was locked in a war with himself. Eira noticed the faint shimmer of magic coiling at his fingertips — barely there, like smoke caught in sunlight. He didn't seem to realize.

"So," Beck said, brushing crumbs from his lap with dramatic flair, "are we ready to go poke at ancient memory repositories that definitely won't give us permanent psychological trauma?"

Anwen closed her satchel with a firm snap. "I triple-checked our pass tokens from the council archives. They'll grant us entry, but the wording was… cautious. We're not guests. We're observers. For now."

"That's encouraging," Beck muttered, rising. "Anyone else feel like we're about to break into a place we were explicitly told we're allowed into?"

Eira stood as well, smoothing her palms down the front of her tunic. Her thread-sense sparked faintly — not warning, but awareness. Something waited. She flexed her fingers once, then again, trying to quiet the flutter in her chest.

Anwen's eyes flicked toward her, steady and thoughtful. "You sure you're ready?"

Eira hesitated just a moment too long. "Of course."

Beck arched a brow but didn't press. "You're doing that thing where you pretend you're not nervous, which means you're definitely nervous."

"She has reason to be," Anwen said softly. "If he's there… you'll feel it first."

Eira looked between them, her throat tight. There was no need to say his name. They all knew who they meant. Caelen hadn't just been a boy from her past. He had been everything. And if he truly was near—if she truly saw him today—

Kael rose without a word. He didn't straighten his coat or reach for his tea. Just stood. When his eyes met hers, she caught a flicker of something beneath the quiet — not fear, but a kind of bracing. Guilt, maybe. Or regret. But it vanished too quickly to name.

They stepped into the hall together.

Beck fell into place beside her and pressed something small and cool into her palm.
She looked down. A charm. Just a tiny knotted loop of copper thread and crystal, strung onto a strip of worn leather. Protective, the weave simple but steady.

"Thought you might need a backup," he said, voice light.

Eira smiled — small, but real. "Thank you."

Always giving pieces of himself away, she thought.

He bumped her shoulder gently. "Try not to get us all exiled before lunch."

The city hadn't quite woken.

Cobbled streets shimmered faintly with dew, and the air held that hush particular to mornings when something is about to begin.

Shopfronts wore shadows like cloaks. A flower cart was being wheeled into place at the edge of a square, petals still furled. The scent of baking bread mingled with the faint metallic tang of magic lingering in the air.

Eira walked with the others in near silence, her boots clicking softly against the stones. The capital was not loud at this hour—but it was layered. Every alley whispered with stories. The weave here was thick with presence, soaked into the stones and stitched into the stillness between footfalls.

The closer they drew to the Archive, the more tightly her thread sense curled around her. This place didn't hum—it *resonated.* Deep and slow, like a drumbeat felt in the bones.

"So… this is the capital," Beck said, stretching his arms wide. His breath clouded faintly in the morning chill. "Lovely, if a bit stone-heavy."

Anwen glanced up at the quiet skyline, where the upper spires caught the sun like teeth. "It's strange not seeing the mist settle here the way it does in Brookwyn."

Eira managed a small sound of agreement, grateful for the change in subject.

"I miss the way it curls around the chimneys," Anwen went on. "Like the town's still dreaming."

"More like the town refuses to wake up," Beck said. "Everything in Brookwyn hits snooze at least twice."

Eira gave a faint smile.

Beck threw her a sideways glance. "It's working, isn't it? You're thinking about fog and breakfast smells now instead of doom and archives."

"Almost," she said, her voice quiet.

Ahead, the Archive rose into view—not tall, but *immense* in its presence. Built of dark stone veined with silver, it crouched on its foundation like a creature at rest. Its domed roof shimmered faintly in the growing light, and sweeping arches framed the broad entrance, open like arms—or jaws. Sigils were carved into every block, old and deliberate: symbols of memory, lineage, containment, loss.

"Built to resist time itself," Kael murmured, falling into step beside her. "Even the stones were etched before they were laid."

Eira didn't answer. The weave here didn't just press—it *called.* Threads brushed against her skin and breath like old names nearly remembered. Her fingertips tingled with it, the air prickling with meaning she couldn't yet read.

They paused at the outer gate. Two sentries—thread-bound and robed—stepped forward from beneath a slanted awning. Their faces were expressionless beneath the embroidered folds of their hoods. One held out a gloved hand, palm up.

Anwen produced the council token from a protective case and passed it over without a word. It shimmered slightly in the early light, the sigils shifting faintly with approval.

The sentries examined it, glanced at each of them in turn, then stepped aside. "You may enter," one intoned. "Your access ends at the sun's height."

"Generous," Beck muttered as they passed through.

Inside, the air shifted. Cooler. Still. Like stepping into a cave that remembered it had once been a cathedral.

The entry hall opened into a vast rotunda beneath the great dome. Light filtered in through a mosaic skylight overhead—not stained glass, but fractured crystal, arranged in patterns that shimmered with every shift in the air. Threads ran like veins across the stone walls and floor, glimmering faintly to those with the eyes—or senses—to see them.

Eira nearly staggered under the weight of it. So much memory. So many echoes. Every breath tasted like something ancient and forgotten. Her knees went soft for a second before she caught herself on the smooth stone rail that circled the rotunda's edge.

Anwen was at her side instantly. "Are you alright?"

"I—" Eira swallowed. "I will be."

Kael stood nearby, watching her closely. His eyes flicked to the inner corridor that spiraled downward from the rotunda, like a staircase carved into a forgotten spiral shell.

"He's here," Eira whispered. "Or… was."

The air still shimmered with resonance. With his. She knew it. Her fingertips curled slightly, instinctively seeking a tether, a thread, anything familiar.

"Then that's where we go," Beck said, not unkindly.

Kael didn't move.

Eira glanced back, confused—until she saw his expression. Not dread. Not concern. Anticipation. And maybe a flicker of regret.

"Beck, Anwen," she said softly, "you two go first."

They hesitated, but didn't argue.

Eira stepped back beside Kael as the others moved ahead. "What is it?"

He didn't look at her. "Places like this remember more than people do."

And then, quieter still: "So do dragons."

The Archivist said little as she guided them beyond the entry chamber.

Her robes made no sound against the smooth stone floors, and her footsteps were unnervingly precise—as if she'd memorized the building's every seam and sigil. She moved not like someone walking through a building, but like someone in conversation with it.

They passed alcoves filled with scrolls wrapped in copper seals, cabinets with drawer pulls shaped like knotted thread. Tapered sconces held dim crystal flames that flickered without heat, casting long shadows that danced ahead of them like whispers.

The deeper they moved, the quieter it became.

Not just hushed, but *weighted.* As though the air itself discouraged speech. As if every sound risked disturbing something sacred, or sleeping.

Eira's senses prickled.

Here, the threads were older. Deeper. They clung to the edges of vision, curling in woven patterns that shimmered only when she wasn't looking directly at them. Some glowed softly. Others pulsed—slow and steady—like breath. She could feel them brushing along her skin, not hostile, but wary. Watching.

The Archivist stopped before an archway framed by a tapestry of pale silver thread. The sigils woven into it shifted with the angle of the light, forming glyphs Eira couldn't quite decipher.

"You are cleared for these upper chambers," the Archivist said. She turned slightly to glance at them—but her gaze landed, and lingered, on Eira. "You may view what the Archive allows. You must stay in this area. You may not take, alter, or touch the anchor weaves."

Anwen stepped forward, calm but firm. "We understand. We'll treat the records with respect."

The Archivist held her gaze a moment longer than necessary. "Sensitive materials respond poorly to unstable threads."

Kael's jaw tightened.

Beck shifted his weight, the movement sharp with unspoken retort, but he held his tongue.

Eira lowered her eyes. She didn't need to ask who the Archivist meant. The implication was as clear as the tension braided into the silence.

They moved into the chamber beyond.

This room was different—round, domed, and hushed, with shelves that curved like the rings of a tree. The air shimmered faintly with thread-signature and memory. Sigils were etched into the wooden panels like growth rings, each line a story, a containment, a warning.

In the center of the space stood a plinth of threadstone: dark crystal laced with veins of pale light, glowing faintly beneath its smooth surface.

Eira stopped short, breath caught.

There it was.

Not a sound. Not a vision. Not even a whisper.

Just... a feeling.

A resonance, deep in her chest—where thread met memory. Where something ancient called without words.

A gentle pull.

Not foreign.
Not frightening.
Familiar.

Her pulse quickened. It couldn't be. And yet—

She took one slow step forward, hand outstretched—not toward any artifact, but into the space itself.

Something stirred. Soft as breath. Fleeting.

Her threads trembled.

Caelen.

She didn't say his name. Didn't need to.

Behind her, Beck and Anwen had both gone still.

Eira's hand lingered just above the thread-veined plinth. She hadn't touched anything—not truly—but her magic had reached farther than she meant it to. Something had answered. Faint. Fleeting. But there.

When she finally stepped back, her balance wavered.

Anwen was at her side in a heartbeat, one hand steadying her elbow. "You okay?"

Eira nodded, though the room swam faintly at the edges of her vision. "Just… dizzy. It's passed."

Kael stood a few paces behind, arms folded, gaze fixed too intently on her. Watching for signs even she didn't understand yet.

Beck let out a low whistle as he peered around the chamber. "So this is what ancient forbidden knowledge feels like. Slightly moldy and mostly ominous."

Anwen didn't laugh. She was still watching Eira, worry shadowing her features.

Her pulse still racing from the thread-plinth, Eira stepped away from the center of the chamber, letting her fingertips drift along the nearest shelf.

A thread tugged at her—subtle, half-there. Not like the pulsing threads of the plinth, but something quieter. Faded. She followed it.

A single threadbook rested tucked among scrolls and parchment rolls, bound in dusky green with a clasp shaped like a half-moon. She didn't know how she knew it was for her. She just… did.

She unfastened the clasp and flipped it open. A name caught her breath mid-thought:

Elander Wyrmsson.

The entry was brief and seemed incomplete— little more than a ledger note — but her fingers trembled as she read.

Controversial scholar. Unsanctioned research into geodecraft. Believed to have been killed during an experiment. Unconfirmed.

That last word lodged like a splinter in her chest. Unconfirmed.

Behind her, Anwen called softly — the Archivist had returned. Time was up.

Eira closed the threadbook and slid it gently back into place, but the ache remained. This wasn't just coincidence. The weave was drawing her somewhere.

The Archivist spoke quietly, her expression unreadable. "You may return tomorrow if you choose. The Archive allows limited hours of inquiry to non-resident Threadcasters."

Eira inclined her head, still not trusting her voice to sound steady.

They followed her through the winding halls toward the exit. The air felt heavier now. Dimmer. Or perhaps it was her senses still unsettled — that echo of something not-quite-memory curling in her mind.

Along the corridor walls, faint glimmers of threadlines pulsed with quiet rhythm. Watching. Remembering.

Near the outer chamber, another robed figure approached from a side passage — a younger woman this time, her braid woven with silver thread. She stepped forward and held out a folded missive, the wax seal of the Council pressed sharply at its center.

"For you," she said, voice soft but firm. Her eyes flicked briefly to the others. "By request of the Council."

Eira took it slowly.
The envelope was thin. No more than a few lines, surely. Still, it felt heavier than stone.

They stepped into the bright courtyard beyond the Archive's doors. The sun had fully crested now, warm on their skin — but the warmth didn't reach the tight knot pulling behind Eira's sternum.

She broke the seal.

Council script. Elegant. Precise. Cold.

Your access has been noted.
While you remain within the capital, do not attract undue attention.
We are watching. Be cautious in your inquiries — and in your company.

No signature. Only the emblem: a threaded ring surrounded by twelve points of flame.

Beck leaned over her shoulder and gave a low whistle. "Friendly."

"Expected," Kael muttered.

Eira folded the paper and tucked it into her satchel, her fingers lingering briefly on the edge. *Let them watch,* she thought. *She was watching too.*

"Let's get back to the inn," she said, glancing around wearily.

No one argued.

CHAPTER TWENTY-FIVE

The note was waiting for them at the front desk when they arrived back at the inn, folded once and marked only as Eira Wynfell.

Once back in her room dropping off her satchel she broke it open the plain wax seal with a thumbnail. Only a handful of words were written inside, neat and measured:

You are not alone in this. Do not lose heart.Continue to pull the threads you found today.

No signature. But a faint shimmer in the corner of the page made her smile— Lysari's sigil, a silver blade, hidden like a watermark that winked and vanished the longer she looked at it.

For a long moment, Eira just stared at the letters. The council chambers had been heavy with suspicion, but here—in the dim lamplight of her room—the words glowed warmer than they should have.

"Does that mean what I think it means?" Anwen asked quietly, entering the room and leaning close.

"That at least one of them doesn't want us burned at the stake?" Beck's voice drifted in from the door. He was nose-deep in his battered journal, quill scratching as he walked without looking. "Add that to the list. *Top Ten Ways Not To Get Exiled,* number seven: 'Be liked by a councilor.'"

"Number eight," he added as his shoulder bumped into the doorframe, "walk into an inn while writing in your journal and concuss yourself to death. Very undignified."

Anwen snorted, Eira exhaled, and the sharpness of the day began to uncoil. The note still pressed cool in her hand, though, its weight urging her toward quiet—toward some place less crowded with eyes and ears.

"Courtyard," she said, tucking the slip of paper into her sleeve. "We need air."

The inn's courtyard offered a brief illusion of peace. Ivy climbed the stone walls in delicate threads, and the midday light fell dappled through wrought-iron trellises overhead. The city's hum pressed faintly from beyond the gates, but here, the air held a quieter tension.

Eira sat on the edge of a low stone bench, the council's cold letter folded tight in one hand and the new note in the other. She hadn't meant to keep them both, but somehow she couldn't let go.

Beck leaned back against a sun-warmed column, arms crossed, expression uncharacteristically thoughtful.

"So… is this where we pretend that creepy letter wasn't creepy?"

"They're not even pretending not to watch us," Anwen said, arms folded. "Which means we have to assume someone is."

Kael stood off to the side, half in shadow. He hadn't spoken since they left the Archive. Not really. But Eira had seen the way his posture changed — the tension that tightened when the seal broke, the flicker of something darker that crossed his face when he read over her shoulder.

“It’s not just about them watching,” Kael said quietly. “It’s about what they’re afraid we’ll find.”

Eira looked up sharply. “You think they know?”

“I think,” he said, eyes meeting hers, “they suspect you can find what they need.”

A hush settled over them, brittle and taut.

Beck broke it with a short sigh and pushed off the column. “Alright, team doomscroll — we need a plan. Preferably one where we don’t all get cursed, stabbed, or turned into memory husks.”

Anwen gave him a sidelong glance. “You’ve been reading too many of those scroll-mystery novels.”

“Only the ones with ghosts,” he said with a wink, then turned back to Eira. “Seriously though. If you want help, we need to know what we’re actually looking for. Vague mystical doom vibes aren’t quite searchable.”

Eira hesitated. Part of her wanted to hold it in — not out of secrecy, but because it felt… fragile. Like naming it would give it shape too soon. But they were here because they cared. Because they trusted her.

So she spoke.

“I think the geodes are changing,” she said quietly. “I think the way they react to me — and Kael — it’s not normal. And I need to understand why.”

Beck nodded slowly. "Okay. Weird magic rocks, step one."

"I don't know what's causing it," Eira went on, fingers fidgeting with the leather cord around her wrist. "But back in Brookwyn, I felt something — a memory that wasn't mine. And with it came a name."

Kael's posture shifted slightly, barely visible, but not lost on Anwen.

"What name?" she asked.

"Elander," Eira repeated. "I didn't just feel it. I found fragments of old records in the Brookwyn library. His name had been… scrubbed out. Sloppily, in some cases. Like someone tried to erase him, but couldn't quite finish the job. Then today just before we had to leave I found a partial record."

Anwen's eyes narrowed slightly, sharp with thought. "You think he's connected to the geodes? Or the instability?"

"I think he's connected to the truth," Eira said. "And the council doesn't want us finding out what exactly that is, just to lead them to it."

Kael said nothing.

Anwen caught the tension in his jaw. "You know something."

"I've heard the name," Kael said. "But I'd rather we find the source before I start speculating."

"Fair enough," Anwen replied. "Then that's our goal. Tomorrow, we split the research. Someone follows mentions of geodes, someone takes council records. We look for anything that connects the name *Elander* to what's happening now."

Beck raised a hand. "Dibs on anything with scandal. Or curses."

Eira exhaled, the smallest breath of relief. "Thank you."

"Don't thank us yet," Beck said, slinging an arm over Anwen's shoulders. "We haven't found the horrifying secret chamber or tragic love letters in ancient ink. That's where the real drama happens."

Kael's gaze lingered on Eira a moment longer, unreadable.

Then he nodded. "We'll find it."

The Archive doors loomed with their usual hush of grandeur, but today their weight pressed differently. Less awe. More warning.

"This is the part," Beck whispered theatrically, "where we split up and get attacked one by one by sentient books."

Anwen leveled him a flat stare. "You've clearly never read a research-heavy novel."

His grin widened. "I've read plenty. They're just boring until someone finds a cursed scroll."

The hall unfolded around them in solemn silence. Shelves spiraled upward, stacked beyond reason, each rung of history slotted with ruthless precision. Iron balconies wrapped the higher tiers, their railings narrow and cold, stairwells winding like threads through a tapestry of shadows. The place was vast—cathedral vast—too sprawling to wander without intent.

Anwen consulted the slip of parchment the registrar had pressed into her hand.
"Our passes grant two hours of unsupervised access. After that, we're required to report our findings and request continued clearance."

Beck leaned close, stage-whispering, "So... don't get caught hiding in the ceiling stacks. Understood."

Anwen ignored him and passed over a second slip with codes scrawled in neat rows.
"You're taking older council proceedings. Anything indexed under 'geode,' 'resonance,' or 'containment.'"

"Containment," Beck repeated, rolling the word. "Definitely not ominous."

"I'll cover magical theory," Anwen said crisply. "Particularly resonance tied to memory imprints. I want precedent for what happened to you—living through a memory that wasn't yours."

Eira nodded. "I'll search the reference wing. Names, magical disruptions, and..." She faltered. "And Elander."

Kael stepped in. "I'll help with that."

Eira blinked. "You want to—?"

"I'm a fast reader," he said, almost too casual. "And if something dangerous links to that name, I'd rather not be blindsided later."

Beck's grin had faded. His gaze lingered on Kael, not distrustful—yet—but sharpened, wary. Watching.

There was something unreadable in Kael's tone, a shade too careful. Eira studied him for a beat, then gave a slow nod. "Alright."

But as she turned toward the shelves, unease lingered. She could feel it in her bones: he wasn't telling her everything.

The carved stone rows deepened as they moved farther from the main reading rooms, into dust-laden chambers where no lanterns burned — only the faint glow of resonance crystals pulsing in the ceiling arches. Kael walked a half-step ahead of Eira, his movements cautious, almost reverent.

She kept silent. The quiet here was not absence but presence — charged, waiting. Threads curled beneath the stone floor, unseen yet brushing her senses, ancient and thick with memory. They scraped across her skin like wind through thorns.

Kael paused beside an alcove. "This section predates the Restoration," he said, voice low. "Most of it hasn't been catalogued in decades."

Eira brushed the edge of a stone ledger. It shimmered faintly at her touch — not with magic, but with memory. Grief pressed from its surface, layered with stubborn resolve. The strength of it startled her.

"This one," she murmured, drawing it free. "It's old, but it's reaching. Like it wants to be seen again."

Kael's eyes narrowed. He didn't touch it, but he didn't stop her either.

She opened the record: a folded slate of etched crystal, nearly translucent, humming faintly. The air shifted, dense with raw memory — tangled, unshaped, like thread torn from a seam.

The script was ancient, but tucked between accounts of long-past disputes and resonance studies was an inserted record far newer, one that didn't belong among the rest. Its edges bore different tool marks, its tone sharper, more urgent — as if someone had hidden it here, hoping it would be overlooked.

One name leapt clear from the entry.

Her breath caught. *Elander.*

The account was sparse: a brief note of his tenure as a professor at the University of Cirellan and his assignment to investigate anomalies in emotional resonance and object-binding. No conclusions. No fate. Just fragments — and one phrase scrawled beneath in a different hand:

Too much taken. Too much left behind.

Eira's pulse fluttered as she traced the words. The threads hummed under her skin, not with knowledge but with grief.

"This isn't just memory," she whispered. "It's truth — a truth someone tried to bury."

Kael's gaze sharpened. He didn't speak.

"You know this phrase," she pressed.

He nodded slowly. “I’ve seen it before. On a scroll I was never meant to find.”

Her eyes lifted sharply. “Where?”

“It belonged to one of Elander’s students,” Kael said after a pause. “A man named Tauren.”

The name struck a chord. “Councilor Tauren?” she asked. “The one who stepped down before my time?”

Kael’s gaze slid away. “The same. But that’s… complicated.”

She waited, but no explanation came. Closing the ledger, she felt the cold seep into her hands. “So we’re not the only ones chasing this.”

His jaw tightened. “No. And I don’t think we’re ahead of him.”

Beck slouched against the edge of a fountain in the outer Archive courtyard, the late afternoon sun catching on the edge of a half-eaten tart he held like a prize. “I swear, these scholars must be allergic to helpfulness. I asked three different people about energy resonance irregularities in central geodes, and one of them tried to sell me a pamphlet on aura alignment.”

Anwen approached, her quiet steps giving her the upper hand — Beck didn’t see her until she sat beside him.

“Of course,” she said, “your great contribution to the day’s research is sugar.”

Beck tore off a bite and grinned. "Sugar sharpens the mind. You should try it."

Her quill stilled. "If that were true, you'd be a council archivist."

He pressed a hand to his heart. "Unfair. They'd never let me in — too much personality."

That earned the faintest flicker of a smile. "Too much frosting, more like."

"Did you have any luck?" he asked, cocking his head.

"Not in the records, but I came across something else. A group at a table in a nearly empty section of records."

Beck took a bite of the tart. "Subtlety's a superpower. What'd you overhear?"

She pulled a small leather notebook from her satchel, already marked with symbols and shorthand notes. "Bits and pieces. There were whispers about someone the council doesn't talk about anymore. A former member who went rogue. They think he had followers. Maybe even a movement."

Beck frowned, straightening slightly. "Like the zealots?"

Anwen nodded. "That word came up. Along with mentions of unstable magic, old rituals… and dragons."

"Dragons?" Beck blinked. "Plural?"

"They spoke like it was a metaphor at first. But then one of them said, 'It was his job to keep the magic bound — to keep the dragon asleep.'" She looked over at him. "I don't think they meant it figuratively."

Beck whistled low. "And let me guess — they didn't actually say any names?"

She didn't answer right away. "Of course not. But the people I overheard… they weren't researchers. Not really. I think they were watching us. Meant to look like scholars, but they were too alert. And one of them had a council crest barely tucked beneath his sleeve."

Beck muttered something under his breath and tossed the last of the tart into the fountain. "Well, that's comforting."

He looked over at her, eyes serious now. "Does Eira know?"

Anwen shook her head. "Not yet. I wanted to be sure."

"Good," Beck said, quieter now. "She sees too much already. Not in a bad way — just… deeper. The rest of us read what's written. She hears what the stone is still trying to say."

They let the fountain carry the silence for a beat. Then Beck leaned back, voice dropping. "Tell me I'm not the only one who thinks Kael's hiding something."

"You're not." Anwen recapped her ink with precision. "Eira knows it too. But she wants to believe him."

Beck gave a low whistle. "Wants to believe him or wants to ignore what she sees?"

Anwen's gaze sharpened, but she didn't argue. "She hasn't mentioned Caelen once. Not yesterday, not today. As if silence could erase that he was important."

Beck's grin faltered. "That's… not encouraging."

"No," she said quietly. "It isn't."

"Right," Beck said, standing and brushing crumbs from his coat. "So we've got secret council spies, magic dragons, and one brooding maybe-spy with cheekbones sharp enough to slice through parchment. That's not steady ground."

Anwen's jaw tightened. "It never is, with threads this tangled."

Beck blew out a sigh, then brightened his tone deliberately. "Well. If it all collapses, at least I'll be here to say 'told you so.'"

Her eyes flicked to him, dry as parchment. "You'll be here eating sugar."

He raised the crumpled wrapper in salute. "And looking brilliant while I do it."

Anwen rose beside him, quiet and composed. "We should find the others."

They stepped back through the stone archway, the echoes of their conversation fading into the hum of the Archive — a place that, like Kael, held more secrets than it seemed willing to share.

CHAPTER TWENTY-SIX

The inn's common room was quieter than usual, lit by the warm flicker of wall sconces and the occasional snap of the hearth. The clatter of dishes had faded to a low murmur, and most patrons had either gone to bed or lingered in companionable silence.

Their group sat tucked into a corner booth. Beck leaned sideways in his chair, a spoon dangling from his fingers, half a bowl of stew forgotten on the table. Anwen sat straight-backed beside him, slowly sipping tea, her eyes scanning the room with quiet precision.

Eira poked at her own meal, appetite absent. Her thoughts kept circling back to the Archive, to the subtle way the threads had shifted around the oldest geode records. Truth stirred beneath the weave, leaving a tremble in her palms that hadn't faded all evening..

Kael sat apart, his arms folded and gaze fixed on the hearth. He hadn't spoken much since they returned.

The innkeeper's son approached with cautious steps, a dark green missive in his outstretched hand.

"For you, miss," he said, voice barely above a whisper.

Eira accepted it with a nod. The seal was unmistakable—and there was an embossed silver thread in the shape of the Council's crest.

She broke it open.

Eira Wynfell,
Your presence is required immediately at the Threadwitch Council chamber. Bring those who accompanied you to the Archive.
—Councilor Darek, on behalf of the Threadweavers Council

Eira set the parchment down slowly. "They want to see us. Now."

Beck raised an eyebrow. "Do they always schedule surprise interrogations between soup and dessert?"

Kael stood immediately. "Let me grab my coat."

Anwen had already gathered her things, sliding her satchel over one shoulder. "Let's meet back here in five minutes."

The walk through the capital was brisk. The evening mist curled at their heels, dissipating more easily here than it ever did in Brookwyn. Streetlamps cast long shadows, and the streets were mostly empty—eerily so.

"I overheard something today," Anwen said quietly, drawing close to Eira. "Two researchers were whispering by the restricted scroll racks. They didn't notice me."

Eira glanced at her, heart ticking faster.

"They said someone was tampering with old seal-threads. That a dragon stirred before its time, that the Archive's protections were cracking.

Beck stepped in on Eira's other side. "So either we're very lucky or very cursed to show up right as things go sideways."

"They summoned us to the capital, they knew what was happening. There's no luck involved," Eira said coldly.

Kael walked ahead, his shoulders tense.

The stone doors loomed before them, carved with sigils older than memory. The air felt thick with fog and tension. As the guards stepped aside to admit them, one held out a hand to Kael.

"Not you."

Kael's posture stiffened. "I was summoned with them."

The guard didn't flinch. "By order of the Council — only those registered under the Archive's official access list may enter."

Eira turned, disbelief rising. "He's a threadmage. That *is* his registration."

The guard's gaze flicked briefly to Kael, something colder in it now. "He's not registered with the capital. Not anymore."

A pause. Heavy. Measured.

Kael said nothing.

Beck stepped forward. "You've got to be kidding—"

"Stand down," Kael said quietly.

His expression had shuttered, but there was something in the tension of his jaw — not surprise, but resignation. Like he'd expected this.

Anwen's voice was soft but pointed. "What does that mean — not anymore?"

Kael gave a slight shake of his head. "It means I'll wait out here."

For a long moment, Kael held her gaze. Then he nodded once and stepped back into the shadows.

As the heavy door creaked open, Eira swallowed the knot in her throat. Beck placed a steadying hand at her back.

"Showtime," he murmured.

The chamber of the Threadwitch Council was carved into the bones of the capital itself—vaulted stone archways, veined with silver thread that pulsed faintly in time with the magic of the city. Seven chairs sat in a half-circle at the raised dais, occupied now by cloaked figures in hues of stormcloud and smoke. Their faces were visible, but their expressions gave away nothing.

Eira stood below with Beck and Anwen flanking her, a small triangle of resolve in a sea of cold marble and judgment. The silence pressed down before a voice finally broke it.

"Eira Wynfell," said Councilor Brannoc, the man in the center. His silver hair shimmered faintly as he tilted his head. "Thank you for coming. We apologize for the… abruptness of this summons."

Beck snorted softly, then masked it with a cough.

"We've reviewed your petition to research the geode anomalies," Brannoc continued, "and we are… intrigued by your findings."

"I haven't submitted any findings," Eira said carefully.

"No," said Mirelle. "But we always have eyes at the Archives and you ask the right questions. The sort of questions that ripple. The kind that open doors we've kept closed."

Councilor Darek, seated on the far left, steepled his fingers. "Where did you hear the name Elander?"

Eira's throat tightened. "I saw it. In a memory. Not mine."

A pause.

"Threadcasting at that level," muttered another, "shouldn't be possible without training."

"She has the training," said Brannoc. "Just not ours."

Eira felt Anwen shift beside her. Beck's posture was casual, but he was watching each movement with sharp focus.

"And what do you know," asked Councilor Darek, "of Elander's student?"

Eira blinked. "Nothing except a possible name. former counsilor Tauren."

The woman in gray—Councilor Ines—smiled thinly. "Then let us offer you an opportunity. You've proven… promising. We'd like to support your research. Grant you access to restricted materials. Specialized tools. Even personalized training, should you wish it."

"In exchange for what?" Eira asked, already wary.

Brannoc's voice was calm. "Cooperation. Openness. We believe your particular talents may hold the key to mending the unstable thread network. There are deeper mechanisms at play than you know."

"And Caelen?" she asked quietly.

That changed the room. Some councilors stiffened. Brannoc's eyes narrowed.

"He is…nearly awake," said Ines. "But altered. The longer he remains in that state—unbound, ungrounded—the more dangerous he becomes. We hoped your presence might stabilize him. But if not…"

"If not?" Beck echoed.

"Then we must reconsider whether he should remain as he is." replied Councilor Mirelle coldly.

Eira's pulse roared in her ears. "You put him there and now you're threatening him."

"We are protecting this realm," Thorne said.

Anwen took a half-step forward. "You barred Kael from this meeting. Why?"

Councilor Darek answered. "Because Kael has grown reckless. He was once a loyal extension of our will. Now he walks shadowed paths. We don't know who he answers to."

Eira's hands were cold. Her voice was not. "You should already know I won't accept your offer without time. Or without answers."

"Of course," said Brannoc, "But the longer you delay, the more frayed the weave becomes."

Councilor Mirelle folded her hands in her lap and added, almost casually, "We trust, of course, that anything you discover in the

Archives — or hear within these walls — will remain strictly within your circle. Discretion is, after all, the oldest thread in our craft."

A pause. A smile that didn't reach her eyes.

Before the silence could settle, Councilor Varric leaned forward, his tone velvet-smooth. "And perhaps some doors are best left unopened, Miss Wynfell. Curiosity has value, yes, but it also has a cost. Not every thread, once tugged, can be rewoven."

His smile was warm, almost charming, but there was a shadow beneath it—an unspoken warning disguised as advice.

"Pull the wrong one," Mirelle said softly, "and everything unravels."

As the council dismissed them, Beck leaned in and whispered, "That went well."

"By council standards?" Eira muttered.

"No. Just in general. We're still breathing."

The heavy doors thudded shut behind them, cutting off the echo of power and politics. Eira walked like her feet were made of stone, each step away from the chamber dragging questions behind it.

Kael was waiting just outside, arms folded, his posture casual—too casual. He straightened when he saw them. "What happened?"

Beck didn't answer right away. He just stared. Not angry. Not surprised. Just… watching.

"They said you were one of them," Eira said quietly. "That you worked for the Council."

Kael blinked once. "I did. A long time ago."

"You never mentioned that," Anwen said, her voice even but wary.

Kael's expression shifted—not guilt exactly, but something close. "Because it stopped being something I was proud of."

"You were their extension," Beck said, quoting Councilor Darek. "You were their shadow."

Kael's mouth twitched, bitter. "Once. When I was younger, I believed them. I was raised outside the capital, in a place the weave barely touched. Magic there frayed constantly—fires, sickness, crops failing. The Council promised they could fix it, if enough of us served. I thought I was helping people."

Eira's brows drew tight. "And you did their bidding."

"I enforced their protections," Kael said. "At first it was simple—containments, seals, keeping unstable magic from spilling into villages. But the longer I served, the more I saw what those 'protections' cost. Families broken apart. Records sealed so no one would ever know the truth of what was taken." His jaw tightened.

He hesitated, then added, voice lower: "My last assignment was Caelen. They needed someone to maintain the wards, to keep him asleep when the first fractures spread. I told myself it was mercy—that he was safer bound than burning out. And for the people in the capital, maybe it was. A dragon awake before its time could have destroyed everything."

His eyes flicked to Eira. "But every time I reinforced those threads, I felt him fighting. I felt him slipping further from who he was. I wasn't sure if the Council was searching for another way, or if they'd decided this was easier—contain him, use him, forget the cost."

"And you stayed?" Beck pressed.

"I tried," Kael admitted. "I told myself I could change things from inside. But binding Caelen was the breaking point. That was when I realized the Council didn't care who they sacrificed—only that the weave looked intact from the outside."

Anwen's eyes narrowed. "And so you left."

"I walked away," Kael said. "But you don't really leave the Council. You just stop following orders and pray they stop chasing you. They never stopped—not completely."

Eira's hands curled into fists. "That's exactly what they said, Kael. That keeping secrets was protection."

The words landed between them like a dropped stitch. He winced but didn't look away.

"They offered her access," Beck said after a beat. "Training. Tools. The whole archive buffet—if she agrees to dance to their tune."

Kael's mouth pulled into a grim line. "I know how that tune ends. With silence. With obedience. With blood."

"Do you?" Eira asked. "Because right now, I'm not sure who you are at all."

For a moment, his expression cracked—tired, raw. "I was a boy who wanted to save his village. I became a man who carried out orders he didn't believe in. And now I'm trying to be something else before the mistakes I made catch up to you."

The doors to the council building opened and two clerks emerged, their footsteps clicking across the marble. Anwen's eyes followed them, sharp and wary. "Not here," she murmured. "Let's walk."

The silence after that was heavy, but truer than any mask he'd worn before.

The evening crowd spilled along the lane, a press of voices and color. Lanterns swayed on iron brackets above the shopfronts, catching on the wind.

Eira kept her stride brisk, though her thoughts lingered on Kael's words, each one turning like a shard of glass in her chest. The conversation Eira wanted — *needed* — to have with Kael had to wait.

They had reached the merchant's quarter when the sound of breaking glass cracked the air.

Ahead, a shop door flew open. A woman stumbled into the street, clutching her arm. Behind her, three figures poured out, their movements sharp, deliberate. Orange cloth wound around each of their upper arms—the mark of the Veilbreakers.

Kael's hand was at Eira's shoulder before she even realized she had stopped walking.

The leader's voice rang out, loud enough to claim the crowd's attention. "You hide behind charms and scrolls while the weave unravels. You think these trinkets will save you? They're lies. They keep us chained to the Council's leash."

Murmurs rippled through the gathered onlookers. The shopkeeper pressed her back against the wall, pale and shaking.

Another Veilbreaker seized a box of folded papers from the doorway and shook it open, scattering charms into the dust. Each one unfurled like a gutted bird, powerless without the hands that made them.

"See?" the leader snarled. "Worthless. And you pay coin for it while families starve." His boot came down hard, crushing a lantern-shaped fold beneath his heel.

Eira's fingers curled against her palms. Every fiber of her wanted to run forward, to snatch up the scattered papers, to shield them from the mockery. But Kael's grip tightened at her shoulder—steady, warning.

Two city guards appeared at the end of the street, halberds in hand. The Veilbreakers didn't flee. They raised their chins, defiant, daring.

It was only when one of the guards shouted for reinforcements that the orange-banded figures melted into the crowd, slipping down an alley before steel could meet skin.

Silence followed, jagged and uneasy. The shopkeeper knelt in the dirt, gathering the ruined scraps of her craft with trembling hands.

"They're growing bolder," Kael muttered, his gaze following the alley. "That wasn't a message for her—it was a message for everyone watching."

Eira crouched beside the woman, helping her collect what little could be salvaged. Threads of ink and paper brushed her skin like whispers of grief. She didn't speak, not with so many eyes on them, but the heaviness in her chest told her enough.

The crowd broke apart slowly, voices low, unsettled. Some carried the Veilbreakers' words with them like tinder waiting for a spark. Others only shook their heads and hurried away.

By the time the guards returned with more men, the shopfront was already swept of confrontation, though the fear lingered, heavy as smoke.

Kael said nothing more until they'd put distance between themselves and the broken charms. Then, his voice was grim. "Now you see why the Council grows desperate. If the weave doesn't hold, these factions won't just shout in the streets. They'll burn them."

"We've done what we can here for now," Eira said, her voice quiet but steady. She stood and glanced back toward Kael. "Let's get back to the inn."

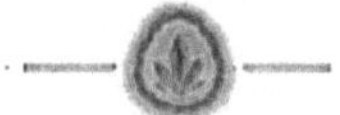

The main room of the inn was dim and nearly empty. The weight of the day—of secrets kept and revealed—pulled them inward.

Beck paused at the bottom of the stairs, rubbing the back of his neck. "If the inn explodes overnight or a dragon crashes through the roof, just let me sleep through it. I'll catch up in the morning."

He gave Eira a crooked half-smile, then trudged upward.

Anwen lingered. Her gaze found Eira's—steady, quiet, knowing. It wasn't a warning, not exactly. But it said: *be careful.* Then she followed Beck, leaving Eira alone in the room's fading light.

She slipped out the back door into the courtyard.

The night was hushed, save for the creak of a shutter and the soft rustle of ivy on stone. Moonlight tangled through flowering branches, spilling silver across cobblestones. A willow bent low over a weathered bench, where Eira sat with her arms folded tight, staring at the sky's pale glow.

Her thoughts were louder than the silence. Secrets and doubts spun like thread in wind—fraying, unraveling.

The door creaked again. Footsteps—measured, hesitant.

"I didn't come to argue," Kael said.

"Good." Her voice was flat. "I'm not in the mood to be lied to."

He stopped behind her. The silence stretched.

"I didn't mean to hurt you," he said at last.

"You keep saying that," she murmured. "And yet, here we are and I'm hurt."

Kael drew a breath, stepping closer but leaving space. "I didn't tell you about my ties to the council because it was complicated. Because I didn't trust them—and I didn't fully trust myself, either."

Eira turned, slowly. "You told me I didn't have to fear you. That you weren't a threat."

"You don't."

"Then why hide the truth?"

His jaw tightened. He looked away. "Because the truth is worse. I helped keep the dragons asleep. I was part of the council's 'solution' to Tauren. We thought it would hold. His voice turned rough, "But those dragons were people. People who wanted to do their part to protect the country, but they were being sacrificed and that's not right."

Eira's just nodded for him to continue.

"My role was small, but it mattered. And when I walked away—thinking I could disappear—I didn't realize how quickly it would unravel."

"You knew about Caelen."

"I was stationed in the Archives. But I came to Brookwyn because of you. I didn't know he was from there. I didn't expect to feel—" He cut himself off, the words hanging heavy between them.

Eira searched his face. "And Tauren? You said you knew Elander had a student, but that's all."

Guilt flickered through Kael's expression. "Tauren was his brightest. Too bright. He pushed where even Elander hesitated—and Elander already pushed too far. After Elander's death—whatever truly caused it—Tauren kept going. The rest of the council didn't even suspect what he was doing. Eventually… he vanished."

"Vanished?"

"He was working in the deeper archives. Forbidden spells. Trying to twist the nature of thread magic itself. When the weave began to fray, they traced it back to him. But by then it was too late."

"And that's when they set Caelen there. To guard it."

Kael inclined his head. "The council tried to stabilize what they could. Part of that was making sure no one reached the back halls again. Caelen became the gatekeeper. My task was to keep him asleep."

Eira stared. "And you agreed?"

"I didn't understand everything. They never gave me the full truth—I think they feared what I'd do if I knew. But I wanted answers. That's why I searched. That's why I started looking for other ways to secure the weave."

Her voice was quiet. "And you're here because…?"

"Because I made a mistake." His words were stark. "And I'm trying to mend it before it costs more lives. Before it costs you."

She sat slowly on the edge of the bench. "You should have told me."

"I know."

The wind stirred petals across the stones. For a long moment, neither spoke.

Then Kael said, low, "If you tell me to leave—I will."

Eira looked up at him. At the shadows under his eyes, the weight in his stance. "I don't want you to go. But I need the truth. All of it. No more fragments."

Kael nodded. "Then I'll give you whatever I can."

This time, when he sat beside her, she didn't move away.

CHAPTER TWENTY-SEVEN

The hum woke her.

At first, Eira thought it was part of a dream — a low vibration threading through the dark like distant thunder rumbling through her chest. But as her eyes opened, the sensation sharpened. Not a sound. Not exactly. A *presence.*

She sat up, breath caught in her throat.

The geode.

It hadn't made a sound in days — not since they had arrived in the capital. It had lain still and cold at her bedside, wrapped in linen and hope. But now…

Now it was humming like it had a heartbeat.

She flung off the blanket and crossed to the side table where she kept it hidden, fingers already tingling with magic. The linen was warm as she unwrapped it — no, *hot* — and as the final fold peeled back, her breath caught.

A new crack split the stone's surface.

Not like the tiny hairline fracture from the day she wove Caelen's memory into it. This one was deeper, jagged, and glowing faintly at the edges — like something inside was trying to burn its way out.

"No," she whispered. "No, no, no—"

She reached for a stabilizing thread, but the geode *shuddered* in her hands.

The hum became a low vibration in the air. Books shifted on the shelf. A loose bundle of thread unspooled across the table as if stirred by invisible wind.

And then — she felt it.

That black strand. Dread settled in her heart.

It hadn't been near for days, but now it slithered through the weave like a whisper with teeth. It coiled at the edge of her vision, thin and sharp, stretching toward the geode like it meant to slice through the heart of it.

Eira reacted instinctively.

She grabbed a flicker-thread — lightborn and etched with warding runes — and snapped it through the air. The thread caught the black strand mid-lunge, searing it with a flash of silver-blue. It hissed, recoiled—

And vanished.

The geode pulsed once. Then twice. The light from the crack dimmed to a dull ember. Not fixed. Just… *pausing*.

Eira fell to her knees, cradling it in shaking hands.

"It was stable," she whispered. "You were fine."

But the stone was trembling. Threads she hadn't woven into it sparked faintly around the edges — Caelen's threads, wild and fraying, fighting to hold together. And it felt like they were losing.

She pressed her forehead to the linen, blinking back the burn behind her eyes.

If it cracked all the way through…

If the memory inside shattered…

She wouldn't just lose him. She'd lose the *chance* of him — the quiet promise that one day, he might remember. Might return.

"I can't lose you again," she murmured. "Not like this."

A decision settled into her chest like cooled iron.

She rose, wrapping the geode in fresh cloth with trembling hands, and moved swiftly around the room — grabbing her satchel, ward-thread, salt pouch, the looped cord she always carried when the path ahead felt uncertain.

She had only one answer.

"I'm going to the Archive."

Eira moved down the hallway with silent urgency, the chill of the inn's stone floor biting through the soles of her boots. The geode was tucked close against her ribs beneath her cloak, its fractured hum pulsing like a second heartbeat. The linen wrapping couldn't muffle the vibration — or the dread curling tight in her chest.

She paused outside Anwen's door and raised her hand to knock.

Before her knuckles could land, the door eased open.

Anwen stood there barefoot, braid sleep-mussed, a knit shawl pulled hastily over her shoulders. Her eyes, though — they were sharp. Awake.

"You felt it," Eira said, voice low.

Anwen nodded once. "The threads shifted. You're going to the Archive?"

Eira held up the bundle of linen. "It cracked again. Badly. I don't know how long I have before it… breaks for good."

Anwen stepped fully into the hall, pulling her door shut behind her. "I'll get dressed."

"I'll get Beck," Eira said.

They split without another word.

Down the hall, Eira stopped outside Beck's room and gave two firm raps.

A groggy thump answered, followed by Beck's voice, muffled but distinct: "If this is about Kael again, I'm going to need a snack and a sarcastic apology."

"It's about Caelen," she said. "The geode's cracking. I'm leaving for the Archive now."

A long pause.

Then the bolt slid open.

Beck's curls were flattened on one side, his shirt wrinkled, and his belt only half-looped through the trousers he clearly yanked on in a hurry.

"I'm coming," he said, grabbing his boots and cloak from the chair. "Give me three minutes and pretend I don't look like death's intern."

Eira managed a tight smile — the first one in hours. "Only if you hurry."

By the time Beck had his boots on and Anwen emerged fully dressed, her braid tight and her cloak fastened, Eira stood in the hallway again — still and silent.

She glanced toward the stairs that led to the lower guest rooms.

Kael's room.

Her jaw tightened.

She didn't want to see him right now. Not after what he'd said in the courtyard and had not said in all the weeks she had known him. Not after the way her heart had tried to untangle itself from the jumble of emotions he caused. There were too many threads between them, and none of them were neat.

But—

He had helped put Caelen to sleep.
He knew things she didn't. Things the council kept from everyone else.
And this wasn't about trust.

This was about *Caelen.*

And time.

Eira exhaled through her nose. "Wait here."

She descended the stairs without magic. Without sound.

At the far end of the hallway, Kael's door was slightly ajar — not enough to see in, but enough to show he hadn't fully sealed himself away. A faint flicker of light came from within, the soft glow of a low-burn ward lamp.

She knocked once, knuckles sharp against the wood.

Silence.

Then a rustle. Footsteps.

Kael opened the door, bleary-eyed, hair unbound and falling loosely around his face. A plain linen shirt clung to him, creased from sleep. He blinked once, taking in her cloak, the wrapped bundle in her arms, the storm behind her eyes.

"It's Caelen," she said. "The geode's failing. I'm going to the Archive."

His gaze dropped to the bundle. He straightened.

"Then I'm coming."

She hesitated.

Only a breath.

Then nodded.

"Get your things."

They met just outside the inn beneath the flickering lantern by the gate. The city was hushed, the cobblestones slick with mist, as if the capital itself was holding its breath.

Anwen stood ready, her ward-thread already looped around her wrist. Beck paced a slow arc behind her, checking his satchel's clasps with more force than necessary.

When Kael stepped outside, cloak half-fastened and eyes sharp with purpose, Beck looked up — and stilled.

For a breath, the two men just regarded each other.

Then Beck gave a slow nod. Not exactly friendly. But solid. Measured.

"Appreciate you being here," he said. "We don't all have to like each other to know this matters."

Kael dipped his head once. "I didn't come to be liked."

"Good," Beck said.

The edge in his voice was light, but the meaning wasn't.

Eira stepped between them, geode secured in the crook of her arm.

"I need to say this before we go," she said, scanning their faces. "What we're doing — this isn't repair work or chasing echoes. We're going to the Archive. The restricted section."

"The one Caelen's guarding?" Anwen asked, quiet but clear.

Eira nodded. "And if he's waking up... or if the sealing is failing... the council won't care what our reasons are. We could be charged with trespass. Interference. Magical destabilization."

Beck let out a low whistle. "So... light treason. Got it."

Eira didn't smile. "And if Caelen is awake and in dragon form there's a very real chance he won't remember me. If anyone wants to stay behind—"

"We don't," Anwen said.

Beck raised a hand. "I'd rather be eaten by a dragon than sit this one out."

Kael's voice was low. "I've already made my mistakes. I don't get to run from this one."

Eira swallowed the ache rising in her throat.

Then she turned toward the road, heart hammering with purpose and fear.

The Archive waited.

CHAPTER TWENTY-EIGHT

The Archive's outer gates loomed in silence, carved from stone so old it no longer remembered the sun. Wards shimmered faintly along the seams, layered with magic that whispered stay away in the language of thread and time.

Eira reached for the locking rune—then paused as Beck stepped forward beside her, cracking his knuckles.

"Let me," he said. "This one's speaking my language."

He crouched by the rune, fingers brushing the spiral of threadline embedded in the stone. "You've got overlapping locks here. Layered glyphs. Council craftsmanship—too proud by half." He muttered something under his breath and tapped a woven charm ring to the surface.

The rune sparked once.

Then again.

And clicked open with a soft pulse of yielding magic.

"Like a key in an old door," Beck said, standing and dusting his hands. "Bit rusty, but still works."

The air inside was colder. Heavier. Like walking into memory itself.

Their footsteps echoed down the corridor — Beck's soft with satisfaction, Anwen's nearly silent. Kael's made no sound at all.

Eira walked at the front.

She could feel it now — the threads humming faintly along the walls, woven into the stone, whispering past decisions and echoes of footsteps long erased.

The deeper they went, the more the magic changed — older now. Less refined. Woven by hand, not spell.

"This shouldn't be here," Kael murmured, brushing his fingers along the corridor's stone wall. "These threads… they weren't here before."

"They grew," Eira said.

"Like vines?" Beck asked again.

Anwen, walking at her shoulder now, pulled a small pouch from her satchel and opened it with a practiced twist. Inside were narrow glass vials, bundles of dried herb, and something folded in oilcloth.

"They're more like roots," Anwen said softly. "When something deep begins to shift, it spreads." She tucked the pouch away again. "I brought sedative blends. And a tonic that might help with shock — magical or otherwise."

Eira glanced at her with quiet gratitude. "You think we'll need it?"

"I think we'll be lucky if that's all we need."

The corridor narrowed, and the stone turned darker. Threadlines etched into the walls began to pulse with a faint golden glow. The energy in the air prickled against skin and threadmarks alike.

Then she saw it.

The final door. Not marked. Not sealed.

Just waiting.

A round of ward-stone circled its frame, with a spiral weave pattern centered in the middle — a sunloop.

The same shape she'd used to seal Caelen's memory.

Her breath caught.

"He's close," she whispered. "I feel him."

She stepped forward and opened the door.

Air rushed out — hot, dry, metallic. Beck swore softly behind her. Kael tensed beside the wall.

Inside, the chamber curved like a hollowed geode, jagged and radiant with thread-veins of gold and crimson. At its center, the stone floor had cracked wide open.

Something shifted in the dark — massive, deliberate.

Stone scraped beneath a claw, black and ridged, curling as if to keep from crushing the floor.

A breath—long, slow, fire-warm—rippled out across the room.

The dragon's eyes opened.

Two massive golden eyes fixed on her.

Eira stepped forward. Her knees wanted to lock, to hold her still, but she forced herself forward, palms open. Every step cracked her heart wider.

"Caelen," she whispered.

The dragon growled — low, uncertain.

Kael stepped forward, and the dragon's entire body turned toward him, wings flaring just slightly in warning.

"Don't," Eira whispered, stepping between them. "Please—he's not the enemy."

The dragon's breath hitched.

Just for a second.

And in that second, she saw it — a flicker of memory ripple through the threads:

Her laugh. His voice. A sunloop drawn in the snow.

He reared back — not in fury.

In pain.

As if the memories *hurt.*

Anwen moved to her side, already unscrewing the cap from a small vial, ready if the dragon collapsed or lashed out.

"No," Eira said softly, tears burning. "Don't pull away. Please… please remember. I promised to help you remember"

A groan echoed through the chamber — the stone beneath their feet shaking as the magic surged.

The geode in her satchel flared once.

And then dimmed.

But the threads didn't fall silent.

They sang.

And somewhere deep beneath the dragon's skin — a thread pulled tight.

The silence pressed with heat and tension. Caelen's gaze pinned her in place — fierce and wary, threaded with something ancient and wounded.

Each slow breath stirred the air like a bellows, crackling faintly with lingering fire. The warmth of it brushed against her skin, *moist and whisper-soft*, like the mist that rolled off the hills back in Brookwyn. Familiar, but changed. Like everything else.

And at last, she truly *saw* him.

He was enormous — taller than the trees they had passed on their way to the capital — feline in his coiled body, a panther poised to spring. Despite his size, he moved with a sleek grace that defied expectation, as if the ground shifted to accommodate him.

His scales were black, ridged like unpolished obsidian, jagged along his back and limbs. But where he had lain for seven years, the stone had polished smooth — gleaming like volcanic glass shaped by time.

No sigils adorned his body. No glowing runes or signs of enchantment. Just the sheer weight of presence, the tension of a being half-lost in memory and magic.

And his eyes — oh, his eyes.

They were golden, deep and luminous, flickering with the faintest echo of the man she had known. There was no fire in them now, only a quiet ache. A soul flickering behind the beast. A tether, frayed but not severed.

Behind her, the others waited.

And she felt it — a subtle shift in the air whenever Kael's presence stirred.

Each time Kael moved, even slightly, Caelen's nostrils flared. The ridge of spines along his back rose a fraction. The tension in his claws tightened, scraping faintly against stone.

Eira turned her head slightly. "Kael."

He stepped forward instinctively, as if to offer help.

But she raised a hand. Not harsh. Just firm.

"Could you… wait outside the chamber?"

Kael's jaw tightened, and for a moment, he didn't move.

"It's not because I don't trust you," she said, her voice gentler now. "It's because he doesn't."

A beat passed. His eyes flicked to the dragon — to Caelen — then back to her.

Kael nodded once, sharply. "Of course."

But she saw it — the flicker of something in his expression. Not anger. Not quite.

Hurt.

He turned without another word, his footsteps echoing dully as he left the chamber and the door eased shut behind him with a whisper of thread.

Eira's shoulders sagged.

Not from regret, exactly.

Just the weight of knowing she was choosing one thread over another. At least for now.

She stepped forward slowly, eyes locked with Caelen's.

"It's just me now," she said softly. "No threats. No lies."

A low rumble rolled from deep in his chest — not hostile, but uncertain.

Still watching.

Still weighing.

Still remembering.

Eira hovered, breath unsteady.

She didn't move at first. Just stood, eyes fixed on Caelen's — those ancient, golden eyes that held no malice, only wariness and something deeper. Something fractured.

A flicker of motion caught in the corner of her vision.

Anwen.

She stood just behind the threshold, close enough to intervene — or to witness.

Their eyes met. Are you sure? her look asked. Eira's nod answered: I have to be.

Anwen gave the barest nod, subtle and steady. Her hands curled loosely around the vial pouches at her belt, ready — always — but not moving.

And so, Eira stepped forward.

One pace. Then another.

The warmth in the air grew with each breath, not uncomfortable but charged. The scent of ash and petrichor surrounded her like a memory.

She lifted her hand.

Caelen did not flinch, though his eyes narrowed slightly. His body remained still, his breath slow and deep.

Her fingers found the smooth plane of his chest — where the obsidian had been worn glassy by seven long years of stillness.

The moment her skin touched his scales—

Flash.

She was barefoot on a sun-dappled path, laughter echoing between trees. Caelen walked ahead, turning just enough to look back at her, grinning like he had no burdens at all. In his hands, a kite of stitched silk tugged against the wind.

Flash.

A library, dust dancing in golden light. They sat cross-legged on the floor, scrolls strewn around them. He passed her one with a quiet murmur — their fingers brushed. The warmth lingered.

His voice low. His laugh joyful. His eyes curious. Hopeful.

Snow fell gently around them. They stood at the edge of a frozen lake, their breath visible in the air. He reached up to brush a flake from her hair, and didn't quite lower his hand. He moved closer and let his lips brush her forehead like a whisper.

Her heart stuttered.

The cottage, glowing with ritual light. Caelen knelt, eyes steady, as Eira traced trembling thread into a waiting geode. Her pulse roared in her ears. Every stitch shimmered with grief. He never looked away.

Then—

Gone.

Eira staggered back with a gasp, as if breaking the surface of water she hadn't known she was drowning in.

Caelen had not moved. But his eyes had changed.

He remembered her. Not fully. Not yet.

But enough.

He lowered his head — not submission, but recognition. Behind her, Anwen exhaled, and the chamber seemed to breathe again.

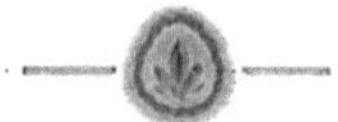

Eira steadied herself, her pulse still echoing in her ears from the memory surge.

She reached for her satchel — already slung across her chest from when she'd fled the inn — and unlatched the small pouch hidden near the center. Her fingers found the geode instantly. It was always warm to the touch, but now it throbbed faintly, like a warning heartbeat.

She stepped forward and held it out in her palm.

Moonlight caught the jagged vein running down the side — a fracture that hadn't been there before yesterday. Not like this.

Caelen's gaze dropped to the stone.

"I don't know what changed," Eira said, voice low, unsteady. "It was stable for months. Since the day I sealed your memories inside it, it's barely flickered. But now…"

She swallowed hard.

"Now it's cracking. And I don't know what happens if it breaks all the way through."

The dragon didn't move, but something in the set of his shoulders shifted. A subtle lowering. A soft rumble escaped him — not warning, but awareness.

Eira tightened her fingers around the stone. "If it shatters, I lose everything. Not just the memories — the connection. The tether back to who you were. And I don't know if I can find you again."

Her voice caught.

For a breathless moment, Caelen was still. Then he lowered his great head until his snout hovered inches from her hand. His breath stirred her hair, warm and damp like Brookwyn mist.

Gently, reverently, he touched the tip of his snout to the geode.

A quiet pulse of heat passed between them.
Acknowledgment. Agreement. Trust.

Behind her, Anwen said nothing — letting the silence carry the weight of the moment.

Eira looked down at the fractured geode, heart thudding.
"We have to unbind it," she whispered. "Before it's too late."

The dragon closed his eyes. Not in retreat, but in memory.

CHAPTER TWENTY-NINE

The air inside the Archive was cool and dry, the scent of ink and parchment sharp against Eira's skin. The entire building felt quieter than it had, as if it, too, were holding its breath.

Eira paced beside the long worktable, the fractured geode cradled in her hand. It pulsed gently.

"It's not spreading yet," she said softly. "But it *feels* like it wants to. Like it's waiting for something."

Beck stood near the door, arms crossed. "So we unbind it. Before it decides to do that something."

"We don't *know* how," Eira snapped, frustration sparking. "I didn't create that weave. Caelen did. I was the conduit."

A silence fell — not angry, just tense. Honest.

Kael's voice broke it, quiet but certain. "There may be a way."

They all turned toward him. He stood with his hands in his coat pockets, eyes on the far wall — the one that separated this part of the Archive from the older, sealed sections behind it.

"I spent time in the back halls," he said. "Before I knew what they really were. Before I understood what the council was *hiding* back there. I didn't get far — not past the third seal. But I saw shelves of forbidden work. Not just ordinary threadweaving, but the specialized branches like geodecraft, time threading, emotional entanglements. Bindings no one speaks of anymore."

Eira frowned. "You think Caelen's method is back there?"

"I think," Kael said, stepping closer, "that if he wrote anything down, if there's *any* chance someone recorded a reverse-weave or even theories about it… it's going to be in the forbidden stacks."

Beck sighed, rubbing his jaw. "Great. So we're breaking and entering again. Why not step up from just light treason."

Anwen didn't smile. She was already pulling a pouch from her satchel. "I brought a few things. In case we needed them. Calming herbs. A pain tincture. Something for dragon breath, if it comes to that."

Beck raised an eyebrow at her. "Prepared as always."

Eira looked down at the geode again. She didn't want to wait. Couldn't.

She closed her fingers around the stone and met Kael's eyes. "Can you get us in?"

"I can get us to the outer seal," he said. "Beyond that, we'll have to improvise."

"Improvising is Beck's specialty," Anwen murmured.

Kael's mouth quirked, but only slightly.

Eira looked between them — not just her friends but her found family, her tether to something lost but not gone.

"Then let's move."

And without another word, they crossed the Archive's threshold and disappeared into the forbidden dark.

The air grew colder as they moved deeper into the Archive. The polished marble gave way to older stone, uneven beneath their boots. Lamps here had long since gone dark, and only Anwen's softly glowing herb charm lit their path — its pale green shimmer casting eerie shadows on the walls.

"This place gives me the creeps," Beck muttered, running his fingers along the cracked mortar of the archway they passed through.

"You'd like it more if it were trying to bite you," Anwen said without looking up.

Kael paused before a thick iron gate etched with threadwork sigils. They pulsed faintly in the dark — not glowing, exactly, but *watching*.

"This is the first seal," he said. "I've come this far before. It's old magic — not lethal, but temperamental. Needs to be undone in the right order."

He stepped aside.

Beck crouched down, brushing his fingers along the edge of the etched runes. "Looks like a lock with too many opinions," he said, then grinned. "Perfect."

Kael handed him a small piece of folded parchment. "I sketched the order once, before the sigils faded. You'll have to feel your way through."

Beck's hands moved with practiced ease, magic weaving through his fingertips like a whisper. Eira watched him work, heart thudding in her chest.

Every moment counted.

With a soft hum and a faint shimmer of blue light, the seal released. The iron gate groaned open.

"One down," Beck said.

Kael nodded, already moving. "The next two are worse."

The second seal was more arcane — a memory-locked threshold that required intent, not just skill. Anwen stepped forward this time, holding a vial of powdered dreamleaf to her nose before speaking a soft invocation.

The doorway pulsed — then melted into mist.

They stepped through.

By the time they reached the third and final barrier, Eira's hands were shaking.

The final seal wasn't carved. It was *woven* — long threads stitched directly into the air like glowing spider silk. Black and red strands bound in a complex knot.

Kael stopped. "This one was different before."

Beck cursed under his breath.

"What does it mean?" Eira asked.

Kael's voice was quiet. "It means someone added protections. Recently."

The group fell silent.

Then Eira stepped forward. "We're already here. Help me unweave it."

Kael hesitated, then nodded.

Together, they moved slowly — not cutting, not forcing — but gently unbinding, coaxing the threads loose with care and magic and fear. Eira's fingers felt numb by the end.

But it worked.

The final seal unraveled with a sigh, and the door creaked inward.

Inside was a small chamber choked with dust and secrets. Tomes lay scattered across shelves and tables, the air heavy with silence and forgotten power.

Kael stepped back. "This is your work now."

Eira didn't wait. She dove in — eyes scanning, hands flipping pages, breath catching when she found diagrams nearly identical to the weave she'd followed to bind Caelen's memories.

Beck stood watch at the door, arms tense.

Anwen stood beside Eira, helping sort scrolls.

Kael lingered in the doorway, eyes shadowed. He didn't speak.

Finally, Eira found something — a marginal note scrawled in sharp ink:

Memory unbinding requires an anchor.

Her hands trembled.

"It seems incomplete, but I think we have to try," she whispered.

Behind her, dawn began to rise.

They cleared space on the floor with frantic care — dragging aside dust-covered scroll tubes and stacks of forgotten tomes, sweeping parchment scraps into the corners. Anwen crushed herbs into a shallow bowl, releasing a sharp, grounding scent that cut through the heavy air.

Eira laid the cracked geode on a folded cloth. Its faint glow pulsed once, as if responding to the change around it.

Eira nodded. "I was the one who bound him. I felt his thoughts. I *knew* him in those final moments."

"And he knew you," Anwen added, arranging small tokens around the geode — a circle of focus.

"And if we mess up?" Beck asked.

"Then the fracture finishes what it started," Kael said. "And Caelen's mind scatters beyond reach."

A cold silence followed.

Eira placed both hands on either side of the geode, drawing a steadying breath. "We won't mess up."

Anwen offered her a soft vial of clarity root. "For focus."

Eira drank, the bitterness anchoring her.

Kael passed her a sliver of thread — no ordinary fiber, but one of the final strands from the original binding.

She tied it around her wrist.

"Ready?" she asked.

No one answered — they just moved into position.

Eira closed her eyes and bent over the geode, voice low and trembling. "Caelen… it's me. You trusted me once. You gave me your story — your strength. And I've kept it safe. But I need you back now. Please. Come back to me."

Her fingers trembled on the cracked surface. The light within the stone flickered — a golden flicker.

Anwen burned a sprig of whisperleaf behind them. The circle gleamed in the dim chamber, its lines smudged from hurried chalk and too many trembling hands.

Eira pressed her palm flat against the geode, heart pounding in her throat. The whisperleaf smoke curled around them, sharp and bitter, while Beck murmured the fragments they'd pieced together from the forbidden notes.

Threads of light trembled through the cracks. At first, it seemed to work. The stone warmed, a deep pulse answering her touch. She felt Caelen — or something of him — straining against the barrier.

"Keep going," Anwen urged, voice tight.

Eira whispered the last line of the chant, pouring every ounce of strength she had into the stone. The geode shuddered. A fissure split wider across its surface, spilling raw light into the chamber.

For a breathless moment, the outline of a man flickered inside the dragon's breast — tall, shadowed, his head lifting as if he could see her.

Her breath caught. *Caelen.*

Then the glow convulsed. The half-shape unraveled like torn thread, scattering back into the stone. The geode gave a soundless crack, then dimmed to a sickly ember.

"No, no, no—" Eira pressed harder, desperate. Nothing answered. The stone was heavier now, its fractures darker, as if they had driven him deeper into the prison instead of freeing him.

Beck staggered back, face pale. "We didn't anchor it. We—gods, we might've just—" He cut himself off.

Silence pressed around them. Eira's hands shook against the geode. She had felt him there, so close, closer than she'd dared to dream—and she had lost him. Worse, she had hurt him.

The circle's chalk guttered out as if the spell itself rejected them.

"What if that was our only chance?" Anwen asked quietly.

Eira closed her eyes. Her throat burned with the answer she couldn't speak.

CHAPTER THIRTY

The candles guttered low, their wax runnels thick with the hours they had burned. Eira sat slumped at the table, her hands still trembling from the backlash of the broken spell. The room smelled of scorched paper and bitter ashroot — failure pressed in heavy as smoke.

"We did everything right," Anwen whispered. She stared down at the blackened scraps of thread, her jaw tight. "The runes were aligned, the incantation exact—"

"Exact, but wrong," Beck cut in, running a hand through his tangled hair. "Whatever that was meant for, it wasn't meant for him." His gaze flicked toward Caelen, who lay curled in uneasy stillness near the wall, dragon form looming in the shadows. The faint fracture down the geode pulsed like a wound.

Eira pressed her palms together, trying to quiet the frantic beat of her heart. If they failed again—

A whisper of movement at the door stilled her thoughts.

"Do not speak loudly," came a voice, cool and firm. "Walls remember what is said within them."

Eira looked up sharply. A figure slipped inside, hood low, robes bearing the sigil of the Council.

Councilor Lysari.

Anwen half-rose, startled, but Lysari's gesture stilled her.

“I should not be here,” she said, voice hushed, eyes flicking toward the shuttered windows. “The Council already suspects. They know you’re in the Archives without permission, though not why. I cannot stay long.”

Her presence felt like a blade balanced on its edge — dangerous, fragile, necessary.

Eira forced herself to speak. “Why risk this, then?”

Lysari’s mouth curved, not quite a smile. “Because I have studied the heart of stone for ten years, and still the Council refuses to act. Because I once traveled to Brookwyn and spoke with Ysolde Wynfell, learning what fragments she would share.” Her gaze fell to the cracked geode in Eira’s hand. “And because I know what happens when the tether fails.”

The words landed like a blow.

Eira’s throat tightened. “Then tell me how to stop it.”

Instead of answering, Lysari slipped something from her sleeve — a sealed letter, edges worn from travel. She set it gently on the table.

“Ysolde placed this in my care long ago, for a day such as this. I swore to keep it safe until I found the one she named.” Her eyes lifted, meeting Eira’s with startling clarity. “That one is you.”

The room went still.

Eira reached out, fingers brushing the parchment as if it might dissolve at her touch. The seal bore Ysolde’s sigil — a lantern entwined with thread.

Her chest constricted. Her mother's hand, across years and distance.

Lysari's voice softened, urgent. "Too many eyes, too many threads knotted close. But within it lies the spell you need — the true unbinding. The only chance you have. And you must do it quickly."

Behind them, Caelen stirred, a low rumble rolling through the floor.

Beck stepped closer, suspicion narrowing his eyes. "And why should we trust you? Why now?"

Lysari met his gaze without flinching. "Because time runs short. And because if you fail, you will not be the only ones to pay the cost. The Council thinks binding and breaking are tools to wield. They do not yet see the storm beneath. I would rather you succeed than all of us fall."

The words held no warmth, only truth sharpened to a point.

She turned toward the door, already fading into shadow. "I must go now. Please keep my visit between us. I must remain on the council to sway them down the right path."

And then she was gone — the latch clicking shut, the silence left raw in her wake.

For a long moment, no one moved.

Eira's hands shook as she broke the seal. The letter unfolded with a sigh, ink strokes steady and sure, as though Ysolde herself stood in the room.

Her mother's voice seemed to whisper from the page: *To unbind without breaking, you must weave the fracture into wholeness. The thread remembers. The heart remembers. But it will cost you more than you think you can give.*

Eira closed her eyes, the words burning into her. The weight of choice pressed down, heavy as stone, bright as flame.

And somewhere within the dragon's chest, a low note of recognition hummed — as if Caelen, too, heard Ysolde's hand reaching through time.

The chamber seemed to hold its breath.

Lanterns guttered in their sconces, their flames strained thin against the stillness. Dust hung suspended in the air, unmoving. Even the dragon—massive, stone-bound, eternal—was silent, its wings folded in a hush that pressed down on every heartbeat.

Eira's hands trembled as she unrolled the parchment. Ysolde's script, sharp and sure, danced across the page in looping strokes of ink. She smoothed the paper flat against the cold stone floor and swallowed hard. The first attempt still burned behind her eyes: threads cut too soon, the spell collapsing into ruin. Caelen's outline glimpsed, then lost again, swallowed by the dragon's prison.

She could not lose him twice.

Not after seven years of silence. Seven years of carrying his absence like a stone under her ribs. Seven years of imagining the sound of his voice, the warmth of his laughter, the way his hand had once brushed hers and lingered a heartbeat too long.

Her throat tightened. She bowed her head, as though Ysolde might hear her across the centuries.

Guide my hands. Please.

She breathed deep, steadied herself, and began.

Threads of light stirred as she traced the runes with her needle, silver glimmer bleeding from the parchment into the chamber's stonework. Lines unfurled like living veins, crawling across the floor, spiraling toward the dragon's bound form.

Beck's hand tightened on his dagger hilt. Anwen whispered under her breath, fingers brushing the air as if in prayer.

Even Kael, usually so unreadable, stood taut and waiting, shadows carved sharp across his face.

The chamber thrummed. The rune-lines flared, gold deepening to white, white to searing violet. The dragon shuddered, scales cracking as if light itself clawed free from beneath. A roar tore through the cavern—ragged, furious, yet edged with something that was almost pain.

Eira pressed on. Needle darting, thread racing, her breath caught between panic and hope. *Hold, just hold—*

The roar fractured. Light burst outward in a torrent, dissolving wings, unraveling talons, until what remained was not a beast at all, but a figure kneeling in the ash of dissolving fire.

Eira froze. Her vision blurred, her knees weak beneath her.

Caelen.

Not scales, but skin. Pale, drawn tight over bones as if carved from hunger. His dark hair fell ragged into his face, his shoulders heaving with the first human breaths he'd taken in years. Slowly, his head lifted. His eyes—those eyes she had memorized in absence—met hers and after a moment flashed with what felt like recognition.

For a long, fragile moment, the chamber was nothing but the two of them.

His lips parted. His voice, hoarse and raw, shaped a single word.

"Eira."

Her heart broke open. She stumbled forward, hands half-lifted, unable to breathe, unable to speak. She had dreamed this moment so many times, but none of them had prepared her for the weight of hearing her name on his tongue.

And yet—

Her gaze flicked sideways, just for a heartbeat. Kael stood at the edge of the light, shadows crowding his face, eyes locked on hers. Something in them caught her, held her, a tether pulling taut. For one searing instant she felt herself split in two: one half rushing toward the boy she had grown up with and loved, the other rooted by the man who had stood at her side through this journey and who had trusted her with his pain.

His jaw clenched just a bit and his blue eyes felt like they bore into her soul. The pull of it left her breathless.

Then the way Caelen's voice had sounded so raw and fragile, pulled her back.

She stepped closer—

—and the chamber doors slammed open.

The sound shattered the stillness, sharp as a blade through glass. Lanterns rattled in their sconces. Dust fell from the high stone beams.

Armed council guards surged in, their boots thunder on the flagstones. Crossbows were raised, swords drawn, shields locked tight.

"By order of the Council!" the lead guard barked. His voice rang against the chamber walls. "Stand away from the creature!"

Eira staggered back instinctively, not from fear of the guards but from the jarring violence of their arrival. The moment—Caelen's voice, her name on his lips—was torn from her hands. Her breath caught sharp in her chest.

The light from the runes flickered. Ash from the dragon's dissolution curled into the air like smoke. Caelen swayed on his knees, one hand braced against the floor, his other reaching toward her—unsteady, but unmistakable.

He was *human.* Flesh and bone, breathing, broken, but *alive.* And yet the guards didn't see him as Caelen. To them, he was still a threat, a relic of dangerous magic, an abomination to be chained.

"Wait—" Eira's voice cracked, but she forced it louder. "He's not—he's *Caelen*! He's—"

"Restrain him!"

The command cut through her words.

Steel rang as half the unit surged forward. Chains clattered, runes already etched into the iron. Beck moved without thought, daggers flashing into his hands. Anwen's lips parted in a word of protest. Kael's expression hardened into something unreadable, his body taut as if preparing for a fight he already knew they couldn't win.

Eira took a step forward, fury sparking in her chest. They had *no right.* After everything—after all the years of silence, all the unraveling—Caelen was finally here, finally *free.* And now—

Crossbow bolts snapped into place. A dozen pairs of eyes fixed on her, on them.

The air grew heavy. The chamber trembled with the weight of the moment, balanced on a knife's edge between miracle and catastrophe.

Caelen's voice broke through, raw but steady. "Eira…"

Her heart clenched as cold iron closed around her wrists.

CHAPTER THIRTY-ONE

The clink of chains still rang in her ears when the guards thrust her forward. This chamber was smaller than the grand council hall she had stood in before, but no less cold. Stone walls, a table too large for the space, chairs carved with quiet precision. Comfortable, somehow—though not welcoming. Eira sat stiffly in one of them, facing all eight councilors across the table like a student called to task.

She wasn't offered tea. Not even water.

Kael, Beck, and Anwen were nowhere to be seen. She had asked. Twice.

"They're being held in the adjacent chamber," said one of the older men—Darek, if she remembered correctly. "Restrained, for safety."

Eira's jaw tightened. "For whose?"A pause — then Councilor Lysari's gaze flicked toward her, just long enough to suggest an answer she could not speak aloud. The others stayed silent.

A councilor with ink-stained fingers — Ines, perhaps — cleared their throat. "The irons were unnecessary. The guards can be… carried away in their zeal."

Eira's laugh was bitter. "Carried away? They shackled him like a beast."

"Caelen is… different," Ines hedged, not meeting her eyes. "But you and your companions should not have been treated so harshly."

Councilor Mirelle folded her hands. "You're not the one under evaluation here, Miss Wynfell. Let's not make this more difficult than it has to be."

Eira's fingers tightened in her lap. She could still feel the hum of magic beneath her skin—wild, unstable, like a current waiting to arc. And not just hers.

They were all afraid. She could see it behind their carefully neutral expressions. Even the ones pretending to be amused.

Councilor Thorne leaned forward, his smile polite and sharp as a blade. "You must understand, Miss Wynfell. The circumstances are… unprecedented. A dragon returned to human form? The Archive nearly compromised? You arriving with a group of outsiders and weaving magic far beyond sanctioned limits?"

"Don't pretend you haven't been watching," she said. "You knew we were in the Archive. You *let* it happen."

A murmur rippled around the table, quickly silenced by a single raised hand from the only figure who hadn't spoken yet—Councilor Halden. Older than the rest. Eyes like burned steel.

He spoke quietly. "We are not here to litigate the past. We are here because something is unraveling. And you may be the only one who can help stop it."

The admission landed with a weight that silenced the room.

Eira didn't flinch. "You're losing control."

That got a reaction—one of the younger women scowled, another councilor's jaw clenched.

"We are trying," Darek said carefully, "to preserve what still holds. There are factions—those who would burn the weave down entirely. They believe the old ways are rotten and must be remade. They're gaining traction. Faster than expected."

Eira didn't look away. "And what do *you* believe?"

"That survival requires strategy," he said. "Which includes knowing when to ask for help."

"And you're asking?"

"We are," said another voice. Councilor Varric, all smooth diplomacy. "But asking is not the same as yielding." His eyes gleamed too brightly, like someone savoring a game only he knew the rules to.

That, at least, was honest in it's own way.

Eira exhaled slowly, like she was weaving breath into control. "You'll get nothing from me until you release my friends."

Silence. A flicker of hesitation. Then Darek again: "They are… important to you?"

She laughed, bitter and quiet. "They're the only reason I'm still here. The only reason the weave hasn't torn wide open beneath your polished floor."

That truth settled into the stone like dust.

No one spoke for a long moment.

Finally, the woman with the braid—Councilor Mirelle, Eira remembered now—sighed. "We will permit a supervised reunion. Limited time. But you will return here for further discussion."

"I'm not a prisoner."

"You're something rarer," Varric said. "You're necessary."

And Eira hated how true that was.

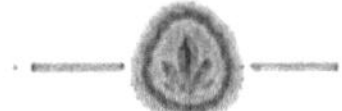

They didn't take her far.

A stone corridor, barely lit. A heavy door with no lock on the outside, only a smooth copper rune that pulsed as she approached. The guard touched it with gloved fingers, and the rune dimmed.

"She has ten minutes," he said.

Eira didn't answer. She was already inside.

The room was windowless and sparse — just a bench against one wall, a table with untouched water, and her friends.

Beck was the first to speak. "About time."

He stood, rubbing his wrists where faint red lines hinted at restraints recently removed. "We were starting to think they'd put you on a leash."

Anwen didn't rise, but her eyes found Eira's and didn't look away. "Are you all right?"

Eira nodded once. "I'm fine."

Kael said nothing.

He was seated furthest from the door, arms loose over his knees, but his magic was a weight in the air — not violent, not panicked, just… coiled.

"I'm sorry," Eira said, barely above a whisper. "They wouldn't let me—"

"We know," Beck interrupted gently. "It's not your fault."

"They're afraid of you," Kael said at last, looking up. "Afraid of us. Afraid of what we might mean."

Eira moved to sit beside him, close but not quite touching. "They want my help. To stabilize the weave. There's more going on than they've admitted. Factions rising. A system collapsing."

"So they need the girl with the needle and thread," Beck muttered. "Typical."

"It's not funny."

"I wasn't joking."

Eira's gaze drifted to Anwen, who still hadn't moved from her seat. "You haven't said much."

"I'm listening," Anwen said. Her voice was quiet, even, but her fingers twisted a loose thread from her sleeve. "I'm trying to decide if we're pawns or players."

Kael let out a slow breath. "Same thing, depending on who's moving the pieces."

A silence settled — not awkward, not quite — but full of things that didn't need to be said.

Then Anwen's voice cut through it, softer than before. "And Caelen? Have they… said what they're doing with him?"

Eira's throat tightened. "Not much. Just that he's being watched. Contained."

"Because they don't know what he is anymore," Kael muttered, bitter. "Or what he might become."

"They won't hurt him," Eira said, but it sounded too much like hope, not certainty.

Anwen's fingers stilled. "They'll use him. If they can."

The rune on the door pulsed.

Time's up.

Eira stood, but turned back at the threshold. "I'll find a way to buy us more time. To figure this out."

Beck grinned, too wide for the situation. "No doubt. You've always been the stubborn one."

Anwen rose at last, her eyes meeting Eira's again. "Be careful what you give them."

Eira nodded.

And Kael?

He didn't speak.

But as she turned away, she felt the hum of thread between them — faint and frayed, but real.

And when the door closed behind her, she swore she could still feel it.

Eira stepped back into the council chamber with her spine straight and her pulse a drumbeat of resolve.

The chamber was no warmer than before. Still stone, still shadowed. Their gazes turned to her as she entered alone—eyes that watched her like a thread poised to snap.

Eira didn't flinch.

They'd taken Kael, Beck, Anwen, and Caelen—separated them, restrained them, treated them like threats instead of allies. And now they wanted her cooperation?

That, more than anything, had sharpened her anger into something usable.

She stepped inside with her head high, the heavy door closing behind her like the lid of a box. She didn't let it show. Not yet.

"You requested further conversation," said the gray-bearded man at the end of the table. Councilor Darek, she suspected—measured and calculating.

"I did," she said, moving to the spot they had left empty at the far end. She didn't sit.

"Sit," said the stern woman at the far left—Councilor Thorne, if Eira remembered correctly. Cold and authoritarian.

A woman with silver rings on every finger tapped one nail against her water goblet. Councilor Mirelle. "You should know—this is not a negotiation. The threads are failing. The Archive is unstable. There is no time."

"Which is why you need me. You want the magic stable," she said, tilting her head. No greeting. No fluff. "You need it, in fact—or your grip on this world, your influence, your precious Archive—all of it crumbles."

Murmurs passed between them. Surprise, perhaps, or offense. She didn't care.

"The weaving I felt in the Archive… it's decaying. You know it. I know it. If something isn't done soon, there won't be anything left to govern."

"And you believe you are the solution?" asked a smooth-voiced man—Councilor Varric, likely. Ambition wrapped in diplomacy.

"Your thread magic is unmatched," said Councilor Brannoc, leaning forward. "But so is your lack of discipline."

Eira let the insult pass. "I believe I'm the only one who can begin to fix it. And you seemed impressed enough with my results back in the Archive."

A few murmurs passed between them.

Councilor Lysari was the first to speak, arms crossed but her voice level. "What do you want, Eira?" Her eyes lingered on her a fraction too long, carrying a weight the others seemed not to notice.

"I need my allies released," she continued, voice even. "Beck and Anwen—you've seen their loyalty. Kael—his magic is tied to mine, whether we like it or not. And Caelen—"

She paused, her throat tightening.

They exchanged glances.

"—he's back, but you don't know what that means. You see a mystery to poke and prod. I see someone who might still be whole—if we stop treating him like an experiment."

"You're not in a position to make bargains," said Varric.

She met his gaze, unwavering. "You're in no position not to."

That, finally, brought a murmur from the others.

She folded her arms. "You want me to reweave the magic holding your entire system together. I think I'm exactly in a position to negotiate."

"I will not proceed without them," Eira said. "And if the structure collapses before you make up your minds… well, I suppose we'll all see how well the council fares when the weave unravels beneath your feet."

Someone coughed—possibly to cover a chuckle. Varric? His eyes gleamed too brightly for someone committed to unity.

Councilor Ines raised a hand to calm the rising voices.

"Let's be practical," she said. "You're powerful. Yes. But this is bigger than any one threadwitch. We need a united front if this has any hope of succeeding. We all must act."

Eira took a breath. "Caelen and Kael can weave too."

That drew another wave of murmuring.

"They're not under council supervision," Mirelle said. "We have no assurance—"

"They're under my supervision," Eira cut in. "And I trust them more than I trust any of you."

Silence fell again.

Councilor Halden, quiet until now, folded his hands. "If we agree to this… what do you intend to do next?"

Eira took the empty seat at last, cloak pooling around her like a shadow.

"I start weaving," she said, her voice steady. "And you start looking for anything and anyone that can help me… after you release my friends."

CHAPTER THIRTY-TWO

Eira stood in the side chamber the council had assigned her, the sharp tang of ancient parchment thick in the air. She hadn't sat. Not out of nerves — she refused to give them that — but because it felt wrong to rest while her friends were still being held elsewhere, even if only in formality.

The door opened with a muted groan.

Anwen stepped in first, composed as ever. Her hair was slightly mussed, a bit of ash on her sleeve, but her bearing hadn't cracked.

"They said you made quite the case," Anwen said softly, crossing the room with calm purpose.

"They gave me an opening," Eira said. "I took it."

Anwen's gaze flicked briefly to the closed door behind her. "They're letting us move forward then?"

"At dawn. We start in the Archive."

The door opened again.

Beck entered with his usual dramatic flourish, arms thrown wide. "Did somebody order a crowd favorite and his grumpy sidekick?"

Kael followed at a more measured pace, his expression unreadable.

Beck threw himself into a chair. "I have to say, that was possibly the least entertaining stay I've ever had in an official council holding suite. Barely any snacks. No complementary robes. I'm filing a complaint."

Eira arched a brow. "Glad to see you're handling captivity with grace."

"Oh, absolutely. We should do it again sometime. Same dusty walls, same awkward silence." He leaned his elbow on the arm of the chair and grinned. "So, what did it cost you?"

"Only a thinly veiled threat and a healthy dose of guilt," she said, folding her arms. "They're reviewing the restricted scrolls now. Trying to find anything that might help stabilize the weave once we begin."

Beck gave a low whistle. "We're down to trusting the council's filing system? We really *are* desperate."

Kael stepped closer but didn't sit. "You bought us time," he said, voice quiet.

She met his eyes. It was the first time they'd truly looked at one another since she asked him to leave that room. Since the moment he'd seen her reach out to calm Caelen — alone.

"I'm going to need your help," she said.

Kael didn't speak right away. Something shifted in his gaze — something wounded, though carefully hidden beneath the stoicism. "You have it," he said at last. But his voice held a cautious distance.

There was a silence that followed. Not uncomfortable — not entirely — but charged. Neither looked away.

Then the door opened again.

Caelen stood in the doorway, one hand braced lightly against the frame. His expression was difficult to read — fatigue, caution, a ghost of something lost behind his eyes.

His gaze flicked to Beck, to Anwen, and lingered there a moment as if confirming they were real. Then it landed on Kael.

"I'm not sure if I should thank you," Caelen said, "or punch you."

Kael didn't flinch. "You wouldn't be standing here if I hadn't done what I did."

"No," Caelen said, voice softer. "But I wouldn't have been asleep alone in the dark for years either."

Another pause. The air between them was heavy, not with animosity, but something deeper — history, regret, the kind of understanding that comes with time and pain both.

"And yet," Caelen said, glancing at Eira, "you didn't stay on the path you were on. You brought them to me."

Kael inclined his head, the barest hint of acknowledgment.

Eira's heart beat faster. Caelen's eyes lingered on her — thoughtful, wary, but warm. And when he looked away, Kael was watching her, too.

Neither man spoke, but something passed between them: recognition, however fragile.

Beck cleared his throat. "So… shall we all pretend this isn't deeply awkward and instead focus on saving the world?"

"I was hoping for at least a cup of tea first," Anwen murmured.

Eira allowed herself a breath, the tension in the room not gone, but rearranged.

"We begin at dawn," she said. "And whatever comes next, we face it together."

The Archive had never felt like this before.

Eira walked the marbled corridor flanked by her friends, the great doors ahead already unlatched. Council scribes hurried past with clipped urgency, scrolls clutched tight, whispers sharp as blades. For all the council's practiced condescension, their fear now was unmistakable — the weave was failing, and no one could deny it.

The central chamber yawned open, vast and echoing. Shelves loomed like ancient ribs, and magic hummed faintly in the stone. Overhead, the great thread mural shimmered, its light pulsing unevenly like a faltering heartbeat.

"Well," Beck said, hands on hips, "this still smells like a thousand-year-old sock drawer. Good to know some things never change."

Anwen nudged him gently. "Try not to antagonize the librarians."

"They adore me," he said. "In that quiet, repressed way where they don't make eye contact and hope I vanish."

Eira allowed herself a small smile, but it slipped as her gaze drifted upward again. The threads. They revealed themselves now — just barely — thin lines glinting through the air like veins in glass. Some stretched taut, glowing. Others frayed at the edges, flickering in and out of existence.

"We need to divide the work," she said. "The scribes are reviewing the restricted shelves, but I want to check the foundation records. Kael, search the north alcove — the early vault diagrams."

He inclined his head in quiet acknowledgment.

"Caelen—" she hesitated. "Will you examine the theory scrolls on magical harmonics? They're dense reading, but…"

"I'll manage." His voice was low, steady. "I've done harder things recently."

Eira turned to the rest. "Anwen, Beck — search the ledger archives. I need any mention of Elander or ward alterations after the last stabilization."

"On it," Beck said, already halfway to the side shelves. "If we find anything cursed, I'm not touching it. That's Kael's job."

They dispersed, vanishing into spines and shadows. Eira moved toward the central records, where a half-dozen scrolls had been set aside for her. She didn't sit. She unrolled the first page and began scanning by lanternlight.

Minutes bled away, measured in parchment scrapes and soft footsteps.

Then—faint, high above—one of the ceiling threads shivered. Eira looked up just in time to see it stutter like a fraying wire.

The air chilled.

Something was coming.

And the weave, delicate as a spiderweb strung across time and space, could not bear another break.

A sound like snapping twine cracked overhead.

Eira's head jerked up as a high-pitched hum vibrated through the stone underfoot. The threads — those faint lines of light strung through the Archive — thrashed in violent arcs. One jolted, then snapped, vanishing in a sharp flicker.

A scholar near the western shelves cried out as scrolls clattered to the floor, dust pluming like smoke.

"Something's wrong," Anwen said, voice clipped, alert.

"No kidding," Beck muttered, already sprinting toward the tremor. "Please tell me this is just an unstable rune and not the beginning of the end."

They converged near the central stairwell where the floor had begun to fracture — not in stone, but in the weave itself. Eira saw it first: a jagged gash of chaotic magic blooming open like a wound. Threads around it unraveled midair, curling back like burned ribbon.

"Move!" Kael barked, reaching out as another violent flicker jolted through the foundation. "It's spreading!"

Before anyone could respond, Caelen stepped forward and dropped to one knee, pressing his palm to the marble. Magic surged from him — raw and strange — like an echo of something long-forgotten. The threads trembled but stilled, as if stunned.

Eira didn't waste the moment. She knelt beside him, hands already glowing with threadlight. Kael joined them without hesitation.

Three pairs of hands, three distinct magics — converging on the tear.

The air buzzed with tension. Caelen's magic pulsed deep and jagged. Kael's steadied it, weaving the stray strands back together like bones being set. Eira stitched the outer threads tight with her precision, her breath ragged with focus.

Behind them, scholars whispered and fled.

"Whatever did this," Kael said quietly, "was no accident."

A single scroll lay abandoned near the fracture — one Eira didn't recognize. She reached for it with shaking fingers.

The seal had been broken. The ink still wet.

"Restricted records," she breathed. "Someone's been tampering."

Beck stumbled up beside them, panting. "There's a passage in the lower stacks — forced open, scorch marks everywhere. And I saw a strip of cloth caught on the hinge." He held up the shred: dark orange, singed at the edge.

Eira's stomach dropped.

Veilbreakers.

"There were council members in the restricted archives," Eira said sharply, already moving.

They ran.

The corridor bent hard and spilled into the private chamber of forbidden texts. The heavy doors sagged on crooked hinges, scorched at the seams. Inside, haze clung to the air, acrid with the scent of magic gone wrong.

Three council members lay slumped across the reading benches, motionless but breathing.

Eira rushed to the nearest — Councilor Ines — and gently turned her over. A pulse fluttered, faint but steady, beneath her skin. Beside her, Anwen knelt, brushing her fingers through the air, nose wrinkling.

"Herbal magic," she murmured. "Sedative, but gentle. No blood magic. No dark marks. They'll wake… within a day, if they rest."

Relief caught in Eira's throat, leaving her breath shaky as it escaped.

Footsteps thundered behind them. More council members surged in through the shattered door — Councilor Mirelle in front, with Darek and Varric close behind.

"What in the name of the weave—" Mirelle's sharp gaze swept the room, lingering on the unconscious bodies. "What happened here?"

"They were attacked," Kael said. "Whoever broke the seal on that scroll wanted the restricted vault and didn't want interference."

Varric lurched forward, face pale, hands spread in a show of outrage. "This is an *outrage*! An infiltration at the heart of the Archive? We are under siege!"

His voice carried too loudly, just a shade strained. The shock on his face was almost *performed*, a mask that slipped at the edges. Beck, leaning in the doorway, gave a quiet snort.

"If I didn't know better," he muttered, "I'd say someone rehearsed that performance."

Eira didn't answer, but her eyes narrowed. Something wasn't right.

CHAPTER THIRTY-THREE

The inn was quieter than usual when they returned — as if even the air knew something had shifted.

Eira dropped into a chair by the hearth in the common room, not bothering to take off her cloak. Her muscles ached, not from any injury, but from the relentless strain of too many threads pulled too tight. Across from her, Anwen sat with a piece of thread looped between her fingers, slowly braiding and unbraiding it while her gaze wandered toward the fire.

Beck was the only one with any energy left. He kicked his boots off dramatically at the door and stretched with an exaggerated groan. "I don't want to alarm anyone, but I might actually be too tired to be charming."

Anwen didn't look up. "So… you're normal now?"

"Excuse me," Beck said, pointing a mockingly wounded look at her. "I am the emotional glue holding this group together."

Eira almost smiled, but the effort caught in her chest. Even Anwen's braid fell apart in her hands, fingers moving too slowly to keep it tight.

Kael leaned against the wall near the window, arms folded. He hadn't said much since they left the Archive, but Eira could feel his thoughts pressing in like heat on the back of her neck. She hadn't looked at him since they'd passed through the inn's door, afraid too much would surface in her expression.

Caelen emerged from the hallway, freshly washed and visibly exhausted, hair still damp. "The room's… comfortable," he said awkwardly, glancing toward Beck.

Beck gave a crooked grin. "It's all yours. Just don't touch the notebook under the bed. It bites."

That earned him a small, reluctant smile from Caelen, but the tension still sat heavy between them — between all of them. Too many questions unanswered. Too many threads tangled.

Eira finally looked up. "Thank you, Beck."

He waved her off. "Honestly, I've slept in the woods with spiders for neighbors. Caelen's got fewer legs, far less webbing, and I haven't heard him hiss even once. Upgrade."

Caelen hesitated, then asked, "You all came here because of Kael?"

Eira stilled.

Kael's posture tensed, but he didn't move.

"Yes," she said. "He found us. He helped us. And he brought us to you."

Caelen nodded slowly. His jaw flexed — something between discomfort and understanding. "Then I owe him… something. I don't know what yet."

Kael finally spoke, voice low. "You don't owe me anything. I kept you hidden, asleep, too long."

"And I'd still be asleep if you hadn't changed your mind," Caelen said. "That's… complicated, but I'm here now. Because of you."

Their eyes met. It wasn't a peace offering. Not yet. But it wasn't a war, either.

Beck clapped his hands once, too loudly. "Well! That was emotional and grown-up. Can we all agree not to do it again?"

Anwen gave him a look. "You're terrible."

"Thank you."

The room settled into silence again. Kael stepped back from the window and sat in a low chair near Eira, but didn't speak. She could feel the weight of what still hung between them — unspoken hurt, things left unfinished.

Anwen broke the quiet. "What now?"

Eira stared into the fire. The flames danced like the threads in the Archive — flickering, fragile, half a breath from breaking.

"We fix what we can," she said finally. "We guard the weave. And we get to them before they strike again.

Anwen shifted, finally setting the thread aside. "Then tomorrow, we make a plan."

Eira nodded, though her body already sagged toward sleep. "Tomorrow," she echoed — a promise she couldn't know she wouldn't keep.

Sleep had claimed them unevenly. Eira slumped near the hearth, cloak still around her shoulders. Anwen's braid lay unfinished, thread curled against her palm. Even Beck, who never seemed to stop moving, had finally gone still in a crooked sprawl across his chair. For a moment, the inn was nothing but the crackle of dying embers.

The knock came just past midnight.

Not a timid tap, but three deliberate raps — loud enough to jolt Eira from half-sleep. She sat up, instantly alert.

Beck blinked blearily. "That better be room service or a dramatic confession. I'll accept either."

Kael was already at the door, hand near the dagger tucked beneath his coat. He opened it just wide enough to see—

A young courier stood there, trembling. His eyes were wide, as if he'd seen more than the message carried. He held a sealed parchment bearing the sigil of the Council — only it was torn, smudged with ash.

Kael took it and shut the door without a word.

"What is it?" Anwen asked as Eira stood beside him.

He broke the seal and read aloud.

"Urgent report. South wing of the Archive breached. Dozens injured. Fires contained. Council members requesting immediate reinforcement and magical support. Suspected hostile spellcraft—possibly coordinated."

A beat of silence.

Eira felt the bottom drop out of her chest. They hadn't even had a chance to breathe, let alone prepare. Tomorrow was gone before it began. "They weren't done," she said quietly. "The fracture earlier was just the beginning."

Beck ran a hand through his hair. "Are they trying to tear the whole thing apart thread by thread?"

"They're trying to collapse it," Kael said. "To unmake what the Archive holds."

Caelen appeared in the doorway of the hall, drawn by the noise. "Where?"

"The south wing," Anwen said. "Where the enchantments are oldest."

Eira looked at Kael. "If those threads come apart—"

"Then the restricted collections won't be the only things lost."

Caelen stepped forward. "We need to go. Now."

Beck stood, already strapping on his boots. "I was just starting to enjoy the smell of this place. Guess we're saving the world again."

Kael's hand brushed Eira's arm, light but grounding. She met his eyes and nodded once.

No more delays.
No more waiting for orders.

Whatever the Veilbreakers had started, they would finish it.

Together.

They didn't make it two blocks before the smoke found them.

It curled in slow coils from the cracks between buildings, the scent sharp with charcoal and burning paper. The sky above the Archive glowed faintly, flickering like a storm trapped behind stone.

People poured into the streets, clutching children, half-dressed and wide-eyed. A woman shouted for her husband. A boy sobbed, clutching a singed blanket. Somewhere nearby, a window shattered as wild magic burst through glass.

"We have to stop and help—" Anwen turned toward a woman trying to douse magical flames crawling up her doorframe.

"No time," Kael said, his voice tight. "If the wards fall, this spreads to the whole city."

"They'll die," Anwen whispered, visibly torn.

Eira grabbed her arm. "We save them by ending this. Every second we lose here means more lives in danger."

Beck looked back at the panicking crowd. His voice was unusually quiet. "I don't like it either… but she's right. If we don't stop this now, there won't be a city left to save."

He swallowed hard, eyes darting to the towers burning against the horizon. "And if it spreads beyond these walls… it's only a matter of time until it reaches Brookwyn."

Another surge of magic rippled through the air — like heat rolling off a forge — and a lantern down the road exploded in a burst of tangled threadlight. Screams followed like an exclamation point on Beck's warning.

Caelen stepped forward, jaw clenched. "We run."

And so they did.

Through twisted alleys and half-collapsed lanes. Past shop fronts where silks had come to life and now coiled like serpents, strangling their own looms.

Past a baker's cart that hovered two feet off the ground, its wares circling in wild orbit.

Past a man staring, horrified, at his own reflection — dozens of them now, each shouting a different word, as the glass cracked wider with every syllable.

The weave was coming undone.

"Almost there!" Beck shouted over the chaos, pointing to the Archive's towers rising ahead like storm-battered cliffs.

The final approach was clogged with debris and panicked citizens. Kael used sharp bursts of threadwind to clear their path. Caelen diverted magical surges with half-formed shielding spells, sweat pouring down his temples.

And still — they ran.

Because behind the smoke and shattered streets was a harsher truth.
The weave wasn't just power, or spells tucked safely into books.

It was breath in lungs, flame in hearths, water in wells. If it unraveled, so would the lives built upon it.

The Council's warnings had never been only about politics or control. For once, Eira understood — if the weave collapsed, it wouldn't just be their authority lost. It would be everything.

They reached the lower gates of the Archive as the first tremor shook the stones beneath their feet.

CHAPTER THIRTY-FOUR

The Archive loomed ahead, half-shrouded in smoke and flickering magic. From a distance, the ancient spires had always looked eternal. Unshakable.
Now, they wept light.

Threadlight bled from cracks in the outer walls like veins rupturing beneath too much strain. Glyphs sparked erratically, like lightning trapped in glass. Doors once bound by spells swung loose on their hinges. Screams echoed from deeper inside.

Eira didn't stop to admire the horror. She ran.

The others followed close, footsteps pounding uneven stone. Kael at her left, Caelen a shadow behind. Anwen brought up the rear, her eyes already scanning the chaos, calculating.

They burst into the entry hall—and staggered.

The devastation was overwhelming.

Shelves that had stood for centuries toppled like kindling. Scrolls smoldered in shattered cases. Statues wept from their eyes, thread magic dripping down marble cheeks like tears. Paper butterflies that once fluttered peacefully now clawed at the air, wings frayed and dissolving.

And through it all, scholars ran frantically, clutching fragments of their life's work. One man cradled a half-burned tome as if it were a dying child. Another stumbled with an armful of scrolls, tripping as parchment scattered, unraveling into ash before it touched the ground. Their voices rose in broken pleas — to save, to salvage, to remember — drowned by the crack of collapsing beams.

"They're trying to save what they can," Eira whispered, throat tightening. "But it's too much."

Kael's jaw flexed. "Too much is already gone."

Near the central stair, two councilors stood amidst the ruin, robes torn, faces streaked with soot. They flung threads desperately into unstable wards, trying to contain a surge of light splitting the walls. The magic lashed back, scorching the stone and knocking one councilor to his knees. The other swore, clutching her burned hand, but kept casting.

"They're losing control," Anwen said. "And if the keystone falters—"

"We stop it before it does," Kael snapped.

They pushed deeper into the Archive, down corridors that had once felt reverent, sacred. Now sabotage marks scarred the floors — hasty sigils of unbinding, scrawled in ash and fury. Doors to the restricted vaults gaped open, forced by brute spellcraft.

"They were here," Kael growled. "Tauren's people."

"They're not just trying to collapse the Archive," Caelen murmured. "They're stealing what they can before they do."

Beck swore. "We can't cover this whole place on our own."

Anwen scanned the glowing glyphs overhead, already unstable. "Then we split. I can keep the northern lines from detonating — for a while. Beck, with me."

"I thought you'd never ask," Beck said, flashing a grin that didn't reach his eyes.

Kael looked to Eira. "We head for the sanctum."

Eira's gaze flicked to Caelen. "Can you handle it?"

"I have to," he said simply.

No more hesitation. They split.

The moment Beck and Anwen vanished down the side corridor, Eira felt the weight shift, like a thread had been cut she hadn't realized she leaned on.

But there was no time for unraveling.

The Archive needed saving. And someone was already deep in its heart, pulling at every thread that held the world together.

The sanctum archway loomed ahead, cracked and humming with unstable power. Protective wards once woven into its stone had been erased, ripped from the weave like threads torn from cloth.

Inside, the air reeked of sulfur and static.

And there, before the keystone pillar, stood Councilor Varric.

Stolen scrolls bulged from a satchel at his side. Fresh spellwork glowed along his hands. The keystone's web pulsed erratically, like a wounded heart.

He didn't flinch when they entered.

"I was wondering when you'd arrive," he said smoothly. "Though I expected you to be… more hindered."

"You did this," Kael growled. "You let them in."

"I guided them," Varric corrected. "There's a difference."

"You betrayed your own council," Eira spat.

Varric's smile widened, eyes bright with conviction. "The council betrayed itself long ago. Clinging to power while the threads rotted beneath them. Censoring truth. Burying history."

"You destroyed half the Archive."

"No," Varric snapped, voice sharpening. "I'm saving it. These scrolls — the ones they hid — show how thread magic was meant to work. Before the shackles. Before the lies. I'm tearing down what's broken to build something stronger."

"Then explain the people screaming in the streets," Eira shot back. "The children hiding in the rubble. This isn't rebuilding. It's slaughter."

For the first time, Varric's gaze flickered.

"Casualties are unavoidable," he said too quickly.

"They're unforgivable," Eira answered. "And if you can't see that, you've already lost."

Varric's lip curled. "You sound like someone afraid of change."

"No," Caelen said. "You sound like someone already lost."

Threadlight flared around Varric, wild and uneven. He raised his hand — not in attack, but in finality.

"You can't stop what's coming. You're not strong enough to hold it together."

He triggered the sigil etched at his feet.

The floor buckled. The keystone screamed with light, shattering its web. The chamber cracked open, stone raining from the ceiling. Kael yanked Eira back, Caelen shielding her from the blast.

And when the flare dimmed, Varric was gone — vanished with his stolen knowledge, leaving only chaos behind.

Eira staggered up, ears ringing. The keystone pulsed erratically, its web fraying faster with every beat.

Kael's eyes went grim. "We're out of time."

"Please tell me you didn't start the fun without me," Beck's voice called from the hall, as he and Anwen reappeared, smoke clinging to their clothes.

Eira's relief nearly undid her.

"You're late," Kael growled, though his shoulders eased.

"Had to rescue a councilor from a bookshelf and an existential crisis," Beck said. "Zero out of ten. Wouldn't recommend."

Anwen's face was pale, her eyes rimmed with fear she rarely let show. But she only nodded. "We're all here."

Eira surged forward, pulling Beck into a tight hug before she could stop herself. He tensed, then softened, whispering, "Ow. Ribs."

"You're okay?"

"Still standing," he said. "Still making bad decisions. Pretty standard."

Eira turned toward the pulsing keystone, the fractured weave snapping in and out like a heartbeat on the verge of failure. "It's Varric. He's let the zealots inside."

"Then we end this," Kael said.

They stepped forward as one.

And for the first time, Beck didn't joke. His voice was quiet. "Then we end it — no matter the cost."

CHAPTER THIRTY-FIVE

The sanctum shook like a bell struck too hard.

Threadlight spat from the keystone in ragged bursts, casting the room in strobing gold and white. The air smelled of hot stone and burned paper. Every breath tasted like ash.

"Pattern three," Eira said, voice hoarse. "Triangulate and pull on my mark—now."

Kael slid to her left, hands already weaving light. Caelen took the right, the cracked geode at his hip flaring in time with his pulse. Anwen braced behind them, eyes fixed on the outer rings of the web, pulse-counting under her breath. Each surge rattled her bones, but she forced her magic steady, binding cracks before they widened, keeping the others from being thrown apart.

They pulled.

For a heartbeat the weave obeyed. Threads tightened, the keystone's pulse steadied—

—and then the whole lattice kicked like a startled animal.

Light snapped back on them. Eira's palms seared. Kael staggered; Caelen slammed a shoulder into the pillar to keep from going down. Anwen hissed and jerked her hands away, fingers smoking.

"It's slipping faster than we can stitch," Anwen gasped. "Like trying to bind a river with twine."

Eira swallowed hard against the throb in her hands. "Again."

They tried a different angle—Kael dropping to a slower cadence, Caelen forcing a counter-rhythm through the geode. The keystone shuddered, then lurched. Stone dust sifted from the vaulting. A fissure raced up the nearest column and bloomed across the ceiling like frost.

Outside, somewhere deep in the Archive, something heavy fell. The impact rolled through the sanctum floor, and the web juddered dangerously.

"We're out of time," Kael said, eyes tight.

Beck didn't answer. He was watching the keystone, head tilted, jaw set—like he was listening for a word only he could hear.

"Beck—" Eira started.

He lifted a hand—wait.

"Your stitchwork is right," he said quietly, eyes never leaving the heart of the web. "But the keystone isn't. It keeps slipping under you. You're sewing a sail in a storm."

"Then we hold it," Caelen said through his teeth.

"From where?" Beck's mouth twisted. "Outside won't do it."

Understanding hit Eira like cold water. "No."

Beck looked at her finally. The old mischief wasn't there. Only a steady, stubborn light.

"It needs a hand on the inside," he said. "A tether that won't yank when the ground moves."

Anwen shook her head, tears springing hot. "That's not a hand, Beck. That's a whole person."

He huffed a breath that might've been a laugh on another day. "Lucky for you, I am one."

"Don't," Eira said. It came out raw. "We'll find another way."

"You already tried." He glanced past her, to where the web trembled like a wounded heart. "If we fail here, there isn't a 'later.' Not for them." His chin tipped almost imperceptibly toward the city beyond the walls. "Not for Brookwyn."

Another tremor rolled through the sanctum. A ring of runes guttered, then went out.

He turned to Anwen.

"Beck, I—" Her voice cracked on the single syllable. She took a breath like she might finally say the thing she'd been holding for years.

He reached up and touched two fingers lightly to her cheek, brushing away a tear. A small shake of his head. Don't. Not here. Not now. His eyes said the rest—I know.

Her mouth pressed into a trembling line. She nodded once—fierce, desperate, and steadying all at once. If he was giving everything, then she would not falter. She would make his hold matter.

"You absolute menace," she whispered, because anything truer would undo him.

"Accurate," he said softly, the ghost of a grin flickering and gone.

Eira stepped in, fingers trembling. "I can—"

"No," Beck said, and for once there was no joke riding shotgun with the word. "You lead. Kael stitches steady because you breathe steady. Caelen can fake brave if you say the word 'now' like you mean it. I'm the one who can hold when everything else is falling apart. That's… always been my bit, hasn't it?"

He squeezed Eira's hand, brief and grounding, then tugged his own scarf tighter at his throat—as if bracing himself against a wind only he could feel.

"Make it count," he said.

Then he turned, stepped into the spill of threadlight, and reached.

The weave swallowed him like surf taking a swimmer—one bright flare, and he was inside it, a figure lit from within, threads pouring through his fingers and around his arms, anchoring, binding. The keystone bucked once. Beck braced and held.

"Now!" Eira shouted, voice not breaking.

They moved.

Kael's stitches came clean and sure, each motion a promise. Caelen drove power from the geode, forcing rhythm back into the lattice, jaw clenched until a drop of blood slid from the corner of his mouth.

Anwen stood at the rear circle, hands trembling but unbroken, pulse-counting the surges. When Kael's rhythm stuttered, she caught and steadied it. When Caelen pushed too far, she braced him before the weave tore wider. When Eira wavered under the strain, Anwen's magic wrapped firm around her like a bandage.

She was the net beneath them all, the healer holding the line while her own heart threatened to split.

Eira took the center. She set her breath to a five-count—the way she taught apprentices with burned fingers and brave hearts—and stitched as if the world depended on it. Because it did.

The sanctum roared. The web flashed and dimmed, flashed and dimmed. Beck's outline blurred as more of the weave wound through him. He never looked away. He never let go.

"Left seam tearing," Kael barked.

"I see it," Eira said, and threw a new thread across the breach. It hit and held.

A wave of backlash punched them in the chest. Anwen went to one knee and clawed her way upright again, teeth bared. Caelen sagged, caught himself on the pillar, and shoved more power through the geode until it sang with pain.

The outer rings began to answer. One by one, wards flickered awake—faint at first, then brighter, runes crawling back into carved grooves like rivers remembering old beds.

Another surge. The floor lurched. Eira stumbled—Lysari's hands caught her elbows from behind before she went down.

Eira whirled. The council had arrived at the arch—robes torn, faces ash-streaked—Mirelle wide-eyed, Thorne grim as stone. Lysari alone moved like she'd been here the whole time, like she'd been watching for this exact moment.

"Steady," Lysari said, low enough only Eira heard. "Five-count. Don't chase the pulse—let it meet you."

Something in Eira unlocked. She nodded, set her breath again, and the next stitch slid clean.

Mirelle stood frozen at the threshold, hands half-raised, watching the weave climb back from the brink. "Stars," she whispered. "They're—"

"Quiet," Thorne snapped, not unkindly. He stepped forward, slammed both palms to a failing ward at the far wall, and threw his weight into it like he was holding up a collapsing beam.

Lysari didn't move to the center. She drifted the perimeter, pressing sigils back into place with quick, precise taps—enough to keep the room from eating the people in it, not enough to pull the task out of Eira's hands. When Eira faltered, Lysari's voice found her again. "Steady. In. Hold. Out."

The web tightened.

"Final lock," Kael said, voice scraped thin.

"On three," Eira said. "One. Two—"

Beck looked at her. Really looked. Even inside the light, even as it burned through him, she saw his grin—the soft one he saved for found-family and fearless mistakes.

"Three," Eira breathed.

They pulled together.

The keystone screamed. Light tore through the chamber and blew every banner on the walls straight out. The weave snapped tight—then cinched, knotting around Beck's anchor point with a sound like a bell brought to heel.

Silence hit so hard it rang.

Dust drifted. Runes glowed in steady, waking lines. The keystone pulsed like a heart that had remembered how to beat.

Eira staggered forward, already reaching.

The place where Beck had stood was empty. Threadlight bled into the stone and vanished. On the floor lay a scorched scrap of yellow and half a silver ring, cracked clean through. The air still held the shape of him, as if he had just stepped out of the room and left his outline behind.

Kael stooped, fingers clumsy, and lifted the scarf fragment. Thorne's mouth tightened; he looked away.

Anwen folded at the waist like she'd been cut, hands braced on her knees, shuddering. She had poured every thread of her love and steadiness into holding the others together, but with Beck gone, the weight of what she'd held back crashed through her at last—raw, merciless, unstoppable.

Eira knelt. The stone was still warm. She touched the ring as if it might burn her and cradled both relics in her palm.

"It counted," she said to the quiet, to the weave, to everyone who would ever ask. "It counts."

Only then did the sanctum breathe.

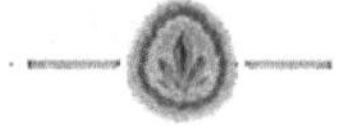

Bootfalls rushed the corridor—more councilors, healers, archivists with bandaged hands and smoke in their hair. Orders stuttered. Questions collided in the doorway and died there when eyes found the web holding, the pillar lit, the four of them—three—still upright.

Darek came first, composed by force. "Report."

"Alive," Thorne grunted, still palming the ward, sweat carving tracks through soot. "Barely."

Lysari didn't report. She slipped beside Caelen and pressed two fingers to the inside of his wrist, then to the cracked geode, reading whatever needed reading. "You've overdrawn. Do not draw again." Her voice carried no argument.

Caelen swallowed, nodded once.

Mirelle's gaze snagged on the empty center of the room—the absence where a person should be—and moved quickly past it, too quickly. "Where is Councilor Varric?"

"Gone," Kael said, all edges. "With stolen work. He opened the way. He armed the Veilbreakers and walked out while it burned."

Mirelle flinched like the truth struck her. "He was with us earlier. He—he ordered—"

"Enough," Thorne said softly, a word like a closed door. He plucked something from inside his scorched sleeve and set it in Mirelle's palm: half of a council medallion, the snap deliberate and mean. "Found near the rear exit."

Mirelle stared until her hand shook. She closed her fingers around the metal and looked to the weave again, to the people who'd held it. "We will answer for this," she said. It wasn't a threat. It was a promise to the dead and the living both.

Lysari's eyes found Eira's over the space between them. No smile. No comfort. Just a nod—acknowledgment and thanks and a vow to stand where she could, when she could, without saying the dangerous part out loud.

Behind them the stabilized web hummed—not triumphant, not safe, but steady. Alive.

"Get them out of here," Lysari said quietly. "Before the healers decide they belong on cots."

"Agreed," Thorne said. "You've done enough." He met Eira's gaze. "More than enough."

Eira closed her fingers around scarf and ring, then turned to where Anwen still swayed, pale and hollow-eyed. For years Anwen had been her anchor, her steady place when the world spun too fast. Now it was Eira's turn. She slipped an arm around her friend's shoulders, steadying her with a gentleness she had learned from Anwen herself, and together they stepped toward the door.

The inn felt wrong without Beck's noise in it.

They laid what they had on his bed: the half-burned scarf, the broken ring. Anwen brought wildflowers from the alley cracks because it was what she had; her hands shook as she placed them, petals scattering. Eira moved closer without a word, brushing her fingers lightly against Anwen's wrist in quiet steadiness, a silent promise: *you're not carrying this alone.*

Caelen set the ring in the center like a marker stone. Kael stood at the window and watched the smoke thin over the city until only the stubborn glow of wardlight remained.Eira took a charred thread from the scrap of yellow and tied it around her wrist with clumsy fingers.

"He always said if he went out, it should be dramatic," Kael murmured, voice rough. "Preferably with fireworks."

"And a terrible pun," Anwen whispered.

"He'd have said, 'Guess I've really… made a lasting impression,'" Caelen offered, and then looked appalled at himself.

The laugh that followed was small and crooked and exactly right.

Caelen drew something from under the mattress, an oilskin-wrapped bundle. "He told me where he hid this before we left for the Archive. Said not to open it unless—" His voice thinned. He held it out.

"His journal," Anwen said, tracing the handwriting on the cover with reverent fingertips. "We'll keep it safe."

Eira nodded, and this time she laid her hand gently over Anwen's for a moment, grounding her. "And when we're home—" The voice shook. She steadied it. "When we're home we'll find a place for him. Water. Wildflowers. Quiet."

"And a sign," Kael said. "Absolutely no dramatic exits."

The sunset slid warm light through the window, turning the smoke to gold. For a long time none of them moved. The city's new heartbeat—slow and stubborn—thudded through the walls.

Outside, bells began to ring. Not for victory. For counting every life the city would not see return.

Inside, Eira closed her eyes and listened to the weave hold.

CHAPTER THIRTY-SIX

The sky over the capital was still hazy, the lingering traces of unbound magic crackling faintly in the air like the aftermath of a summer storm.

Eira stood just outside the Archive, her hands resting on the stone balustrade of the broad outer steps. The building behind her still buzzed with movement—council staff and scribes working to assess the damage, rescue teams tending to the wounded, and magic-weavers checking for ruptures in the foundational wards.

But for the moment, Eira was alone.

Not entirely alone, she corrected herself. She could still feel the threads of Kael and Caelen, pulsing faintly at the edge of her awareness like distant stars.

And Beck...

Her hands tightened on the stone. She hadn't allowed herself to cry. Not yet. Too many people had needed her calm, her clarity, her strength.

Now, in the stillness, that wall began to buckle.

Footsteps approached behind her. Familiar, steady.

Anwen stopped a pace away, silent for a moment. Then: "He would've hated the memorial service they're planning."

A short laugh escaped Eira—more breath than sound. "Too quiet. Too formal. Not nearly enough snacks."

"He left a note in my satchel." Anwen held it out with a shaking hand. "One of his… ridiculous backup plans. He had them in case we survived. Or didn't."

Eira took the folded parchment. It read, in Beck's unmistakable hand:

If I bite it gloriously, someone better cry. Bonus points if someone throws a chair in my honor.

Eira choked on a laugh and let the tears come.

Anwen sat beside her on the cold stone steps tears flowing down her cheeks. Neither of them spoke for a long time.

Eventually, Anwen whispered, "I can't help wondering if I could've stopped it… if I'd gone with him…"

"You couldn't have," Eira said, making eye contact with Anwen, her voice firm despite the crack in it. "He knew what he was doing. He chose it."

Anwen nodded. "Doesn't make it hurt less."

"No," Eira agreed. "It really doesn't."

The wind shifted. Distant bells rang out across the city, calling citizens to a public address from the still-fractured council. A different world, now. One Beck had helped forge.

Eira glanced toward the horizon where smoke still rose faintly. "We're still here," she murmured. "So we make it count."

The meeting chamber hadn't changed much—the same stone floor, the same long table, though one corner bore scorch marks where the ceiling had cracked and collapsed. Temporary scaffolding crisscrossed parts of the chamber, lending the illusion of repair. It felt less like a seat of power and more like a wounded beast, barely breathing.

Eira stood at the far end, not at the seat they'd once left open for her, but beside it. Upright. Tired. Finished.

Only four council members were there to greet her—Mirelle, Darek, Brannoc, and Ines. They looked worn too. Varric was gone. His home cleared out during the chaos the zealots had caused. Nobody had seen Tauren, and it was unknown how much he had been involved in the planning and execution of the attack.

Eira folded her arms as the door clicked shut behind her. "You asked for a word?"

Councilor Mirelle inclined her head. "We wanted to thank you. Without your intervention—without all of you—the weave would have shattered."

"You're welcome," Eira said. She didn't soften the edge in her voice.

Councilor Darek cleared his throat. "We know you have no desire to remain in the capital, but we hoped you might stay on a bit longer, advise as we rebuild—"

"No." Calm. Firm. "This was never my home. And I have a town to return to. A shop. People who count on me."

Brannoc leaned forward, resting their hands on the damaged table. "The magic still needs stabilizing."

"I've given what I could. Risked what I could. This council has access to the Archive, to records and spells older than anything I've seen. You can carry the burden forward."

"And the traitors?" Mirelle asked, voice clipped. "If you learn anything of Varric or Tauren's whereabouts—"

"I'll send word," Eira said, already shaking her head. "But I won't chase them. That's your responsibility now."

Silence pressed down, thick and jagged.

Ines shifted, fingers twining tightly in her lap. "You're leaving."

Eira nodded. "I've done my part. The weave is holding. The Archive is alive. The rest—it's yours to tend."

Mirelle's lips thinned, like she'd bitten back a retort. Brannoc's eyes dropped to the ruined table, tracing the scorch marks. Darek sat straighter, as if her words were both accusation and challenge.

She turned toward the door, then paused, hand on the handle. "I hope you do better. For the next generation of threadwitches. And for yourselves."

Then she left, not waiting for their reply.

Eira found herself wandering the garden courtyard behind the inn, where the evening light filtered gold through the climbing ivy. It was quiet here—removed just enough from the chaos to feel like another world.

She sat on the edge of the old stone fountain, fingers trailing in the cool water. The ache in her chest hadn't dulled, but it had changed shape. Grief had a way of doing that. It bent inward, hollowing out the edges of every other feeling.

Footsteps on gravel reached her ears. She didn't look up.

Kael didn't speak at first, just settled on the fountain's edge a few feet away, close enough to share the silence. For a while, they simply sat.

It was Kael who broke the quiet. "I wasn't sure if you wanted space."

"I didn't know what I wanted," she admitted. "I still don't."

He nodded slowly. "When you asked me to leave the chamber… during the weaving… I understood why. But it still felt like—like being shut out."

She winced, not at the accusation—because there wasn't one—but at the truth in it. "I didn't mean to hurt you. I just… needed Caelen calm and room to think. Without anyone pulling at me."

"I wasn't trying to pull," he said softly. "I was trying to stay close without undoing the fragile thing we were starting to build again."

She looked at him then. Really looked. His eyes were rimmed red, exhaustion dragging hard at the corners. He hadn't cried—not where anyone could see—but she wondered if he would let himself at all.

"Beck would've hated this part," Kael murmured suddenly, voice rough. "The quiet. He'd have made a terrible pun just to break it."

The corner of her mouth twitched. "He'd have called it his 'solemn duty.'"

Kael huffed out a breath that might have been a laugh. "Exactly." He rubbed a hand over his face. "I keep expecting him to walk around a corner and say something stupid. And then I remember."

Eira's throat tightened. "I know."

Silence stretched again, but it was a different silence—warmer, shared.

"I don't know if I'm ready," she said finally, the words tumbling out before she could stop them. "For anything more than… this. Whatever this is."

He offered a half smile. "That's more than I had before."

A breeze stirred the ivy, and her fingers brushed his on the fountain's edge. His hand twitched, like he almost reached for hers—but he didn't. Not while her grief still bled raw. Not while Caelen lingered in every unspoken corner between them.

"I don't want you to stay in the capital," she said, barely more than a whisper. "But I can't ask you to come with us."

Kael looked down at their hands. "I've been thinking about staying. Help rebuilding, maybe. Starting something useful."

She hesitated. "That sounds… right. For you." A pause. "But I'll miss you."

"I'll miss you too." His voice cracked, just slightly, and this time he didn't hide it.

The moment stretched. She wanted to reach for him, to say something that would make it easier—but she couldn't. Not yet.

Then Kael stood, exhaled slowly, and said, "You'll let me know if you ever want more than this."

She nodded, eyes stinging. "I will."

He walked away quietly, not looking back.

She didn't stop him.
Not yet.

The inn room was silent but for the dull creak of wood as Anwen tightened the straps on her satchel. Eira folded one of Beck's scarves—the ridiculous one with little suns stitched into the ends—and placed it gently inside her bag.

Caelen sat on the edge of the bed. He hadn't spoken since they returned from the Archive, but his eyes followed Eira more than his hands did. He rolled bandages, slipped a small healer's kit into his pack, movements practiced, almost mechanical. Something to keep his hands from shaking.

No one spoke of what they'd lost. Not yet. Not while the ache was still raw and swollen.

"He always packed last," Anwen murmured, fingers frozen on the buckle of her bag. "He'd act like it was some strategy. Said we were predictable and that's how you get pickpocketed."

Eira let out a sound—something like a laugh but heavier, like it had been caught in her chest for too long. "He'd toss half his stuff in my bag anyway."

Anwen gave a quiet huff of agreement. "Mine too. Claimed he had 'emergency cheese' that needed temperature regulation."

That cracked something in Anwen. She sat down hard on the bed, covering her face with both hands. "I keep expecting him to swing the door open and make some stupid joke…"

Eira knelt in front of her. "I know." She touched Anwen's knee, grounding her, giving back the steadiness Anwen had so often given her.

They didn't reach for each other—not yet—but grief knit them together anyway.

Caelen cleared his throat and handed Anwen Beck's journal. "You should keep this," he said, voice low, with unshed tears in his eyes. "There's things you should read."

The morning sun filtered through the curtains, casting gold across the floorboards. It was too bright for the way they felt.

Eira stood, brushing her palms down the sides of her coat. "We should go."

Caelen gave a tight nod. "I checked with the stables. The council arranged a carriage."

"Nice of them," Anwen muttered. "Now that everything's broken and fixed again."

They left the room in silence. At the threshold, Eira turned back one last time—eyes scanning the space for anything Beck might've left behind.

Just a scrap of ribbon tucked in a drawer. She pocketed it without a word.

The streets were still lined with ash, but people had begun to sweep, to salvage, to plant hope again. As their carriage pulled away from the capital, Eira leaned her head against the window, watching the skyline shrink behind them.

Brookwyn waited.

The Veilbreakers waited. She had handed the burden to the council, but her gut whispered what her heart already knew—this fight would find her again.

The hardest words she would ever have to say still waited too.

CHAPTER THIRTY-SEVEN

The streets were still lined with ash, but people had begun to sweep, to salvage, to plant hope again. As their carriage pulled away from the capital, Eira leaned her head against the window, watching the skyline shrink behind them.

Mist wrapped close, not menacing but insistent, as though the very air of Brookwyn had reached across the distance to pull them nearer.

The road into Brookwyn looked unchanged.

The wildflowers still lined the fenceposts. The crooked sign still leaned at the edge of the lane. The hill still crested just before the town came into view — roofs and chimney smoke, ivy-covered stone, the flicker of market flags in the breeze.

Caelen's voice was quiet as he walked beside the cart. "Even after all this time, it looks the same."

Anwen's fingers tightened against the bench. She shook her head, eyes fixed on the town. "It doesn't feel the same."

Eira didn't answer. Her chest ached with both their truths.

The cart rattled behind them as they made the final turn. Silence settled — not empty, but heavy. Grief threaded with exhaustion. Relief tangled with dread. The kind of silence that felt like a held breath.

Heads turned as they entered town. A hammer stilled mid-strike. A broom leaned against a wall, forgotten. Children went quiet, peering from behind their mothers' skirts. A few waved. Most just watched.

Eira forced a smile. She lifted her hand in a small wave, but it felt like lifting a stone. Her whole body wanted to curl in on itself, to disappear before the questions came.

At last, they reached the familiar path between her shop and the cottage. The cart came to a halt. Caelen helped Anwen down, then offered a hand to Eira.

She took it without meeting his eyes.

For a long moment, they stood there — quiet in the shade of the trees, the cottage just ahead, the weight of return pressing close. The mist curled around their ankles, cool and insistent, like Brookwyn's breath.

And then, without a word, they stepped forward together.

The scent hit her first.

Lavender. Woodsmoke. The faintest trace of elderflower tea. Eira's hand hovered on the cottage door handle, just for a breath, before she pushed it open and stepped inside.

The warmth of the room wrapped around her instantly — not heat, exactly, but memory. The worn wooden floors. The bundles of herbs drying in the rafters. The soft clink of a windchime on the back window. Everything was familiar, but quieter. Older.

A rustle came from the far room.

"Mum?" Eira's voice cracked more than she meant it to.

There was a pause. Then the sound of a stool scraping back, and soft, steady footsteps.

Her mother appeared in the doorway, shawl draped over her shoulders, silvering hair pulled into its usual neat knot. For a second, she simply looked at Eira. Not with surprise, or even relief. Just eyes wide and brimming with the kind of love that didn't need words.

Then she moved.

Eira barely had time to cross the room before Ysolde reached her. Her arms wrapped around Eira with surprising strength, one hand cradling the back of her daughter's head as though she could hold every broken piece together.

Eira's breath hitched.

"I'm here," Ysolde whispered. "You came home."

And that was all it took.

The sob burst from Eira's chest, uninvited but unstoppable. Not just grief for Beck, or fear from the battles they'd fought — but the release of holding everything in for too long. She clung to her mother, fingers twisted in the back of her shawl like a child again.

Behind her, Anwen entered silently, her eyes glistening. She didn't interrupt. She just sank down at the old table and rested her hands on the wood like it might anchor her.

Ysolde pulled back only enough to look Eira in the eyes. "You're hurt."

Eira shook her head. "Not like that."

"I know." Ysolde cupped her cheek for a moment longer, then looked past her to where Caelen stood in the doorway, hesitant, not quite stepping over the threshold.

"Welcome home" she said softly.

Caelen nodded once and stepped inside, removing his cloak as he entered. For all his strength, he looked tired — not in the body, but in the soul. And when Ysolde turned her gaze to him fully, something unspoken passed between them. Old grief. Older affection.

"You still make poor decisions," Ysolde said lightly going to embrace him. "But at least you keep good company."

A ghost of a smile touched Caelen's lips. "Some things never change."

Ysolde turned back to her daughter. "Come. Sit. Tell me everything — or nothing. Whatever you need."

Eira looked toward the familiar chair by the hearth, then hesitated. She didn't want comfort, not quite. What she wanted was to breathe. To not have to be anything at all for just a few minutes.

"I'll make tea," Ysolde said, already reaching for the tin of dried leaves. "Then we'll sit."

As she moved around the kitchen, she glanced once more toward the door — toward the empty space where two others should have been.

Her voice was soft, almost too quiet to carry. "I was hoping to see five returning."

Eira stilled.

Ysolde didn't press. She just let the words settle in the air like steam from the kettle, and returned to her work.

Caelen's expression didn't shift, but something in his stance closed in.

Anwen lowered her gaze, hands still folded on the table.

Eira drew in a breath that felt too large for her chest. "We lost Beck."

A pause. A look of grief passed over Ysolde's face for just a moment.

"And Kael?" her mother asked gently.

Eira hesitated. "He's not lost. Just… gone. For now."

Ysolde nodded slowly, the motion full of unspoken sorrow and understanding.

"Then we'll keep the lamps lit," she said simply, "for both."

Ysolde laid four cups on the table, then, without thinking, set down a fifth. Her hand lingered on the rim before she slowly slid it back into the cupboard. She poured the water into the teapot, the scent of dried mint and chamomile curling through the room like memory.

And just like that, the spell of return softened around them — not undone, but held with care. The grief would still be there. The questions, the choices, the weight of what came next.

But for now, there was home. There was tea. There were arms that had never stopped holding space for them.

And there was time to begin again.

The town square filled slowly. Word had spread quickly once they returned, and by the time they reached the center of town, neighbors were already gathered — waiting, watching, murmuring to each other in low, uncertain tones.

Ysolde had gone ahead earlier to speak with Beck's family, to share the news with the kind of care only she could offer. Eira was grateful — fiercely, achingly grateful — not to have faced that moment herself. But the relief twisted sharp inside her, too close to guilt. Knowing the words had already been spoken, that the grief had already reached them, made it harder to breathe. Like the loss had become more real the moment it left their circle and entered the world.

Eira stood near the old fountain, her hands clasped in front of her, thumb brushing the faint threadburn scars across her palm.

Caelen stood to her left, arms folded, his face unreadable. Anwen hovered just behind her, hands tight in her sleeves, jaw clenched to hold back tears.

Children were ushered toward home. Shopkeepers closed their doors early. And as the square filled, silence fell.

"We promised to bring him home," Eira said softly.

She didn't need to name him.

A ripple passed through the crowd. Some faces crumpled. Others just closed their eyes.

"There was an attack at the capital," she continued, voice barely louder than a thread's whisper. "The magic—the weave that holds everything together—it was unraveling. We worked to stop it, to save as much as we could. Beck…"

Her voice caught. She swallowed hard.

"Beck gave everything to make sure we did."

Someone let out a broken sob. Mrs. Torren—her hands pressed to her mouth, shoulders shaking.

Eira didn't flinch. Didn't cry. She held steady because Anwen couldn't, not now. Because Caelen wouldn't, not here. Because someone had to.

"He saved us," she said. "He saved so many more than us. And it wasn't fair. It wasn't right. But it was who he was."

A long silence stretched. No one moved.

Then, finally, someone stepped forward.

A young boy — Tomas, one of Beck's students from his impromptu knotwork lessons behind the bakery — approached Eira with a trembling lower lip and a woven braid clutched in one hand. It was crooked and uneven, the kind of thing Beck would've declared "a chaotic masterpiece."

"He said I should give it to someone brave," Tomas whispered. "You can have it."

Eira took the braid with both hands, blinking rapidly.

"Thank you," she whispered.

Mr. Yarrow stepped forward, hands tucked behind his back the way he always did when uncertain whether to scold or comfort. His eyebrows were drawn, but not in his usual gruff annoyance — more like he was trying to smooth them into something gentler and didn't quite remember how.

"Wasn't always easy, that one," he said, voice low but clear enough to carry to Eira. "Had a gift for chaos. Once turned my entire rain barrel into a frog nursery just to prove a point."

A few people chuckled softly. Eira blinked hard.

"But," he added, after a beat, "he had a good heart. One of the best I've seen. I'll miss the lad."

He gave a nod — awkward but sincere — and stepped back into the crowd.

Others began to step forward too—one by one, offering small things. A carved whistle. A wildflower bundle. A note written in smudged ink. Pieces of a community mourning one of its own.

By the time dusk fell, the base of the fountain was covered in memories, the wild, uneven kind he would have loved.

The room above the apothecary was quiet, tucked away from the murmuring crowd outside and the chaos of unpacking. Anwen sat cross-legged on the floor, surrounded by the remnants of their journey: cloaks draped over chairs, half-emptied bags, a worn travel kettle cold on the windowsill.

She was digging through Beck's pack.

Eira watched from the doorway, heart clenched tight. She hadn't been ready to touch it before — not the pack, not the reality of what wasn't coming home with them. But Anwen moved with intention, not to chase pain but to make space for it. To honor him.

Anwen pulled it free slowly, reverently — a leather-bound notebook, the corners frayed, the spine cracked.

Beck's journal.

Eira crossed the room and sat beside her. Anwen passed the book over with a look that asked permission without words.

Eira nodded and opened it.

The first few pages were chaotic — notes, doodles, snippets of poetry so bad it made her laugh under her breath. A drawing of Anwen with "MOST TERRIFYING PLANT LADY" scrawled underneath. A half-drawn magical rune beside a reminder to "buy more socks."

But further in, his handwriting steadied. His thoughts grew clearer. Hopeful. Reflective.

"If you're reading this, I guess I'm not around to explain it all. Sorry about that. I was really hoping for the dramatic survival arc — you know, hero gets the girl, opens a cheese shop, names every variety after his friends."

Eira swallowed hard. Anwen leaned in, silent tears streaking down her cheeks.

"But if it came to a choice, I'd make it again. No regrets. Not when I got to stand beside you. Not when I saw what we were trying to protect."

There were pages about each of them — Caelen, who he still didn't fully understand but had come to respect. Anwen, who he described as *"the spine of our little patchwork family."* And Eira…

She blinked hard, vision blurring.

"Eira — if you're reading this, I hope you're okay. You carry too much. Always have. But you're not alone, no matter what your overworked brain tells you. I believed in you. Still do."

"Tell Kael he was a better man than he thought. Tell Caelen I wish I could've gotten to know him again. Tell Anwen I left the recipe for 'fire stew' in the back and to please never make it again."

"And if you ever need a laugh… just look for the page where I tried to sketch Caelen's dragon form. Sorry in advance."

Eira flipped to the back. There it was — a wildly inaccurate doodle of a dragon with a top hat.

She laughed through the tears.

When she finally closed the journal, Anwen laid a hand over hers.

"We'll carry him with us," Anwen whispered. "Always."

Eira nodded. "He'd probably complain about the weight."

They sat in silence for a long while, the journal between them like a tether to something still warm, still real.

Outside the window, the stars began to appear — quiet, steady, unchanging. Eira imagined him somewhere among them, still grinning, still making terrible jokes at eternity's expense.

The moon was high when Eira stepped around the corner of the cottage to visit the garden, the cool night air brushing her skin like a question left unanswered. She had lingered in the apothecary with Anwen for hours until Anwen had cried herself to sleep, and the journal — Beck's words — still echoed softly in her heart.

She didn't expect to find Caelen in the garden.

He sat on the low stone bench near the herb beds, hands resting on his knees, eyes on the sky. His posture was still too formal, too careful, like he hadn't figured out how to be in his own skin yet.

She froze at the edge of the light. Her eyes caught on familiar lines — the jaw she had once traced with ink-stained fingers, the set of his shoulders, steady even now. But there was something else too, something heavier that hadn't been there before. His silence was shaped by absence, his gaze sharper, older. He was familiar and foreign at once — like a melody she almost remembered but couldn't quite sing.

At last he turned. "Couldn't sleep either?"

Eira shook her head. "Too many ghosts."

A faint smile touched his lips. "Beck left me a dragon with a top hat in that journal. I've been insulted in more flattering ways."

She snorted despite herself, stepping closer. "He meant well. And had no drawing talent."

A pause. She continued, "He liked you. Said he wished he'd had more time to get to know you again."

Caelen looked down at his hands. "I liked him too. He had heart."

The silence stretched again. Not awkward — just full.

"I never asked," she said softly, "but… why did you choose it? Becoming the dragon?"

He didn't answer right away. His shoulders shifted, his mouth opening as if to speak, then closing again. Finally: "Your mother and I… we knew the council was circling you. Watching. Waiting. When they came she was afraid they'd take you to use as a tool. With the magic becoming unstable and them suggesting I go to the capital as a guardian, we saw an opportunity to keep you protected."

Her breath caught.

"I was afraid too," he said after a long pause, voice raw. "But I could protect you, if I became something they needed more. So I disappeared from Brookwyn and went to protect the Archives."

"You disappeared from me," she whispered, aching.

He flinched — not at her words, but at the truth under them. "I know."

Her heart twisted. "Seven years, Caelen. You can't just tell me it was for my sake and leave it at that."

His throat worked. Silence stretched, fragile as spun glass. At last he shook his head. "There's more to say. But not tonight. I don't have the words yet. Not ones that wouldn't break something we just managed to hold together."

Her chest ached at that — at the choice to leave it unsaid, even when her whole body begged for more. "I didn't forget you," she whispered. "Not really. Not even when I told myself I had."

"And I didn't stop wanting to protect you," he murmured. "Even asleep, even lost to the dragon… I still felt your threads brushing close. I knew I was keeping something important safe."

She blinked hard. "And now?"

Caelen stood. The movement was quiet, measured, as if he feared startling her. "Now, I don't know who I am yet. But I want to find out. Not just as a dragon. Not just as a protector."

His eyes met hers, old and wounded and full of something that had once been love, and maybe still was.

“And if that path doesn’t lead back here?” she asked, voice breaking.

His answer came quiet, but steady. “Then at least I’ll have been honest this time.”

The silence that followed was not empty, but full — with ache, with old love, with everything unsaid. The garden lay hushed around them, mint and thyme carrying their fragrance into the night air. Above, the moon held its vigil, cool and unyielding, while neither of them reached to break the stillness.

CHAPTER THIRTY-EIGHT

The pond was tucked in a clearing just outside Brookwyn, ringed by tall birches and dappled in late-afternoon sun. The kind of place where children might catch frogs in summer — or tired parents might steal a quiet moment.

The kind of place where Beck would've absolutely fallen in, then insisted he meant to.

Eira sat cross-legged near the water's edge, the breeze lifting her hair as she rubbed the fraying thread around her wrist — a single strand from Beck's scarf. The last thing she'd taken from the archive. The first thing she hadn't let go of.

It felt strange, how still the world had become. Stranger still that it kept turning at all.

She opened her mouth, closed it again. The words swelled in her chest, too heavy, too clumsy to speak into the quiet. But the silence hurt more, so at last she let them fall.

"I miss you," she said quietly, the words barely loud enough to stir the air. "More than I thought I could miss someone who never shut up."

The smile that touched her lips cracked just enough to let a tear slip through.

"I could really use you right now. Not for the jokes — though they helped. For the... weirdly insightful things you'd say when no one expected it. I'm so tired, Beck. I feel like all my pieces are here, but not put back together yet. And I don't know how to fix it."

She laughed once — not because it was funny, but because it wasn't.

"I care about them both," she whispered. "Kael. Caelen. I keep trying to untangle it, to make it neat, like there's supposed to be a right answer — a single thread that leads to the truth. But there isn't. Not with them."

Her fingers curled tighter around the thread at her wrist.

"Kael sees me in a way I didn't think anyone could. Like he's not afraid of the mess. Like he wants the parts of me I don't even understand yet. And Caelen..." Her breath caught. "Caelen was safety. First love. The person I would've followed anywhere — and maybe I still would, if things were different. But I don't know who he is anymore. I don't know who I am with him."

Her throat tightened. "It doesn't feel like a choice between right and wrong. It feels like standing at two doors that both lead to pieces of myself — and whichever I walk through, I'll lose the other."

The tears came again, quiet this time, like something too deep for sobs.

"And I'm so scared," she said. "Of choosing wrong. Of hurting them. Of being hurt by them. Of being too much, or not enough, or exactly enough and still not being chosen in return. I hate this part. I hate that it hurts to love people who are still alive."

Her voice broke on that last word, and she pressed a palm to her chest as if it might hold her together.

"I wish you were here, Beck," she whispered. "You'd know what to say. Or at least you'd distract me with something ridiculous until I could breathe again."

She rested her chin on her knees. The sunlight rippled across the surface of the pond — a thousand tiny glints like scattered thread.

"If you were here," she added softly, "you'd probably say something annoyingly perfect. Like... 'You already have the answer. You just don't trust yourself to hear it.'"

Then she smiled, truly smiled, through her tears.

"Followed immediately by: 'Also, never fall in love with two broody magical men at once, Eira. That's just poor planning.'"

The laugh bubbled up before she could stop it, and for a moment the ache felt lighter.

She reached up and tightened the thread around her wrist.

A breeze stirred through the clearing — soft, sudden, and just cool enough to raise goosebumps on her arms. A single birch leaf fluttered down from a tree that hadn't shed all day, spinning slowly in the golden light.

It landed on her knee.

Tangled in the stem was a bit of red wool.

Eira stared at it, breath caught.

The thread wasn't from the trees. Wasn't from the forest. It was unmistakably his — the same kind of soft, chaotic yarn Beck had once tried to dye with berry juice and accidentally stained half the inn's laundry.

She laughed, a wet, startled sound, and swiped at her cheeks with both hands.

"Subtle as ever," she murmured. "Thanks, Beck."

And in her mind — maybe memory, maybe imagination — she almost heard him again: *Don't tug too hard, Eira. The right thread will hold.*

Then she stood, brushing off her skirt, the leaf and wool tucked gently into her pocket. She looked back over the path she'd taken. Brookwyn waited just beyond the trees — her cottage, her shop, the threads left unfinished.

She turned toward home. Toward the loom waiting for her hands, the threads waiting for her heart.
And walked forward, where the next weaving — hers, theirs, the world's — would begin.

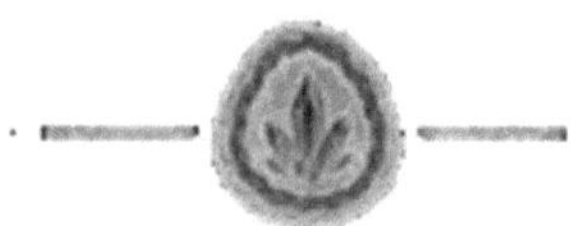

Bonus

Content

From Anwen's Journal

Herbal Blends & Brewing Notes

Tea Blends for Every Occasion

Dreamer's Rest:
lavender + chamomile — for calming the mind and guiding peaceful sleep

Morning Clarity:
ashroot + starpetal — a grounding blend to start the day with focus

Courage Brew:
emberroot + lemonbud — sharp and energizing, for difficult conversations

Hearth Comfort:
bramble + gingerroot — for grief, heartache, or homesickness

Soothing Tonic:
dawnleaf + silverfloss — to ease spell fatigue and steady the voice

Veilwalker:
moonmint + shadowfern — taken before dream-threading or meditation

Brewing Notes & Techniques

1. Boil water to a rolling bubble (not too early or the herbs wilt).

2. Layer herbs in a fine mesh sachet or floating strainer.

3. Pour water slowly to avoid splashing volatile elements.

4. Cover with a cloth and steep 3–7 minutes depending on herb type.

5. Remove herbs and stir once counterclockwise with a wooden spoon.

Anwen's Notes:

Watch the time. Ashroot goes bitter if left too long. Layered blends (like lavender + chamomile) should steep no more than 5 minutes. Trust your nose—if it smells too strong, it probably is. Also: Beck once added pepper leaf. Never let Beck add anything.

From the Private Journal of Beck Witherford

<u>List of Suspicious Brookwyn Persons Potentially Engaged in Espionage</u>

1. Old Man Ferren – Never blinks. Not once in the ten years I've known him. Very suspicious. How do his eyes not get dry?
2. Madam Estelle (seamstress) – Knows everyone's measurements without ever taking them. Definitely a mind reader.
3. The goose at the east pond – Not technically a person, but highly aggressive and chases everyone.
4. Eira – always chanting and scribbling notes, she has to be up to something. Plus, she can spot a lie a mile away. Very suspicious.
5. Little Frey – Seven years old and already knows how to pick locks. Why? WHO TAUGHT HER?
6. Hollis the baker – Pastries too good. Possibly enchanted. Further testing required.
7. The woman with the blue shawl – Always watching. Never speaks. Appears in unexpected places.
8. Myself – For thoroughness. If I were a spy, I wouldn't suspect myself either. Clever.

Thread Crimes I've Witnessed

1. Using glow in the dark thread for stealth magic (whoops)
2. Knotting an emotion weave with 3 ex-lovers present. Such a triagnle.
3. Creating a love charm with alpaca yarn. So much static.
4. Crocheting a sentient tea cozy that refused to let go of the tea kettle. It didn't get lost, but it did get a little burnt.
5. Mixing memory thread with glitter. We still find random glitter.
6. Attempting spells while mildly tipsy.

Not recommended

Eira's Private Journal Entry

This is ridiculous, but maybe it will help to see it written out.

Kael

Pros

- Makes me feel seen-even when I try to hide
- Threads respond to him like they know him
- That smile when he's not looking
- Came clean about his past, eventually

Cons

- I still don't know much about his past
- How much of his interest in me is because of my magic

Caelen

Pros

- My first everything
- Knew me better than I knew myself
- Sacrificed his future to keep me safe
- Trusted me to protect his memories

Cons

- He left without telling me the whole truth
- I was broken for years after he left
- He doesn't feel like he knows who he is no

FROM THE AUTHOR'S FILES

NOTES ON THE THREADWOVEN MAGIC SYSTEM

THREADS

Threads are the fundamental lines of magical energy that bind the world together.

Some are literal strands a threadwitch can grasp and manipulate; others are invisible but sensed through affinity, emotion, or intuition.

Threads connect:

- objects
- memories
- places
- people
- natural forces

They are the underlying weave of the world's magic — delicate, powerful, and deeply responsive to emotion.

AFFINITY

Every threadwitch has natural pull toward particular types of threads.
Affinity is a combination of:

- innate talent
- emotional resonance
- practice and discipline

Affinity shapes how magic feels, how it manifests, and how easily a practitioner can sense or manipulate specific threads.

No threadwitch excels equally in all types — even the strongest have specialties.

Magic users perceive threads differently depending on personal affinity. Some see faint glowing filaments. Others feel warmth, vibration, or subtle shifts in air or emotion. A rare few hear threads as tones or resonance.

Types of Threads

Flame Threads

Volatile, intense, emotion-fueled. Used to ignite, heat, or burn. Responsive to urgency or anger.

Frost Threads

Cooling, preserving, clarifying.
Favored by users who value precision and restraint.
Quiet threads, brittle when overstrained.

Wind Threads

Threads of movement, force, and redirection.
Often sensed through touch. Useful for defensive or utility spells.

Whisper Threads

Soft, secretive, used for carrying messages or subtle illusions. Easy to miss unless one is trained or attuned.

Memory Threads

Hold emotional resonance and recollection.
Used to preserve, transfer, or alter memories — powerful but unstable when tampered with.

Lifebind Threads

Threads of healing, growth, and connection between living things. Often bonded to herbs or plant-based materials; used in apothecary magic.

Warding Threads

Protective grids that shield, repel, or anchor. Strong and difficult to move once placed — common around archives, homes, and ancestral spaces.

Binding Threads

Used to seal, hold, or lock objects and energies. Versatile but prone to backlash if pulled too tightly.

Threadlight Threads

Rare, luminous threads used in ceremonial work. Reveal hidden truths and trace magical origins.

Risks and Backlash

Threadburn

Overstraining unstable or emotionally charged threads can cause a backlash known as *threadburn*.
This often leaves:

- silvery scars
- temporary weakness
- magical exhaustion
- chills

Geodecraft

A rare and potent branch of magic involving the storage of threads within geodes.

Geodecraft allows a threadwitch to:

- preserve spells
- activate delayed magic
- store volatile threadwork safely
- store a person's lifetime of memories

But breaking a charged geode can release magic that is distorted, damaged, or lost entirely.

Eira's journey is far from over. The threads of fate still twist and turn, and her heart remains torn between two paths. As the shadows of the past resurface, new dangers loom on the horizon, and Eira must face the consequences of choices she hasn't made yet. Will she embrace the truth, or will the weight of her love be too much to bear?

Find out in Book 2 of the Threadcrafted Series, ThreadMended.
Coming early 2026.

Acknowledgments

First off, to my family: thank you for putting up with me disappearing into my keyboard for hours at a time, forgetting what day it is, and occasionally answering questions with “hang on or I’ll forget this.” Your patience and reminders to eat made this book possible.

To my beta readers and proofreaders — you brave, brilliant souls — thank you for poking holes in my plot, pointing out the extra spaces and missing words, and reminding me that what made sense in my head didn’t *always* make sense on the page. You helped me shape this story into something stronger, and I couldn’t have done it without you.

And to everyone else who cheered me on in big or quiet ways: I noticed. Every “you got this,” every emoji, every nod of encouragement made me keep going when it felt impossible. Stories may be written in solitude, but they grow best when shared.

Also, if you found any typos or missing commas after all that? Please pretend you didn’t,

About the Author

Brynne Aisling-Rowan writes cozy romantasy stitched with magic, craft, and just enough chaos to keep her characters on their toes. When she isn't writing about threadwitches, enchanted geodes, or mysterious lighthouses, she can usually be found crocheting, hoarding yarn "for future projects," or drinking tea from mugs so large they could double as birdbaths.

She lives in the Midwest with her family and two canine beasts who are convinced they run the household (and probably her author career, too).

Threadwoven is her debut novel.

www.ingramcontent.com/pod-product-compliance
Lightning Source LLC
Chambersburg PA
CBHW060816310726
48980CB00002B/316
* 9 7 9 8 9 9 4 0 8 3 7 2 7 *